CALFAIN
the
Dreamweaver

G L Stead

Published by Barnfold 2008

A catalogue record for this book is available from the British
Library
ISBN 978-0-9561511-0-0

CALFAIN the Dreamweaver

For Catherine

Special thanks to
Lucy

and

Gavin

CALFAIN the Dreamweaver.

Chapter One.

'Do you want a dream or don't you? It's an easy question, my friends. How long does it take to decide whether you wish to continue with your humdrum, boring little lives, or come with me and let me give you a taste of what my dreams have to offer.'

Calfain the Dreamweaver stood, glancing expectantly at the crowd of people that had gathered around him in the market place since he had started to talk some ten minutes ago.

Cynical old men smiled ruefully at what they perceived to be some sort of confidence trick. They knew it; they reckoned he knew they knew it. It was just a matter of them discovering how he was fooling them. Then, they could all go to the tavern and laugh about how they had thwarted him.

The not so worldly wise however, listened to him with open mouths and wide eyes. As Calfain expertly glanced around, he instinctively knew that these were the ones he should single out and pay particular attention to.

Calfain knew not to push his audience. Give them enough rope, was his motto.

Presently, someone in the crowd, a middle-aged man tentatively raised his hand.

'Ho!' he shouted. When no one sniggered at him or made any rude comments, he continued with a little more confidence in his voice, 'What can you offer me, then?'

1

Calfain's head swivelled on his shoulders like an owl hearing the squeak of a mouse,

'How much are you willing to pay, friend? A few copper pennies will buy you a pleasant enough interlude,' he smiled wickedly, 'or for a little more, I'll supply you with anything your heart ever desired. I'm not just giving you that funny feeling you wake up in the morning with and is gone the moment you get out of bed. I'm giving you the chance to obtain an ever-lasting memory. As though you really lived through it. As though you were there. As if – it had only happened to you.'

The middle aged man glanced around at his peers, some were grinning at him with an unspoken encouragement to proceed, a couple of others openly laughed. A few more simply shook their heads at the fool who was about to be fooled.

'What can I have for five pennies?' the man bravely asked.

Someone guffawed at the back, 'More than you deserve.'

That raised a few more chuckles and sniggers. The man had lain himself open to ridicule now and he knew it. Having come this far, he may as well go all the way, he reasoned with himself.

The dreamweaver knew he had a client now for sure, 'You sir, can have the distinction of being the first in this marvellous village to be taken wherever I chose to take you,' Calfain swept his hands wide, 'come my friend, step forward.'

Bravado now took control over the middle-aged man as he began to move through the crowd towards Calfain. One or two souls made snide whispers and comments as the man passed by.

Then, the crowd parted and suddenly, he was there. Exposed to the gaze of his peers, he began to feel his face becoming very hot. He smiled nervously and wiped his sweating palms down the sides of his trousers.

He quickly discovered that speaking from the anonymity of a crowd was very different from being the focus of attention at the centre of a circle.

Calfain stood waiting, smiling his most winning smile that said to the entire world, 'Trust me…I'm the dreamweaver.'

He gently took the man's arm and steered him towards a large wooden high-backed chair that he had persuaded a nearby shopkeeper to loan him for the day…at a nominal remuneration of course.

As the man sat, Calfain moved theatrically around the chair and placed both of his hands over the backrest and onto his subject's shoulders. Then, he scanned the crowd, patiently awaiting their silence and full attention.

The buzz of excitement began to die away as first one, then another and another realised that nothing would proceed until they had fallen silent.

Calfain raised his chin and glanced majestically around,

'I will write on a piece of paper what dream I shall instruct our friend here to have. Then, I will fold the paper and give it to one of you to hold. Then and only then will I place the dream thoughts inside his head? When he awakes, he will tell you all what his dream was about.'

Still standing behind the man, Calfain took a sheet of thick paper from within his cloak. He held it up for all to see, turning it slowly, showing both of the plain white sides. Next, he took a thick black charcoal pencil and began to write. He folded the paper several times and held it aloft once again,

'Who amongst you will hold this for me?' Calfain gazed around. He did not want to be accused of having a partner in the crowd. 'Pick someone you all know.'

'Give it the boy there,' one voice spoke up.

'Aye, Bennok, give it to, Bennok.'

Calfain looked around. Most of the assembly were now nodding their heads in approval at the choice

'Bennok it is then,' he said, passing the folded paper to the lad. 'Here boy, take this and hold it safe.'

Bennok grinned. In his little way, he felt superior to everyone else at having been chosen to perform such an important task.

The dreamweaver returned to his position behind the still sitting man. Without another word, Calfain gently took the man's head in his hands and gracefully swept them over the top of his head as if he were smoothing the hair backwards.

The man closed his eyes without being instructed. He had intended to keep them open, if only to expose the dreamweaver as a fake, but as soon as those cool, almost sensual fingers touched him, he could do no other than fall into a deep involuntary sleep.

'How long will it be?' a woman's voice asked.

'Only until he wakes up,' some unknown wag answered, causing sniggers and giggles.

Calfain smiled, he had heard them all before, a thousand times each. He allowed them their moment of humour. It kept them friendly.

'Any moment now, My Lady,' he advised the unknown woman. Calfain let them linger another moment longer.

The man's eyes flickered open. He looked sharply around, apparently unsure of his surroundings.

'Good nap, Mogga?' a friend shouted from somewhere in the crowd. Several of the spectators laughed.

'Where…where am…Oh dear Lord!' Mogga spluttered, attempting to rise from the wooden chair.

'Steady, careful now,' Calfain advised him. He knew where Mogga had been and he did not want the man stumbling from the chair.

'Tell us, Mogga. Tell us what you saw,' one observer shouted.

Mogga wiped a hand over his face and seemed to look a little green. 'I…I think I was er, yes! I was on the ocean. Sailing with pirates!'

4

The crowd erupted into roars of laughter at his revelation.

'It's true!' Mogga shouted above the din, 'I really was. It was so real! I still feel sick.'

The throng laughed again, even more heartily. Some clapped; some sneered at the suggestion. The old men simply waited.

Calfain turned, swirling his robes about his legs. He looked towards the boy,

'Bennok!' he called, 'open the paper and let someone read it, if you cannot.'

Bennok hastily unfolded the paper and passed it to a woman of about forty. He could not read the words and he saw no reason to let this crowd embarrass him for his lack of education.

The woman read the words carefully to herself, mouthing each one as she did. Presently, as she finished, her eyes went back to the top and she read aloud,

'I am sailing on the sea. On a pirate ship called…'

'The *Fairwind!*' Mogga shouted out, cutting her off before she had the time to finish.

The crowd collectively gasped, 'It that the name?' Calfain asked the woman.

The woman glanced at the paper again, confirming what Mogga had said. She nodded vigorously and grinned back at Calfain.

'He really is a dreamweaver!' a voice called.

'I'm 'avin' some of that!' Said another.

'And me!'

'And me!'

It went on and on. The majority of the assembled onlookers began to dig into their pockets and count up the money they had. Arms rose into the air demanding to be served with a dream of their choice.

For the rest of the day, Calfain, the weaver of dreams, busied himself attending to a steady stream of customers, desperate to view and retain in crystal sharp memories, their own, personal piece of magic.

As each recipient of Calfain's attention sat down and whispered their desires to him, he charged them according to what he described as a sliding scale of prices, which he actually made up on the spot after assessing the persons worth. As usual, he made a tidy pile of money.

The old timers shook their heads and slunk off to the tavern to discuss the merits of this seemingly harmless little ploy to entertain the locals and part the gullible from their coins.

Chapter Two.

Calfain sat quietly eating from a large platter of cooked meats and vegetables in one of the local taverns. He always selected a corner that was dark and away from the other patrons. Several had attempted to engage him in conversation when he had sat, but he had politely rebuffed them saying his work was done for the day and all he wanted was to relax with a little food and drink.

'Excuse me, sir,' a small voice suddenly interrupted his concentration on his food, 'would you be the dreamweaver, Calfain?'

Calfain glanced up to see the outline of what appeared to him to be a servant girl of no more than fifteen or sixteen years.

Calfain smiled wearily, 'Come back tomorrow child, I only work during the day.'

The young girl persisted. 'My mistress is eager to speak with you about your er, ability.'

The dreamweaver stabbed a slice of pork and placed it in his mouth. He studied the girl while he chewed. This may well be his bonus in this outpost of civilisation, he thought. If a servant girl had been sent to seek him out by her mistress, then logically, that mistress would have plenty of money – otherwise - she would not be employing a servant.

Calfain swallowed his meat, 'And just who is your mistress, my girl?' he asked amiably.

'Sir, my mistress is the Lady Peltene. She lives in the manor house, less than a mile distant. She requests that you would call on her to discuss your fees for performing your services.'

'How charmingly put,' Calfain smiled warmly, 'please tell your mistress I would be delighted to attend her house to discuss her requirements.'

The servant girl returned the smile, relieved that he had not been a pernickety old goat who only wanted to peek down the top of her blouse. 'If it pleases you sir, tomorrow at noon would be acceptable to, My Lady.'

'Tomorrow at noon it is,' Calfain confirmed, at the same time reaching into his robe for a few copper pennies to give the girl.

'Thank you most kindly sir', she said, taking the offered coins and turning smartly before he could speak again.

Excellent, thought the dreamweaver. Things were beginning to look up after all. He ordered another tankard of ale to celebrate his anticipated good fortune.

Calfain walked the mile distance to the manor house. He had set out deliberately early in order to survey the area for any other possible avenues of endeavour. If nothing else, life had taught Calfain to be receptive to any eventualities. To spot an angle, an opening, anything whereby he could achieve his lifelong ambition of acquiring an obscene amount of money.

As he strolled along the road, which led out of the village, he took notice of the occasional houses that stood slightly back from the road. Calfain had discovered years ago the curious little practice that rich people had of building their homes along the roads out of towns and cities. The richer the person, the further out of town they seemed to live. Calfain smiled to himself as he walked, it would appear the Lady Peltene, living a whole mile outside the village, would be extremely wealthy

After a short while, the dreamweaver came across a small rickety wooden signpost at right angles to the main road. It pointed along a path and advised all who wished to know, that down the leafy, tree-lined lane was a place called Tennay Manor. This had to be it. Calfain glanced around once more then proceeded along the lane.

The lane was quiet and secluded, the sun filtered through occasional gaps in the tree's canopy, casting long shafts of golden light that danced in the slight breeze. Then, in front and off to his right, Calfain spotted the big house, once hidden by the trees, it now revealed itself to him.

He stopped momentarily to gaze at the magnificent structure. It was big, really big and stone built too. Calfain licked his lips in anticipation. A house of that size would have dozens, if not scores of servants and that, in Calfain's eyes meant wealth…great wealth.

Calfain walked on, a bounce suddenly in his stride now. He kept his eyes firmly fixed on the house to his right as he began drawing near. Suddenly, he halted again. Something was wrong, he thought. He stared at the big house for several minutes. It looked quiet and peaceful enough. Perhaps too quiet and too peaceful, as if no one was at home. Calfain shrugged his worry away, he was just being too cautious, he told himself, but then, had not his cautiousness' kept him out of prison all these years?
He walked on, inspecting the house much more intently.

Another twenty yards and Calfain came across the gate that led to the front door of the big house. The lane continued on for some distance more, to where, he did not know or care. He was just about to turn right through the gates when he caught sight of some fellow further down the lane walking towards him.

'Are you Master Calfain?'

It was a woman's voice, deep and rich with a slight local accent that Calfain had been hearing during his brief stay in the village.

When he had first spotted her, he had only glanced; she wore dirty, soil stained trousers and a grubby looking heavy jerkin, her hair was tied back tight against her head. He realised now his mistake.

'Good morning,' he smiled at the woman, 'yes, I'm Calfain.'

The woman smiled, seemingly relieved to see him, 'Good morning, Master Calfain, I'm Peltene.'

Calfain looked closely at her. She was a little shorter than he, but not by much. Her hair was blonde with natural highlights that served to accentuate it, tied back as it was, he could not determine its true length. Her eyes were of the palest blue and her complexion was smooth and fair. She was, by any standards, an attractive woman. He gauged her age at around forty years, perhaps one either way.

She offered her hand for him to shake.

Odd for the Lady of the manor, he thought, Normal custom was for her to offer the back of it for him to kiss lightly. Nonetheless, he took it, noting immediately that it was not of the texture expected of a Lady. It was hard and almost rough as if she had spent years working with them, but it was not an unpleasant hand. Her fingers were long and gripped him firmly.

'Good of you to meet me at the gates, My Lady' Calfain said as he gently shook her hand.

She smiled, he glimpsed a row of perfect white teeth, 'It wasn't intended, Master Calfain, I was busy in the garden and lost track of the time, until I saw you walking down the lane.

'Oh!' he answered, feeling stupid at his own supposed importance.

She saw his expression and guessed correctly what had gone through his mind. She laughed. 'Would you like a drink? Tea perhaps?'

Calfain nodded gratefully.

The Lady Peltene turned and unexpectedly began walking back along the lane from where she had come. Calfain stood staring after her, confused.

She halted after a few steps, realising he was not accompanying her. She turned back to him, a questioning look on her face.

'It's this way, Master Calfain,' she pointed along the path.

Calfain lifted his chin, 'Ah! Yes, of course.' Fine, he thought, if I have to enter the house through the servant's entrance, then so be it.

As they walked together, she asked several bland questions about his travels and how long he intended to stay in the area. He answered with equal blandness, having never seen the sense in revealing too much of his future plans.

It also gave him a chance to study the woman in profile, she certainly was attractive, and he had already established that. Now he could just make out the contours of her body underneath the jerkin and trousers. The clothing did nothing to heighten her physique. As she walked, she had an easy stride, confidant of who she was and relaxed.

Whilst he was surreptitiously committing her features and her voice to memory and she was still speaking, Calfain failed to notice that they had walked past the big house and were now almost level with a row of cottages to his left.

Suddenly, Lady Peltene stopped walking. Calfain continued, mesmerised now by his companion. After two steps he realised she was gone. He stopped, turned and quickly located her. She stood just behind him, smiling

'Here we are,' she lifted her hand and pointed to the row of cottages.

Calfain's head snapped around, he looked at the old buildings, obviously in need of some repairs here and there, then, his head swivelled. He was attempting to locate the manor house.

'But...I thought...' he burbled, half-heartedly pointing towards the grand building that loomed over the hedge more than sixty yards away.

Lady Peltene smiled sympathetically at him, 'Er, I think there are some things you should know, Master Calfain,' she stepped up to the little door and pushed. It squeaked open on un-oiled hinges.

Inside, the little porch it was warm from the heat of the sun, Lady Peltene led the way through to the kitchen and went straight to the big black kettle, placing it on an already lighted stove. She gestured to a wooden stool at the kitchen table and Calfain dutifully sat.

Whilst the kettle boiled, Lady Peltene busied herself spreading butter on several scones, which she placed in front of the dreamweaver and bade him eat.

Presently, when the tea was poured, she sat opposite him at the table and smiled radiantly.

'Thank you for coming. I didn't know if you would.'

Through a mouthful of her delicious scone, Calfain replied, 'Always ready and willing to allow a Lady to have her dreams.'

Peltene shook her head, 'Ah! Er, no, actually it's not me who wishes a dream. No, that's not right. It is me, but I'm not the one...' She stopped talking and smiled self-consciously, 'I'm not talking sense here am I?'

'Um, no, not quite, My Lady.' Calfain sipped his tea, allowing her time to gather her thoughts into some semblance of order. She fidgeted with her hands and Calfain had the distinct impression she was actually nervous.

'Why don't you just tell me what you do want of me, My Lady,' he said, feeling magnanimous.

Lady Peltene looked closely at the man sitting opposite. He appeared to be about the same age as her. Possibly a few years older, it was hard to say. He was tall; at least six feet with a reasonably athletic looking body from what she could tell. His dark brown hair was a bit ragged, definitely in need of a haircut. It hung down to his shoulders but she thought it somehow suited him. He was sort of handsome, in a rugged way, but the things that drew her, were his eyes. He had kind, trusting eyes. And now, they stared gently back at her, waiting for her response to his suggestion.

'Do you really have the ability to give people their dreams? To put them into their heads as I've been told you can?' She asked in a plain forthright manner.

He answered her in the same way, 'Yes.'

Lady Peltene placed her elbows on the table and nibbled at her fingernails, unsure as to whether or not he was telling her the truth. Calfain had seen that look hundreds of times before; he had found the best way to convince people was to give them a little demonstration. He reached out and without asking, he took one of her hands in his.

Suddenly as if an unseen, un-speaking force had gripped her, her eyes closed without her permission and she was asleep, but only for a fraction of a second. Her eyes opened as soon as he withdrew his hand from hers. She was wide-awake again. She gasped.

'Oh my! Where did I just go? What did you do?' she asked breathlessly.

Calfain smiled at her. 'Tell me what you dreamt of, My Lady?'

A wistful look passed across the Lady's face, as she recalled her dream.

'I was, er, I mean, I saw myself in the garden, well, a garden…full of roses and honeysuckle and hundreds of other beautiful flowers.' She shook her head to clear her thoughts.

'Does that convince you?' he asked softly.

'How do you do that?' she demanded.

'It's a gift, My Lady.'

'That's not what I asked.'

'That's all I can tell you.'

'Have you always been able to do it?'

He nodded, 'For as long as I can remember.'

'It was so real,' she mussed,

'That's what I try to tell people, although I call them dreams, I really sell memories. I create experiences as if they had really happened. You'll remember it always.'

'Can you create any memories? Anything at all? She asked him earnestly.

He smiled again and nodded, 'I'm only limited by your own imagination.'

Lady Peltene sat up straight. Her face and her mood became instantly businesslike. 'Master Calfain, Are you averse to ahem… how shall I say…'

'Say it, as it is, My Lady. I always find it's the best way.'

'Very well,' she nodded, 'I will. Are you averse to earning a handsome reward for not exactly legitimate work?'

Calfain did not allow his face to alter. He gazed steadily back into her pale blue eyes. 'That depends on how *ill*-legitimate the work is.'

She looked at him earnestly, attempting to assess just how much she could trust him.

'My son has been taken from me. I want you to find him and bring him back.'

Now Calfain's face did betray his surprise. 'Erm, Lady Peltene,' he shook his head, 'this was not exactly what I had in mind when you asked me here. That's really not my line of work.'

Lady Peltene reached across the table and grabbed his hands in hers. The suddenness of it and the touch of her cool fingers shocked him slightly, 'Please, Master Calfain,' she searched his eyes, 'listen to what I have to say. Your talent may be my last and only chance.'

'I place dreams into people's minds, Lady - and - that's all I do.' He steadfastly stuck to his motto of volunteering for nothing.

14

Lady Peltene clung onto his hands, 'And that's exactly what I want of you,' she was beginning to sound a little desperate.

'I don't quite understand, Lady,' he replied, a confused look spread across his face.

Lady Peltene released her grip on his hands and leaned back slightly, he felt somehow sad that she had let go her hold on him.

'My husband, Lord Tennay, and I parted from each other almost four years ago,' she began and took a deep breath seeming to gather herself for a protracted explanation that she knew, would bring bad memories to the surface, 'As a concession, he allowed me the use of this cottage on the proviso that our son, Dennel, should live with him in the manor house. I could not refuse, it was the only way I could be near to my son, otherwise, I would have had to seek accommodation in the village.'

Calfain interrupted her, 'Why did you not seek custody of the boy through the courts, you're his mother after all. Surely they would have allowed it?'

'I did. I even pleaded my case with King Austis personally. He agreed with me, but my husband is very powerful. When the king ruled in my favour, my husband beat me so badly I was taken to my bed for a month. He said he would kill me if I attempted to take Dennel away from him, or sought the king's help again.'

Calfain's heart sank; this was not, defiantly not, what he had expected from this encounter. A quick dream planted into the mind of some wretched Lady of the manor, who was desperate for a little excitement or even a fantasy with a young virile stud, was what he had envisioned. Someone who had more wealth than they knew what to do with it. Charge them a fortune and be on his way. Job well done! Everybody satisfied - especially him.

15

'I'm sorry, Lady, I really don't see how I can help. Snatching children from their parents is not in my repertoire.'

'No, Master Calfain, I'm not asking you to snatch Dennel from his father, I will take that responsibility. Your job will be to make my husband dream that he never knew his son…or me.'

Calfain blinked rapidly, 'You mean…erase all his memories of the two of you?'

'Exactly! Can you do it? Can you perform that task?'

Professional pride spurted from Calfain's mouth even before his brain could stop it.

'Well, yes, of course I can,' then his brain suddenly caught up, 'but…'

'Will you do it for me?' she pleaded, again, reaching across the table once more, to clutch his hands in hers. Again, that shock as she touched him jolted through his body.

'I…I don't…'

'Name your price, Master Calfain,' she insisted.

For the first time he could ever remember, Calfain was at a loss to make an instant decision. Half of his mind said back away, refuse her pleas, the other half wanted to negotiate a price that could make him a wealthy man. His heart however was issuing different instructions. There was something about this woman that drew him to her. She had grit and determination, certainly. She was attractive, definitely. She also had a quality that portrayed vulnerability and that, he knew, would be his undoing.

Many years ago, he had fallen head over heels in love. He was badly smitten, as she was with him. But all too soon, it ended. He was crushed, she had meant the world to him, and he would have died for her if she had asked. Instead, she had chosen to take a lover.

Eventually after a time, Calfain discovered the truth and swore he would never allow a woman into his heart again.

Several years later, he found another and for

a time he convinced himself that this was his true love - the one that mattered. History, as it has a strange way of doing, repeated itself and once again, he found himself alone and with a broken heart. He vowed before all the gods, that there would never be a third time.

As he studied her face, Calfain calculated the odds of him succeeding at the task she was asking him to perform. Of his ability to erase a man's memory of a particular subject, he had no doubt. Of the events leading up to that and immediately afterwards, he was unsure. There was more to this than she was telling, he felt certain of that.

'Where is your husband now? In the manor house?' he asked.

She shook her head, 'No, he took Dennel to Tapp City in Paland almost two years ago now. He has business interests there.

Tapp City was, as far as Calfain was concerned, at the other side of the world. He pulled a face.

'Is that a problem?' she asked, concerned by his expression.

'Well,' he said cautiously, 'it adds to the price.'

'How much do you ask?'

No point in beating about the bush, Calfain thought. Everything is negotiable.

'A hundred thousand gold crowns.'

Lady Peltene let his hands slip from hers. She looked aghast at his demand.

Calfain watched her face closely. He had set his price purposefully high to allow her room to manoeuvre, that way they could reach an agreement that both of them would, hopefully be happy with. Now it was up to her.

'I'm sorry, Master Calfain,' she replied apologetically, 'I don't think we could ever reach an amicable price.'

It was now Calfain who was crestfallen, although he did not show it. He had not expected her to withdraw so easily from the negotiations, given that she appeared so adamant about wanting her son back with her.

On the one hand, he was willing to be cajoled a little. On the other, some nagging feeling told him that this whole thing was not quite what it seemed and that it may not be a bad thing if he walked away, even if he did so, empty handed.

'I'm sorry we couldn't reach an agreement, My Lady.'

She sighed heavily and looked away, 'I'll find another way, Master Calfain. It is not your concern.' She looked directly at him, he could plainly see the tears she was holding back from the disappointment, 'Thank you for your time, I'll see you out.'

She stood and began moving to the door. Calfain remained seated; one half of him was tugging at the other again. He shook his head and told himself it was the right thing to leave now. He stood and followed her to the door.

Outside, on the front step, he turned to her. As she stood on the step their eyes were at the same level, he looked into hers and he smiled weakly.

'I wish you success in your venture, Lady Peltene,' he said genuinely.

'Thank you.' She replied in a small voice and returned his smile weakly. Then, she took a step back and closed the door.

Calfain stared at the door for a second. Then he made up his mind. 'This is not your problem, Cal my boy and furthermore you'd wind up getting physically hurt, or worse.'

He strode back down the lane and did not turn his head once to look at the magnificent manor house as he passed it by.

Chapter Three.

By the time the dreamweaver had reached the village it was
much too late in the afternoon to attempt to draw a crowd in the
market place. Instead, he wandered around the village idly
seeking out possible potential customers who may wish a
private demonstration of his talents. None came forward. As he
stood looking absently at a fishmonger's stall, wondering where
it would be possible to catch such enormous catfish like the ones
on display, a hand gently touched his sleeve. He turned his
head, expecting to see his next customer. He was surprised to
see the servant girl who had sought him out the previous night.

'Hello young lady,' Calfain said with a broad smile.

The servant girl was clearly not used to being addressed by a
man in such a polite way; she blushed scarlet and lowered her
head slightly.

'Is something wrong?' Calfain asked the girl, sensing that
there was.

'Sir,' she looked up at him, 'I saw you here and just wondered
what you had said to the Lady Peltene to make her so
distraught.'

Calfain was shocked. He had assumed the Lady would be a
little upset, annoyed even, that he had asked such a high price
for his services, but distraught was something he had not
thought she would be.

'Young lady, I assure you I meant her no ill will. It was
simply business. A contract that failed to transpire.' For some
strange reason, Calfain felt compelled to explain his actions to
this girl.

'Yes sir, I'm sorry for troubling you,' she shrugged her shoulders.

'You really do have concerns for you mistress don't you?' he asked

The young girl smiled weakly, 'I've known the Lady all of my life sir, she has been like a mother to me. I just can't bear to see her hurt any more.' The girl's eyes filled with tears as she spoke. She wiped them savagely away with her hands and glanced at his face defiantly, 'I'm sorry to have troubled you, Master Calfain. Please forgive me.' She brushed passed him and ran along the narrow street disappearing around the next corner. Calfain stood, staring after her for several seconds.

Later that evening, he ate alone again at the corner table in the tavern. As he chewed his food, his thoughts were on the Lady Peltene. The woman disturbed him. It had been a long time since he had allowed any female to get under his skin. Yes, there had been a few passing acquaintances over the years that had followed his two major heartbreaks. All had been pleasurable interludes in his life. Some had occupied his attentions for weeks if not months, others had been more casual. But he rigidly stuck to his principle of not getting involved. The Lady Peltene was different. There was something about her. Her presence, her aura – her - Give it up, he told himself. She's a woman and women have a way of stealing your heart, making you feel like you are the only man in the world and then, when you had succumbed, they would reach into your chest grab your heart and rip it out at the roots, trampling it underfoot, laughing and leaving you for dead.

Calfain smiled ruefully to himself as he took another sip of ale. He made himself sound as if he hated women when in fact the opposite was the truth. He respected them, not only as women, but also as people, as fellow human beings. His trouble he told himself was that he just could not trust them any more. Trust no one, was his motto - especially the female of the species.

Calfain slept fitfully that night. Every time he knew sleep was about to seduce him, her face appeared before his eyes. She smiled. She cried. She touched his hands and he found himself involuntarily jumping in his bed as he imagined her.

He abruptly sat upright. This was ridiculous, he thought. The game was over. It had never actually begun. She had rejected his fees. As far as she was concerned, he was no longer required. She would find another to steal her son away from his father and that would be that. It had been a business transaction. Nothing more!

But the father would come looking to retrieve his son and heir. Without Calfain there to erase his memory, he would do the Lady harm. Perhaps even carry out his threat to kill her.

Calfain climbed out of his bed and began to pace the darkened room.

'So what?' he said aloud,

'So, her death would be on your conscience,' he answered himself.

'No it wouldn't. Because as from tomorrow, you're riding out of here and never looking back. She means nothing to you, Cal. And furthermore – most important of all - she's obviously not rich!'

He sat back down on his bed. Problem solved! He always found it helped to talk through these little problems with someone. Even if it was with himself. He lay down and pulled the sheets over his body. The last thing he mumbled aloud before he closed his eyes was,

21

'Always look forward, never back. That's my motto.'

The Lady Peltene was kneeling down, tugging with her bare hands at a large stone the size of a bull's head that stubbornly refused to move from its hole in the ground and she was growing tired with the effort. Suddenly, she sat back on her haunches and cursed. She had ripped a fingernail so badly it was bleeding profusely and it hurt. She stuck her finger into her mouth and sucked, attempting to stem the flow of blood and ease the pain at the same time. Extracting her battered finger, she looked more closely at it and bitterly cursed again.

'Any soldier in Yarland would be proud of you, Lady,' Calfain said from behind the kneeling woman.

She spun her head around on hearing his voice and looked up. He stood above her with the early morning sun on his back. Peltene shaded her eyes with her injured hand and squinted at his darkened form.

'Master Calfain!' she exclaimed. For some strange reason, her heart missed a beat. She ignored the feeling, putting it down to him simply surprising her. 'What brings you back here?' She had gathered herself now and there was a slight hardness in her voice.

Calfain sensed it and inwardly winced. This is a big mistake, he told himself. Tell her you're leaving today and just wanted to say goodbye.

'How much can you afford, My Lady?'

'I'm sorry?' she frowned under the hand that she still held to her forehead.

When she tells you she only has a thousand gold crowns, tell her it's absolutely not enough and walk away, he urged himself.

'How much can you afford to pay me to retrieve your son,' he repeated patiently.

22

She took a deep breath.' Alas, no where near the amount you were seeking, Master Calfain.'

'How much?' He persisted gently. He simply *had* to satisfy his curiosity before he left forever.

'Perhaps four hundred crowns, five at the very most.' She admitted weakly.

There you are! A paltry five hundred crowns for risking life and limb. I told you so! Now it was out in the open. The woman was officially a pauper. Say goodbye now, Cal. Say goodbye and walk away and live a happy and safe and long life.

'I suppose I could get by with that.' The words tumbled from his mouth and he instantly regretted not having cut his tongue from his head whilst shaving that morning.

The Lady of the manor blinked and gasped, as she suddenly understood the meaning of his words. She leapt from her kneeling position in one fluid movement and threw her arms around his shoulders hugging him tightly.

'Oh Master Calfain! You truly are a wonderful man.'

No you're not, Calfain! He told himself, you're stupid and you have a death wish that even the Grim Reaper would be proud of.

'I know,' he sighed softly into her ear, 'but don't go telling everyone. I have a reputation to protect.' He could feel the warmth of her body and its closeness. It disturbed him greatly.

The scones came out again and Calfain nibbled on one whilst Peltene made drinks of hot tea.

'I really do think it will be a simple matter, Master Calfain,' she said lightly as she poured the dark liquid into cups, 'we ride to Tapp City and...'

'We?' his head snapped up showering crumbs across the table. 'We as in you and me?'

'Why, yes, of course I'll be coming with you. I want to be sure my husband will never try to take Dennel from me again.'

Calfain sipped his tea. This was a bonus in itself, he mused. Tapp was a long, long way away. Things might not be so bad after all.

'Why don't you just have him, er, erased permanently?'

She laughed at the suggestion, 'Believe me, Master Calfain, I've thought about it long and hard. But I'm no murderer. Are you?'

'Er, no Ma'am.'

She smiled warmly at him over the rim of her cup. 'No, I know you're not.'

'You can never tell, Lady. Even the most unsuspecting of people can surprise you sometimes.'

'Oh, I know you're not. I trust my instincts.' She gazed intently into his eyes over her cup. He began to feel hot and disturbed again.

'Anyway,' he rapidly changed the subject, 'we need to lay out a plan and work out the logistics of this trip.'

She set her cup down on the table and became as businesslike as he, 'What's to plan, Master Calfain? We travel to Tapp. Find Dennel, you erase my husbands memory and we come home.'

'Well, first off, you have to stop calling me Master...'

'What do you prefer?' she said huskily.

'Calfain is fine. Cal even, but not Master. It makes me feel older than I am.'

'Cal. That's a nice name,' she whispered and repeated it several times.

'Please, My Lady, don't wear it out.'

'I'm Peltene, or Pel, whichever *you* prefer, Cal,' she lingered over his name delicately. She was teasing him now and having fun. It had been a long time since she had flirted with a man and she was not quite sure if she could remember quite how it was done.

24

'Secondly,' Calfain took a deep breath, 'we really have to prepare. Because that's my motto - be prepared!'

Calfain returned to the tavern and collected his things, paid his dues and took his horse from the stables. He rode back to Lady Peltene's cottage where she had already laid out linen for him in the cosy little guest bedroom. It would be easier they had agreed, if he were nearer to her.

That first evening they sat by a large log fire discussing plans and drinking a local wine Calfain had never heard of but, after a couple of sips, quickly decided that he could get used to it.

The dreamweaver sat in a comfortable chair. The Lady of the manor sat on the floor close to the fire, legs pulled under her chin.

'Have you always had your gift, Cal?' she asked, after exhausting their planning meeting.

He nodded, sipping the wine, 'I think so. It always seems to have been with me, although I really only discovered I had it when I was about fourteen or fifteen years old.'

'How did that happen?' she asked, leaning her head onto her knees and watching him intently.

'I had a friend called Hestone. He was my age but he had always been a sickly lad. Never seemed to want to or be able to do what the other boys of our age did, usual things, watch girls, steal apples, whatever. Then he began to get worse, so bad; he was confined almost permanently to his house. The doctors said he would be lucky to see his eighteenth birthday.'

'What was the matter with him?' Peltene asked, concerned.

Calfain shrugged, 'He had diseased blood they said. There was no cure.'

'How sad,' she said with feeling.

25

Calfain nodded his agreement and continued, 'I used to visit him and we'd sit and read or tell stories together. You know - pirates, or knights and dragon slayers. Maidens in distress, that sort of thing.'

She nodded and smiled.

'Well, one time, we got really involved in our little story. I was pretending to be a big bad knight and Hes was a good knight. I could see everything so clearly in my head it was as if I was really there, somehow, I accidentally touched Hes and he jumped back and sort of fell asleep for a few seconds. I know now that that's what happens, but I didn't then. I thought he'd fallen and knocked himself unconscious - or worse. Anyway, when he woke up, he told me he'd had a dream about us being knights. It was exactly as I had been imagining it.'

'And that's how you discovered your gift?'

'Well, I didn't quite understand it for what it was, until a few days later. I was standing outside my house watching the kings soldiers go by. A whole regiment of them. I was imagining how exciting it would be to be dressed like them and riding one of those war-horses. A boy next to me got a bit close, we bumped and he fell asleep, just dropped to the floor. When he woke up and saw me standing over him he said he'd had the strangest dream. He said he'd just seen me riding on one of those horses dressed as a soldier.'

'So, what did you do with your new found powers?'

'Well,' he grinned broadly, 'I'd like to say that I used it for the good of mankind, but the truth was, I went to the university in Yarlis and didn't really think too much about it.'

Peltene shifted her weight and drank the last of her wine. Calfain leaned forward to refill her glass.

'No, not for me, thank you. I really should be going to bed now.' She stood up and smoothed her dress, 'Feel free to finish the bottle though if you wish.'

26

With that, she bade him goodnight and wandered off to her bedroom leaving Calfain with his thoughts and a half-full bottle of wine.

Calfain filled his glass again and stretched out in the comfortable chair, his feet only inches away from the hot little fire. He drank and smiled to himself. 'I could get used to this,' he thought. Then, his thoughts returned to Yarlis University all those years ago.

The studies had been easy to him. So easy in fact, it had never seemed like work, more a game. He had spent most of his time daydreaming about an idle life of leisure with plenty of money to spend. But he quickly realised the only way he would ever achieve that was to work and earn it, marry into it, or steal it. Over the years, he had accomplished two out of the three.

Chapter Four.

The following morning, Peltene was up and about at first light. She busied herself with preparations for the journey ahead.

Calfain took a leisurely stroll around the gardens that surrounded the cottage in which she lived. Had anyone been observing him, they would have thought his interest in the plants and shrubbery quite normal. In actual fact, he wandered closer and closer to the ancient manor house that loomed up from the other side of the hedgerow.

It was as he had thought a magnificent structure obviously at least four hundred years old, probably more. As he sauntered closer his interest became more aroused by the architecture of the building. He stood for a while staring at the old ramparts and thought to himself that one day; he would like to own such a house. One day!

'Calfain!' It was the Lady calling him from some distance off. He reluctantly turned away and headed in the general direction of the Lady of the manor.

'Ah! There you are,' she said smiling as he approached her.

'Good morning, My Lady. I was just taking the air, admiring your gardens.'

She stood, waiting for him, dressed in black trousers and a black blouse topped off with a calf leather jerkin.

Her highlighted blonde hair caught the early morning sun and seemed to sparkle as if wafted slightly in the gentle breeze. Her pale blue eyes danced with the anticipation of the day ahead. She looked stunning, he thought.

'I'm ready whenever you are,' she said lightly.

He grinned at her, 'I'll get the horses.' And left her to collect together her small travelling bags.

The servant girl, Lissie, had hugged her mistress and wished her success, then; she turned to Calfain and asked him to bring her mistress back safely. He promised that he would and they had ridden down the lane without looking back.

They took the North road that would eventually lead to Yarlis City, but they were going to turn west and head along the border road that ran to the south of Peane and served as the demarcation line between Yarland and Dolomes.

Calfain and the Lady Peltene had ridden six miles when their first problem manifested itself.

Sitting by the side of the road was what seemed like an innocent bundle of rags. Calfain had spotted it from some distance off and, being a constant traveller, he was well aware that seemingly innocuous 'bundles' sometimes had a way of turning themselves into trouble. Usually of the worse kind!

Calfain manoeuvred his horse so that he and his mount were between his companion and the upcoming bundle.

Peltene had, as yet, not seen the mass of rags let alone considered Calfain's actions anything other than a simple change of scenery.

Suddenly and without warning the bundle of rags came to life, leaping into the air and gripping Calfain's left arm and tugging, threatening to dismount him and bring him crashing to the ground.

Calfain had witnessed this exact trick numerous times before and had taken the precaution of tightening his grip on the stirrups and pulling free from his belt, the nasty double-edged long bladed that he carried. He pointed it at his attacker's throat and said not a word.

The attacking bundle of rags saw the weapon and then felt a sharp prick on his neck. He immediately released his hold on Calfain's arm.

'I only wanted to borrow some money,' the attacker yelled in a manner that suggested firstly, Calfain should have known this and secondly, as if it were his right to solicit money in such a way.

Lady Peltene had become aware of the commotion only as the attacker spoke, the rest had happened too quickly.

She pulled her reins tight and backed up her horse to draw level with Calfain who was still mounted.

'What's happening?' she asked anxiously, now seeing the bundle of rags for the first time.

'We were just about to be robbed.' Calfain replied, staring threateningly at his assailant.

'I wasn't robbing yer!' the bundle of rags said indignantly, 'I just wanted a loan.'

Calfain almost smiled, 'Is it me?' he asked, turning to Peltene then returning his gaze to the bundle of rags, 'or don't manners like "Excuse me" exist anymore?'

'Yer wouldn't 'ave stopped if I'd said that,' the surly response was immediate and accusing.

'Who is he?' Peltene asked. A look of concern for the talking rag bundle clearly on her face.

'Just one of the local thieves,' Calfain replied casually.

'I'm not a thief!'

'I beg to differ.'

'I am not!'

'You are!'

If it had not been for Peltene's intervention, the two men would have argued the point long into the night.

'Boy's, boy's let's just calm down.'

She looked down from her horse at the man who was wrapped in rags. His hair was long and greasy and unkempt.

His face smeared with grime and she could smell him from where she sat.

'What is it you want, sir?' she asked politely.

'Our money for one thing,' Calfain snapped.

Lady Peltene glanced quickly at the dreamweaver,

'Cal, give him a chance to…'

'Give him half a chance and he'll slit our throats.'

'Calfain! Hush!'

'I'm not a murderer either!' the talking rags snapped.

'How much do you require?' she asked softly.

Calfain opened his mouth to speak but she cut him off with a hard glare, then she returned her gaze to the rags.

'How much?' she asked kindly.

The man shuffled. His indecisiveness was evident. He had not ever been asked this question before and he was struggling to find an answer. Eventually, he did.

'Two gold crowns!' he stammered expectantly.

'That was a bad move, My Lady,' Calfain said disgustedly.

Peltene ignored him and looked again at the rags. 'If I give you one gold crown will you promise me you'll have a bath, buy some new clothes and eat something?'

Calfain turned in his saddle to look at her, 'Peltene!' he uttered in exasperation, 'we both know that won't ever happen. Where have you been living all of your life?'

'There's always a good side to everyone, Calfain,' she replied with conviction.

Peltene rummaged in her purse and extracted a single gold crown. She held it out for the man to take. He moved quickly around the rear of Calfain's horse and reached up, gratitude now on his face.

Peltene snatched back momentarily, 'Now you promise me you will bathe and get fresh clothes won't you?'

'Yes ma'am, I promise.' He held out his hand waiting and hoping he had sounded convincing enough.

Peltene dropped the heavy coin into his hand. The man turned it between his fingers and then placed it between his teeth. Satisfied it was the genuine article he looked up, grinning, his blackened teeth looked like twigs in his mouth.

Calfain shook his head in despair. He had to do something, he thought; if he did not, then she would probably give away all her money to every thief, waif and stray between here and Peane City. He leaned over in his saddle and lightly touched her neck. In the second it took Peltene to feel the touch, she had fallen instantly asleep. Her head slumped slightly, but she remained upright.

Calfain quickly jumped from his saddle and caught the thief who was by now back on the roads' edge. Calfain had the knife out and in his hand again.

'Now, we both know you aren't going to spend that crown on silly extravagances like clothes and a bath are you?'

The man stared dumbly at the knife pointed at his mid-section, then at Calfain, then at the Lady on her horse.

'She's just taking a nap right now; so don't bother trying to attract her attention. Give me back the crown!'

'No!'

Calfain took a step nearer to the man and the stench made him wrinkle his nose,

'If you don't, I'll put up with your stink while I'm cutting you into little pieces.'

Suddenly the man broke down. He began to weep uncontrollably.

'I'm not falling for that one either,' Calfain snapped.

'I need to buy mushrooms,' he wailed, 'Just a few.'

Calfain let the knife drop marginally. Now he knew. 'Mushrooms, as in "Happy Mushrooms"?'

The man nodded glumly.

Calfain grinned wickedly, 'Give me the crown and I'll give you something a hundred times better than mushrooms, friend.'

The man reluctantly handed over the coin. Calfain secreted it in his belt, holding the knife in his left hand he touched the man on his temples and said. 'Those mushrooms will kill you, and this is far better for you.'

The man dropped to the ground and was instantly asleep. Calfain leaned over him and grabbing his collar, or what passed for one and dragged him behind a large thorn bush, well out of sight.

Next, he climbed back in his saddle and touched Lady Peltene on her neck again.

'Ooh!' she said swallowing hard, 'did I just nod off?' She gently rubbed her eyes

'Not at all, My Lady,' Calfain crooned, 'sometimes riding does make you feel as if you did, though.'

Peltene glanced around, 'Where's that poor beggar gone?'

Calfain's face was deadpan, 'He's shot off looking for a bath and a tailors shop.'

She turned to the dreamweaver and smiled. 'You see, Cal, if you treat people nicely and give them a little dignity, they'll respond.'

'Thank you, Peltene,' he replied humbly, 'in future; I'll remember to treat them as I find them.'

'Exactly,' she said smiling as she nudged her horse into life.

As they rode away, the would-be thief lay sprawled where Calfain had placed him. Three green and brown dragons entered his head and breathed fire on him. He screamed and shrieked with the effort to get away from their hot fire spewing mouths. The dragons changed colour slowly mixing blue with red and then purple. The one thing that remained constant was the searing heat from their breaths.

A white cloud rose up from somewhere, water evaporating perhaps and enveloped the mighty beasts. They disappeared from his view momentarily only to reappear as black and pink winged serpents. Still the fire issued forth and still the man screamed. Then, as suddenly as they appeared, they had gone. He was now floating on a cloud of yellow mist, looking down at the countryside many hundreds of feet below.

The thief suddenly decided he could fly like a bird. He rolled from his protective yellow cloud and soared into the heavens like an eagle riding the air currents.

Four days later, Calfain and the Lady Peltene came upon the river ferry that crossed the Boe Minor, The smaller of the two Boe Rivers that flowed into the Bay of Tansa.

Calfain dismounted from his horse and went to help Peltene from hers.

'If the ferry is late, we may have to camp under the stars tonight, Pel,' Calfain explained.

They had spent the previous nights in different inns that they had managed to reach before each nightfall. This night however, he worried, might prove less comfortable.

'That'll be nice,' Peltene remarked with a wide smile.

'You think?'

'Of course, why ever not?'

'Well, for one thing, it gets cold in the middle of the night. It's still only early summer, don't forget. And,' he lingered, 'we'll have to make our own breakfasts.'

'Cal, if I didn't know better, I'd say you were either getting soft or old.'

'Probably both,' he grunted looking longingly across the river, silently praying that the ferry would return soon.

As they stood watching out across the water, Calfain thought he heard a noise back along the road. He turned quickly, just in time to see a figure dive into the trees. For an instant, Calfain thought he recognised it then shook his head. No, impossible!

Then, there was a muted cry of pain, he turned his head again. Nothing!

'Did you say something, Cal?' Peltene inquired, taking her eyes from the river for the first time.

'Er…no, but I do need to er…'

'Do need to what?'

'You know…'

'No?'

'The call of nature, Peltene,' he said desperately.

She smiled, knowing full well what he was meaning,

'Oh…right…yes of course.' She smiled again at his anguished look.

Calfain marched away towards the trees. As he approached the spot where he was sure he had seen the figure, he entered them.

Hidden now from her view, he reached once more to his belt for the knife he carried.

There it was! A rustling in the undergrowth! He crouched slightly and tried to pinpoint the noise. Calfain crept forward and as he did, he came upon the back of the man in rags. He was watching Peltene through a break in the trees, his attention fully on her.

The dreamweaver crept silently forward until he was an arms length away. Then he coughed softly. The man in rags whirled around like a startled doe caught by a wolf. He instantly saw Calfain's knife.

'Don't stab me!' His voice had a tremble in it.

Calfain stood to his full height,

'And why shouldn't I? After all, you are getting to be a nuisance.'

'Because,' the man began but faltered, losing his voice slightly, 'because…I wanted to talk with yer.'

'And I with you, friend,' Calfain retorted quickly, 'this is definitely your last chance to stop following my companion and me...'

'I will! I will,' the man snapped, 'just give me whatever yer gave me the last time we met.'

Calfain cocked his head slightly, thrown by the man's desperate voice.

'You can have some pennies, but definitely not a gold crown,' Calfain began.

'No! No, I don't want yer crowns, I want that feeling again.'

'What feeling?' Calfain was confused now.

'That feeling in me 'ead. I don't know what yer did or 'ow yer did it, but I want it again...*please.*'

Then, the torch was lit in Calfain's head. He realised what the man was talking about.

'A dream? You want another dream?'

The man nodded eagerly, He did not care what it was called today or what it would be called tomorrow. All he wanted was the pleasure that it brought.

'Yes! Yes!' he said eagerly. 'If that's what it was, it's better than any mushrooms or plants I've ever 'ad.

Calfain sheathed his knife. 'Friend, if you don't get to grips with reality, those plants will kill you.'

'I'll never use 'em again, I swear. Just do what yer did...one more time.'

Calfain grinned at the man and shook his head. Reaching out, he touched the man on his temples and again, the man fell to the ground, instantly asleep and travelling to some strange corner of the universe where dragons are green and clouds are yellow.

Chapter Five.

They slept that night at an inn along the great western old road, having been fortunate enough to persuade the ferry master to turn one more time that day. The boatman seemed reluctant to do so until Peltene took control and turned on her charm, convincing him that the payment would be exceptionally good if he turned just once more.

Calfain had been forced to listen to this exchange and elected to stand particularly close to the boatman as he poled his flat-bottomed craft across the river. The dreamweaver asked many pertinent questions about the mysteries and workings of being a ferry boatman whilst secretly relieving him of the absurd amount of money that Peltene had paid him.

'Peltene,' Calfain began as they rode towards the nearest village to find lodgings, 'have you always been so casual with money?'

'I'm not casual with it,' she protested, 'I just think it's right to pay a fair price.'

'Yes, very commendable I agree, but you just gave that man ten times what the going rate is for crossing the river.'

'Nonsense,' she snorted, 'the poor man had to turn around and bring us all the way over here, didn't he?'

'Well, actually, we could have argued and got passage for free or at the least, a reduced rate.'

'No we couldn't.'

'Yes we could, Lady. He lives over this side, so he had to come back to get home.'

Peltene made no further comment and they rode on in silence.

After a mediocre breakfast they were on their way once again and heading west with the sun on their backs, it had the makings of a pleasant day's ride ahead.

'So, tell me a little more about your husband, Peltene,' Calfain casually asked as they trotted along the dry highway.

'What would you like to know?' she asked equally casually.

'Well, what sort of a man is he?'

'Horrid!' she spat the word out.

'Surely he wasn't always so bad. He must have had some good qualities that first attracted you to him.'

Suddenly Peltene smiled wistfully, 'Well, he was very handsome, but ours wasn't a marriage made from love and affection. We had been brought together by both of our parents. It was more a marriage to consolidate two great families.'

Calfain's ears pricked up. 'Which families are those then?' he tried to ask the question as innocently as possible.'

'My husband's family is the Tennay. Originally from Relpa and mine are the Mercels from Thone.'

Calfain's mind was sifting through all the great family names that he had ever read about or come across. He knew of the Tennay dynasty. They had originally owned most of the ore mines in and around Relpa town plus their own fleet of ships. They were indeed a highly respectable family and filthy rich.

As for Peltene's family, Calfain had not heard of them, so, he surmised, they were either not particularly well heeled or they kept their wealth very quiet indeed.

'I've heard of your husband's family,' he said, 'they have a lot of interests in Yarland.'

'Even more, when we married and all our combined assets came together.'

'Combined assets?' Calfain croaked. His mouth suddenly felt dry with anticipation.

Peltene nodded, 'Alas yes, it was part of the terms of marriage. As my father understood it, we would put the two estates and other assets together and share the administration and of course, the profits.'

'But...?'

Peltene turned her head away from him, sighing deeply remembering the bitterness and hostilities of long ago. She remained silent.

'Your husband and his family reneged on the contract.'

She nodded her confirmation.

They rode on in silence, each lost in their own thoughts. Peltene relived the dark early years of her marriage whilst Calfain practised his mental arithmetic, trying to calculate the combined wealth of hers and her husband's families.

Midday and they allowed the horses a brief rest. Between the road edge and ploughed field, a small brook babbled its way to some unknown destination of a larger stream or river. They hobbled the horses and sat on the lush green grass by the brook.

Peltene had brought apples and early pears and they sat and ate, sometimes squinting at the water as the sun bounced its dazzling rays in every direction.

'I didn't mean to pry earlier,' Calfain said after finishing the last of his fruit

'Don't worry about it, Cal; I get too emotional about it anyway.'

Suddenly she lifted her leg and pulled off her boot, then did the same with the other.

'Come on, let's freshen up our feet.' She stood up waiting for him to do likewise.

'You go ahead, I'm fine,' he said easily.

Peltene acted as though she had not heard him. She bent and grabbed at his boot, quickly and deftly tugged it free of his foot.

'Peltene!' he said sternly.

'Oh come on, Cal. don't be a grump.'

'I'm not a grump. I just don't want to get my feet wet...and cold.'

Peltene bent again and snatched his other boot. Then, holding both, she tripped to the brook and took a tentative step into it.

She drew a deep breath at the sudden shock of the cold water.

'Told you it'd be cold,' Calfain said smugly.

'Well it isn't, Master Know-it-all, it's just right.'

'Where are you taking my boots?' he asked as she waded halfway across the little stream.

'You *will* dip your toes or my name isn't Peltene.'

Then she tossed them lightly to the far bank and turned back to him, grinning like a wicked child.

'Your name will be of no consequence if you don't fetch my boots back,' Calfain growled half-heartedly.

'When you're big enough and old enough to threaten ...come back and we'll talk,' she laughed

Calfain shook his head in mock annoyance. He pushed himself up and walked on his knees, the three or four feet to the edge of the brook, then, reaching in he scooped a handful of water and threw it towards her.

Peltene squealed and tried desperately to avoid the ice cool liquid. He scooped up water again and again until he was satisfied she was well and truly soaking. Peltene had tried her best to reciprocate with her feet but found it difficult because of the pebbles and stones on the bed of the stream.

Peltene gave in and reclaimed his boots from the far bank. She lay on the grass allowing her clothes to dry in the noonday sun.

'You know,' she said almost to herself, 'I haven't done anything as silly as that since my son was little and we'd play in the trout stream behind the manor house.'

Calfain stretched out and propped himself up on one elbow, 'How old is the boy now?'

'Twelve,' she replied, 'Thirteen in three month's time.'

'Well, when we get him back, you'll have all the time in the world to go splashing in the water with him.'

40

She rolled onto her side and propped herself in the same manner as he,

'I made it all sound so easy, back at my cottage.' She bit on her bottom lip nervously, 'Will it be easy, Cal? Can we do it…get him back?'

Calfain looked into her blue eyes, 'Is there something you've not told me, Peltene?' sensing that there was.

Peltene chewed on her lip again, gazing anywhere but at him.

'Peltene?' he said her name slowly.

Peltene looked at him for a long moment, indecision written across her face,

'He's…not actually in Tapp City,' she reluctantly admitted, then breathlessly she added, 'but he's close. Not very far at all - really.'

'Where is he?' Calfain asked darkly.

'Only a short distance - honestly. No more than a day - two at the most.'

'Where, Peltene?'

Peltene glanced down at the grass, 'The Island of Cipeus,' she whispered so softly he hardly heard her.

Calfain looked at her blankly, 'Where's that then?'

Clearly the name of the island held no significance for him. Peltene looked up, searching his face, trying to determine the extent of his ignorance.

'It's in the Great Tamlay Gulf,' she answered cautiously, expecting him at any second to recall with horror the name of Cipeus. His expression remained blank. She felt a rush of relief, but soon realised that the awful truth would eventually come out. If she could manage to suppress it at least until they reached Tapp City, then she could perhaps convince him to continue with their quest to rescue her son.

They rode for most of the afternoon discussing the changing scenery of lower Yarland. Calfain told her of some of his journeys around the country and the sights he had seen.

'Do you make a good living from giving people dreams?'

He smiled, 'It pays the rent I suppose and it's better than working for a living.'

Peltene laughed lightly. She felt completely at ease with this man. He was companionable, intelligent and charming, plus, he was reasonably handsome in a rugged sort of way. Underneath all of that however, she sensed he would be cunning, ruthless even. Someone who would do whatever he had to do, in order to survive, but her instincts told her he was a good man, unlike her husband who had become a force of pure evil. Peltene hoped most of all that she was not asking this man to give his life for her.

'Hello!'

Calfain's voice drifted into her thoughts, she visibly jumped.

'Oh! I'm sorry,' she apologised sheepishly, 'I was miles away for a minute.'

'Is my conversation so boring?' Calfain asked indignantly.

She laughed again, 'No, silly, of course not.'

Calfain continued his offended manner, 'Nobody else ever listens to me either, I don't know why I bother, I...'

'Oh hush!' she cut in, 'you know I hang on your every word.'

Calfain did not reply, his attention was drawn to the medium sized town that had come into his view as they rounded a small hill.

'Baseroyl!' he said, after consulting his mental map of Yarland. 'Now tonight, My Lady, we'll dine in the finest eating house we can find and, rent the best rooms this place has to offer.'

Peltene frowned as she stole a glance at him,

'Who's paying?' she asked, remembering his words about her lack of caution with money.

'My treat,' he grinned.

He had remembered something also. He still carried the gold crown she had given the thief and also the ferryman's exorbitant payment.

Baseroyl Town, population three thousand, was a bustling border town that had miraculously escaped the ravages of the evil Lord Grith and his invading forces from Thandis almost three years ago.

For hundreds of years, the townsfolk had existed in a climate of live and let live with the Dolomians two miles away. It had occasionally suffered raiding parties but now, after the new relationship Queen Aramella had forged with King Benenayas, the town was enjoying a boom in its trading economy. It was rapidly becoming a major gateway for trade.

Calfain had been here several times on his travels across the country and he knew the best - and the worst places Baseroyl had to offer. He gave the more salubrious end of town a wide berth.

They rode up to a large tavern, which boasted sixty bedrooms, all with fresh linen and water and hot meals served throughout the day.

Calfain ordered two rooms and stabling for their horses. Peltene stood close to him all the while. A young boy took their saddlebags to their respective rooms and they agreed to meet downstairs within one hour.

Calfain had bathed, shaved and changed and sat patiently waiting for her at a table in a darkened corner that he customarily preferred.

He drank from a tankard of cider and watched the crowded tavern, attempting to ascertain just what the revenue from owning a place like this would bring.

'Excuse me, is this seat taken?' Peltene's soft voice cut through his thoughts and brought him back to reality.

He glanced at her and was immediately struck by her beauty. Her hair was tied up and scraped tight. She wore a long, elegant dark blue dress of some satin like material cut low at the neck. It fitted her perfectly, accentuating her curves magnificently. Around her throat was a pendant of the most exquisitely hand-beaten gold Calfain could ever remember seeing. He jumped from his seat.

'It would be an honour if you would grace this table with your presence, My Lady.' Calfain said formally, but grinned broadly.

Lady Peltene held out her hand for him to take whilst he ushered her into the seat.

'This is all rather nice,' she remarked, glancing around the room at the other patrons as she settled into her seat.

'Would you like a drink, My Lady?'

'Ooh! I think a glass of wine would be appreciated.'

Calfain scuttled off to the bar and returned with a large glass of fine red wine, which he placed in front of her with great ceremony.

'You do know how to treat a girl, don't you?' she laughed.

'Only the beautiful ones, Lady.' He smiled into her eyes.

They toasted the future and sat drinking and watching the others in the tavern as they came and went.

'I can't remember the last time I did this sort of thing, Cal. I'd forgotten just how much fun it is.'

They had another drink and then Calfain suggested they moved from the tavern to eat. Although the place boasted a reasonable cuisine, the dreamweaver advised her that it was not what he had in mind.

Further along the street was an eating house, which specialised in almost every kind of fresh fish imaginable. Calfain had salmon; Peltene ate some exotic flatfish from Dolomes, the name of which, neither of them could pronounce.

They drank and dined for almost two hours, each immersed in the others company and enjoying every moment of it.

'Night-cap?' Calfain asked as they returned to the tavern, which was by now almost deserted, save for a group of men sitting and gambling in a secluded corner.

'No, thank you, Cal. I've had quite enough for one night. I don't think I could take any more. It was wonderful though and I really have enjoyed myself.' She leaned forward and lightly kissed him on his cheek.

'You're sure?' he asked anxiously.

Peltene grinned flashing those perfect teeth and her eyes twinkled mischievously, 'If I didn't know better, I'd swear you were trying to get me drunk for some reason.'

'I am,' he grinned back at her.

'Well, it won't work, Master Calfain,' she patted his arm affectionately, 'I can drold my hink with the best of them.'

They both laughed. 'Bright and early, My Lady or I leave without you.'

Peltene kissed his cheek lightly again and said goodnight. As she turned to climb the flight of stairs to her room, Calfain glanced towards the group still sitting playing cards. He had already calculated what the cost of two rooms in the tavern would be, plus the evening's meal and decided there was no sound reason why he should not give those fine fellows the chance to help him pay for it all.

'Good evening gentlemen,' he said pleasantly, 'Am I too late to have the privilege of taking some money from your good selves?'

With a few wry smiles, he was invited to join the little party.

Chapter Six.

By the sixth day Calfain and Peltene reached the fork in the highway that led either to Belos or on towards Paland and Tapp City.

Calfain had said they were getting behind and that they should speed things up a little, so they had ridden hard, speaking only when they stopped to rest the horses.

Belos, although not on their route, was about as far West as Calfain had ever travelled. His mental map had now been exhausted and he began to rely on instinct.

'It looks as though we camp under the stars tonight, Pel,' he said reluctantly.

'That'll be nice,' she replied, 'I haven't done that for years.'

He looked at her with a pained expression. 'And just where did you camp out?'

'In the garden of course. Where else?'

Calfain took a deep controlled breath,

'My Lady, we're right smack in the middle of nowhere, here. Probably, miles away from civilisation and the ground comes alive at night with all sorts of unpleasant things that crawl and bite. Not to mention bigger things on four legs that like to eat meat.'

'Then do not fear, Master Calfain,' she smiled reassuringly, 'I will protect you.'

They found a quiet spot well away from the road and shaded by a large oak tree. Calfain chose the place because of its natural advantage on a small raised piece of ground. He could scan the surrounding countryside easily and without obstruction apart from the tree.

Whilst Calfain busied himself lighting a fire, Peltene set about slicing up the dried meats that she had brought. That, along with a few vegetables and other things she extracted from her saddlebags gave them a small banquet.

They talked for awhile until it grew dark. Calfain laid out the bedrolls, one on each side of the fire and they climbed into them.

'The stars are very pretty tonight,' Peltene whispered presently.

'Some say they are the pin cushion of the Goddess Serrephay.' Calfain whispered back.

'I think they're really chinks of light shining through from another world.'

'Let's hope it's a better place than this.'

'Oh, it's not so bad, especially since the Nayals defeated Grith and Queen Aramella has begun to get the country back together again.'

'She has a mighty uphill task, Pel. Others before her have tried and failed.'

'Perhaps…but she has a secret weapon none of the others ever had.'

'Oh! Really…what?'

'She's a woman.'

'Good Night, Pel.'

Peltene lay quietly, watching the stars twinkle. Despite the circumstances she now found herself in, having to travel across a continent to reclaim her son, she decided that she had not been as contented as this for years. Riding free as the wind, with a man she found herself liking more and more. Dressing up and going out to eat with that man and engaging in delightful and sometimes witty conversation with him. And now sleeping under the stars with him. It all combined to help her shrug off her past life and look forward to pastures new and perhaps, for once, a little kindness and love in her life.

'Cal?' she whispered.

'Hmm?'

'You were right…it is getting a little cold.'

Through the darkness, she heard a rustling and then she felt the weight of a blanket being laid over her own.

'I didn't mean you to…'

'Don't worry; I'll use the horse blanket.' He replied

Peltene could just see his outline kneeling above her in the darkness. Suddenly, without really giving herself time to think, she folded down one corner of the blankets.

'We'd be warmer together,' she whispered.

Their lips met. Tentatively at first, exploring the touch of each other, feeling the softness, both nervous of the new sensations, then each gradually growing bolder, testing, teasing and tasting one another for the first time.

Calfain reached out and gently put his hand on her face, stroking it, caressing her soft skin. She responded, eagerly wanting more of his lips to kiss and folding her own arms around his neck as if desperate not to lose him.

Without warning, Calfain broke away from her lips.

'What is it?' she whispered.

He moved his head away from her, upward in an attempt to locate the sound he had heard.

'I don't know yet,' he replied in a low voice, his senses still tuned to the world outside the confines of the warm blankets.

'It's the wind, that's all,' she said, grasping his neck and pulling him closer to her mouth once more.

She kissed him passionately but he did not respond equally. Instead his mind was elsewhere.

'Cal…I want…'

Snap! The twig broke clean and loud. Calfain disentangled himself from her clinging arms and was out of the blankets and standing in a split second, the knife he carried was in his hand ready and threatening. He crouched, turning slowly, scanning the surroundings as best he could in the weak starlight. Peltene held her breath; she remained motionless, watching him as he slowly turned full circle.

One of the horses shuffled and moved as if it had been disturbed. Calfain leapt towards the animal and the dark outline of a figure came into his line of sight.

'I 'ave no weapons! I 'ave no weapons!' a voice from the darkness shouted out.

'Stand away from the horses!' Calfain demanded menacingly.

Calfain became aware of Peltene behind him, far enough so as not to restrict his movements, but near enough to hear her breathing.

The figure moved cautiously away from the animals. Calfain heard Peltene gasp,

'It's him!'

Calfain recognised him at exactly the same time. It was the mushroom addict they had met a few days ago. The dreamweaver relaxed slightly.

'Are you following us again?' he snapped angrily.

'Again?' Peltene asked, shocked by Calfain's outburst.

'He was in the bushes when we crossed the river.'

'I…I need…I really need some more of what yer do. Just one more time…*Please!*'

'No!' Calfain snapped, 'what you need is help that I can't give you, friend. Go seek your dreams elsewhere.'

'What is he talking about, Cal?' Peltene asked, not understanding anything of what had just transpired.

Calfain glanced at her. 'Our friend here is addicted to mushrooms and plants. The kind that makes your head go funny. That's what he wanted money for…to buy more, not clothes and food.'

50

'Please Mistress,' the man pleaded, 'tell 'im to give me one more of what 'e does.'

Peltene looked anxiously at the dreamweaver, 'What did you give him?' she asked, eyes wide with amazement.

'I put a dream into his head. One that would be ten times better than anything his mushrooms could give him, but at least mine won't kill him.' He continued to stare hard at the man in rags.

'When did you last eat, sir?' Peltene asked the man.

He shrugged noncommittally.

'*Pel!*' Calfain burst out.

'Oh hush! Can't you see the poor man's hungry,' she turned to the man, 'come and sit by the fire. Cal will fetch more wood and I'll make something to eat. Come please…'

'This is ridiculous,' Calfain protested, 'He'll slit your throat as soon as look at you.'

'No I won't - I'm no murderer.'

Peltene put her hand on Calfain's shoulder, 'Cal…please…for me.'

The dreamweaver grunted disgustedly and made a move to go and find what wood he could in the darkness. As he drew alongside the man in rags, he stopped and whispered,

'One, just one move that I don't like and you're a dead man.'

The man glanced hesitantly into the dreamweaver's eyes,

'I believe yer,' he replied seriously.

'So, what can we call you?' Peltene asked as the man accepted a hurriedly put together sandwich of dried meat and honey.

'Twill, Mistress. That's me name.' He replied through a mouthful of food.

'Well, Master Twill, welcome to our little family.' She greeted him with a warm smile.

'Thank yer kindly, Mistress, I does appreciate it.'

He glanced around furtively trying to locate Calfain. When he could not see him, he turned back to Peltene and asked quietly,

'Do ya think yer 'usband will fix me up again?'

'Fix you up?' she asked innocently.

'Y'know, wi one of them things 'e does?'

Er,' she stammered, 'I'm not altogether sure what he did for you, Master Twill.' Then, as an afterthought, she added, 'Oh! And, he's not my husband. He's just a friend.'

'I understands.' Twill said with a wink, 'whatever. But can ya convince 'im to do it to me again…just one last time… I promise.'

Peltene ignored the implied wink and replied, 'I'll have a word with him. But I can't promise. Calfain is his own master.'

'*Calfain?*' Twill blurted out the name so quickly; bread tumbled from his mouth, '*Calfain the Dreamweaver?*'

Twill's outburst had taken Peltene by surprise, she blinked rapidly and looked around for Calfain, He was nowhere to be seen, but she knew he would not be too far away.

'Yes, that's what some call him. How have you heard of him?'

'Oh, 'e's been around for awhile, travels all over Yarland performing 'is tricks.'

'Oh no, I don't think they're tricks, Master Twill, I think he really can give you whatever dream you want and apparently, you've seen them first hand.'

Twill stopped chewing and thought about Peltene's words. She was right, up until a few days ago, Twill had indeed thought, like many people, that the dreamweaver was just another clever performer, now of course, he knew differently.

'I once saw 'im in Bushe,' Twill said distantly, remembering the time in his mind, ''e 'ad short hair then an' didn't look as scruffy. That's why I didn't recognise 'im. Folks there chased 'im out of town. They said 'e was a charlatan or something,' he

52

screwed up his face trying to remember if he had the correct description.

'Well, charlatan or not, I believe in him.' Peltene said, rising to the dreamweaver's defence.

At that point, Calfain returned with his arms full of wood for the fire. He placed a few branches into the dying fire and gently blew on the smouldering ashes until the new wood caught hold. Then he sat back and gratefully accepted a drink of tea, which Peltene offered him.

'Cal, this is, Twill,' Peltene said in an effort to cut through the hostility she could plainly feel emanating from her companion.

Calfain glanced at the man and merely grunted.

'I'm 'onoured, sir,' Twill held out his crumb covered hand, glanced at it, then wiped it on his rag-like clothes and offered it again, 'I've seen yer work.'

'Oh! Where?' Calfain asked gruffly, ignoring the offered hand.

Peltene nudged him in his ribs, but he still refused to shake hands.

'Bushe, maybe six or seven years ago, and what ya gave me personally t'other day.'

Calfain grunted again. Peltene nudged him again.

'Where are ya 'eaded?' Twill asked innocently, attempting to soften the dreamweaver's attitude a little.'

'Dol,' Calfain said hurriedly before Peltene could give the true answer.

'Dol? Dol City? Ya could 'ave reached Dol by a more direct route than this.' Twill replied knowledgeably.

'We like to travel,' Calfain said.

Twill suddenly grinned, placing another lump of bread into his mouth; he spoke as he chewed. 'Unless of course, yer trying to give somebody the slip,'

Calfain's head snapped around quickly and he glared at the man.

'No! No! I don't want to know yer business,' he said hastily, seeing the dreamweaver's expression, 'I was just meaning, if yerself an' 'er, the Lady 'ere is, er, well…ya know…wanting to be alone like…'

We're not "wanting to be alone like" at all, we have business there. All right?'

'Cal…' Peltene tugged on his shirtsleeve.

Calfain turned to her and gave her a look that said keep quiet. She withdrew her hand. He returned his gaze to Twill.

'Now then, Master…Twill is it? If I fix you up tonight will you please stop following us? Because if I see you again, I'm afraid your next dream will be your last. Understand?'

Twill nodded eagerly. Right now, he would accept any conditions that were placed upon him. Not that he intended to honour them. The dreamweaver's gift was just far too good to let go of.

The rag-covered traveller finished the last of his drink and just as he placed his pot down on the ground, Calfain reached out and touched his shoulder. Twill fell instantly asleep where he sat. His head slumped forward slightly and he began to snore.

'That was a little unkind,' Peltene remarked.

'It's the best thing that could happen to him right now, Pel and anyway, it's what he wanted.'

'Yes, I know, but…'

'Let him sleep. I'll fix him in the morning so that he sleeps for a few days. That way, he should lose our trail.'

Peltene sighed, 'He wasn't that bad really, Cal.'

'Believe me, Peltene; you don't want to get mixed up with his type. If he goes without those funny fungi for more than a day, he'll do anything to get hold of some - including killing the both of us. Trust me on this one.'

She sighed again, 'Well, I suppose you know best.'

'Never ever trust anyone who sticks plants up his nose. That's my motto.' He wagged a knowing finger at her.

'Will he be all right like that?' she nodded at Twill's upright form.

'I'll stand a bit of guard duty. He may have others with him.'

Peltene got up and went to her blankets. As she passed the dreamweaver, she bent and kissed his cheek softly. Then she was gone.

When Peltene awoke she did so hearing grunts and other noises associated with heavy work. She opened one eye and peered out over the top of her blankets. Calfain was busy hoisting the dead weight of Twill into the oak tree near to them. Peltene watched fascinated as the dreamweaver struggled with the still sleeping man.

Satisfied that he had the addict secure on a wide branch, Calfain tied a leather thong around the man's leg as a further precaution to stop him falling and hurting himself. He climbed down from the branches sweating and breathing hard.

Seeing that she was awake, Calfain went straight to the still burning fire and poured her a cup of early morning tea and took it over to her. As he squatted on his haunches he offered the steaming cup.

'Will he be all right up there?' she asked, concerned.

'Good Morning, My Lady. Oh yes. He'll stay absolutely rigid I think, but I tied him in just in case.'

'Good Morning,' she replied smiling and taking the offered cup of tea, she sipped at it.

'We should be going in…say a half hour.'

'More than enough time,' she smiled.

'I've never known a woman yet who has enough time with a half hour,' he said half jokingly.

'And just how many *have* you known?' Peltene asked him, watching him closely. She was not joking.

Calfain gazed at her steadily for a few seconds, then smiled, 'Enough to know half an hour is a time limit that women just don't understand the meaning of.'

Determined to prove him wrong, Peltene was up, packed and ready well within the constraint that he had imposed upon her.

'I'm impressed, My Lady,' he said truthfully.

Peltene narrowed her eyes and thrust out her chin in a superior fashion saying not a word as she climbed into her saddle.

Chapter Seven

They rode steadily west, passing through a few villages and even smaller hamlets. The terrain began to slowly give way to more open grassland as they went further away from the more populated eastern side of Yarland.

'How many more days do you think?' Peltene asked, really only trying to make conversation more than anything else.

'Perhaps another four, maybe five. This is unknown territory to me, Pel.' He admitted.

As the sun began to wane, Calfain decided that they should begin to look for a place to camp for the night. As he searched the open plains for somewhere practical, his attention was drawn to a thin plume of smoke rising in the distance.

'Perhaps we can get lodgings there,' he said hopefully pointing towards the smoke column.

'It'll make my day if I can get a bath,' Peltene added.

They trotted their horses until the group of buildings came into view. It was a cluster of some twelve houses and farm buildings. Obviously, thought Calfain a large prosperous farmstead.

'Good evening to you sir,' Calfain greeted the man who came to the door as they rode up to the biggest house in the group. 'My Lady and I wondered, can you provide lodgings for the night?'

The short round man studied them closely. Visitors out here were few and far between and so, naturally wary of these two riders.

Peltene saw the look on his face and attempted to allay his fears.

'We can pay whatever the rate you think suitable, sir.' She flashed him a smile that would melt even the hardest of hearts.

The man gave a little, he smiled back at her. 'We have a room we can let you have. It's not much; we don't get many people out here.'

'You're very kind, sir, thank you.' She smiled again.

'Will you be wanting food? If you are then you'll have to eat with my family and me. It's nothing much, just plain and simple cooking.'

The man instructed Calfain as to where he could stable the horses, and then he took Peltene inside. The man's wife was a jovial little woman of about fifty years. She saw the travel dust on Peltene's clothes and immediately set about boiling water for a bath.

'It's no trouble honestly dear,' she fussed, 'we don't often see folks out here so any new face is a chance to catch up on gossip and you look like you could do with a nice hot tub.'

Peltene thanked her gratefully and readied herself for the pleasure to come.

The simple meal that the farmer had promised turned out to be a veritable feast of succulent roast meats and vegetables, all grown on the farm. Calfain remarked that if this was simple fare, then he had never eaten its better.

The farmer and his wife had three children, all in their teen years and all helping on the farm.

The meal was a noisy, happy affair with everyone chattering to everyone else, all at the same time. The farmers wife listened avidly to Peltene as she told her of the latest news from Yarlis, The only daughter, a girl of no more than seventeen, asked about the fashions and what the boys were like and how they treat the young ladies.

Peltene had to confess, it had been at least four years since she had been in Yarlis, but she imagined there was little change in the clothes being worn there and especially no change in the way the boys behaved.

The farmer picked up on the talk of the capital city and turned to Calfain,

'We heard about the great fire they had there. Have you been there since?'

Calfain nodded sombrely, 'Yes, it was a mess. It destroyed more than a quarter of the city, mostly the poor end of town. All the buildings were packed together so tightly they just burned like one huge bonfire.'

The others around the table fell silent as the dreamweaver spoke of the conflagration.

'Is it true that a wicked woman caused it all?' one of the younger sons asked.

Calfain smiled at the boy. 'Well, that's what they say. She was the mother of the woman who was trying to steal the queen's throne. It's said she set fire to houses in a bid to escape the city.

'It is true that the queen is a Nayal too?' the boy persisted.

'Yes, she was born in the Atan Mountains just like the others and yes, she can use a sword. Some say that she personally fought and killed six soldiers while defending the palace, during the invasion.'

'I don't know if I believe all this stuff about knights with green glowing swords,' the farmer interjected gruffly, 'it's all children's stories to me.'

'Well, up until King Austis discovered they were alive and well, everyone else thought that too.' Peltene answered him, 'But the Nayals have a long history and now, thankfully, they're back. Yarland can only be a better place for having them around.'

Getting back to the subject of Yarlis, the farmer turned back to Calfain, 'Is the city going to be rebuilt?'

'I believe work has already started,' Calfain answered, 'Queen Aramella has a woman in charge of getting it all rebuilt, but they say this time everything - every building is going to be made from stone and with enough distance between them so no fires can ever spread.'

'A woman? A woman in charge of building?' the farmer gasped in alarm.

'And what's wrong with that, husband?' his wife snapped.

'Yes, father, what's wrong?' Belda, his daughter echoed.

Peltene smiled at the poor man. 'I think it's a wonderful idea. At least we know things will be done properly.'

The farmer snorted and looked morosely at Calfain for support.

'Sorry, my friend,' Calfain smiled weakly, 'we're outnumbered. At times like these, I find it's best just to say nothing.'

The conversation went on for a while and then as the women gathered up the dishes, the two men continued to talk quietly. The farmer asked casually where Calfain and Peltene were travelling. Calfain told him truthfully, Tapp City on business for the Lady.

'Are you two not, er...' the farmer wagged his head.

'Er, no. No actually we're just friends here on business together.'

'Ah!' the man exclaimed as if he should have known and had now made some terrible assumption.

'I'll have a word with the wife and tell her to make up another bed.'

Calfain nodded his gratitude. Although, he thought, it would have been nice...

'I have a worker here who's from Tapp.' He said abruptly changing the subject. 'I'll introduce you in the morning. Nice enough fellow, but he talks funny.'

'Oh! In what way?' Calfain asked easily.

'Full of thee's and thou's. Really old fashioned way of speaking - like as if he used to be a monk, or something.' The farmer laughed at his own attempt at humour.

The farmer and his family played host to their guests on the next morning. They ate a large breakfast of ham and eggs lashed with honey and piles of toasted bread. Afterwards, the farmer took Calfain to meet with the hired hand that worked for the farmer.

'This is Venden,' the farmer introduced the dreamweaver to a tall, well-muscled man of about thirty years. He had a lopsided, yet friendly face that glowed healthily from toiling out in the open in all weathers and his sandy coloured hair fell about in every direction. His big hands were gnarled and hard with calluses.

''Tis a pleasure, Master Calfain,' Venden grinned warmly at the dreamweaver as they shook hands.

Calfain grinned back, 'I understand you hail from Tapp, Venden. How long since you were last there?'

The muscled farm worker screwed up his face in concentration, 'Twas a whole year five months ago since mine own self last visited there, sir.'

Calfain nodded, 'Tell me, have you ever heard of an island called, Cipeus. It's just off...'

'Mine own self dost know where Cipeus lay, Master Calfain,' Venden said darkly, his friendly mood changing instantly.

Calfain caught the change and looked closely at the man. Venden was now agitated and looked uncomfortable. His eyes darted around, seeking a reason for no longer being here with Calfain.

'If it pleases, Master Calfain, I hath much work to perform this day.' He nodded at his employer and walked briskly away.

61

The farmer pulled a face, 'I don't understand, he's usually the most affable of men.'

Calfain shrugged, 'It must just be me. I sometimes have that effect on people. Give me a minute alone with him and I'll apologise.'

The farmer shrugged again and turned towards the house.

Calfain strode after Venden, who had headed off in the direction of the cowshed. He caught up with him just as the man picked up a large wooden bucket filled to overflowing with a foul smelling brown slime. Calfain wisely stood a few paces away.

'Venden, I'm sorry if I said something to upset you…'

'Taketh mine advice, sir, dost naught travel to that island, for harm wilst befall ye for certain.'

'Harm?' Calfain asked warily.

Venden wearily placed the bucked down and stood upright His face bore a stern, troubled look.

'That island be home to the most ignoble of all holy men. The Cipean monks themselves.'

Calfain shook his head blankly, 'Never heard of them, Venden. Are they not nice people?' he asked trying to set a tone of levity.

Venden took a step nearer to the dreamweaver. He set his jaw and gazed into Calfain's eyes with such intensity that the dreamweaver had a hard time retaining eye contact.

'If thou art determined to travel there, then mine heart wilst pray long and hard for thee.' His voice was no more than a whisper.

'Unfortunately, Venden, I have no choice, my companion seeks to retrieve her son who was taken there by his father.' For some reason, Calfain found himself being totally honest with this man.

'A woman? A female wouldst seek to set foot upon the island?' Venden asked, alarmed at the revelation

'Well, yes, the Lady Peltene with whom I travel.'

Venden shook his head forcefully and stared at the ground. He suddenly looked up.

'Nay, naught female wouldst ever be allowed presence on that island. She will surely die if she attempted such.'

Concern now grew inside Calfain. This man appeared to know a lot more about Cipeus than he was saying. And the little that he had said did not rest easy with the dreamweaver.

'You seem to know a lot about the place. Have you ever been there, Venden?'

The weatherworn man stiffened, 'Aye, Master Calfain, I surely hath,' he replied with a distant look in his eyes, 'And it is naught a place mine own self wouldst recommend to thee.'

'Will you tell me about it? And these monks you speak of?'

Venden studied Calfain's face for a moment as if he was weighing the dreamweaver's sincerity. He took a long deep breath, then said,

'The Isle of Cipeus hath been under the control of the monks since the time of Thentuedal the Convert, almost these two thousand years past. The Convert was banished to the barren isle with neither water nor bread, by the ancient elders of Paland. His crime was the attempted conversion of the populace from the old faiths to that of his own calling. His followers were detained and they too were placed on the isle. The passage of four score years saw those outcasts build with their bare hands a private place of worship. Their monastery.'

Calfain stood and listened in silence to the almost incantation like tones of Venden.

'Who were they worshipping? The Devil?'

Venden fixed him with a steady gaze, 'Nay, Master Calfain, naught the Devil, but one of his many cousins. Ciptransu himself!'

Calfain searched his memory, he screwed up his face in concentration, finally defeated by his lack of knowledge, he shook his head, 'He's a new one on me. Never heard of him.'

'Ciptransu wouldst also be known as the soultaker. In return for his protection, he demandeth the souls of new converts to be offered unto him on the eve of the cycle of Ensalin.'

Calfain cocked his head slightly, *'Now that* - I have heard of,' he said jubilantly, 'Ensalin is some sort of religious period that lasts for, er, er....' Calfain tapped his forehead in frustration at his lack of memory.

'Two years two months and two days,' Venden said helpfully.

'Yes, that's it.' Calfain confirmed needlessly, 'when does it begin?'

Venden almost seemed to smile, 'Twelve nights from this very night, Master Calfain.'

Calfain suddenly felt an overwhelming fear that somehow, Peltene's son, Dennel, was about to be offered up in some way to the soultaker god, Ciptransu. He looked intensely at Venden,

'Tell me Venden, what happens to the persons who are offered to Ciptransu and how do these people get to Cipeus?'

'Some wouldst offer themselves freely and are stripped of their own minds. They become subservient to the monks and eventually pass into the order after a period of learning. The monks also do hath agents who acquire recruits for each new Ensalin.'

'You mean they just take people off the streets?' Calfain asked incredulously

Venden nodded slowly.

'How do you know all this, Venden?'

'I didst provide fresh souls on three successive Ensalintides.' He replied simply and truthfully.

'You were one of them?'

Venden nodded sadly, 'Tis naught a revelation mine own self proudly boasts, Master Calfain. There was a time, in those

64

misguided years that mine own self truly believed with all mine heart that the way of Ciptransu was the only way,' he looked down, ashamed of his admission, 'I realise now, mine own mistake in such beliefs and take every opportunity to repent. I surely do.'

'Are you nearly ready?' Peltene asked as Calfain walked towards where she was standing by the horses.

As Calfain closed the distance between them, he watched her face intently. Then, as he came to stand in front of her, he looked into her eyes,

'Pel, is there something you've not told me about the island of Cipeus? Some little detail that may have slipped your mind, perhaps?'

Peltene stared back at him, a blank expression on her face. Calfain held her gaze. Then, she folded, she could not continue with him staring at her in that way.

'I...er...that is...well,' she stumbled over her words, a guilty expression began to form on her face, she cast her eyes downwards, not able to look at him directly. 'I... well, you wouldn't have come otherwise,' she blurted out in a fair approximation of defiant reasoning.

'Damned right I wouldn't have come, Pel,' he snapped at her, 'and I'm having serious doubts about carrying on.'

Her head snapped up on hearing that, 'Oh, Cal! No, no, please don't say that.' She reached out, placing her hands on his chest, 'No, you mustn't stop now, we're almost there, Please, Cal,' Desperation crept into her voice.

'Peltene, I've just discovered that there are some extremely not nice people on that island and they do things to men's minds. Far worse than I could ever begin to imagine and I have a vivid imagination. I don't know if I can do what you ask.'

'Cal, I must get my son back. I'll do anything to get him away from there.' Suddenly, a new strength came to her voice, 'I'll give you fifty thousand crowns to help me.'

Calfain was visibly shocked by her offer. It was not the offer of money as much as the admission that she had more of it at her disposal.

'I thought you said you only had five hundred?' he asked, watching her reaction.

A weak smile flitted across her lips, she shrugged slightly.

'It was an opening offer. I never imagined you'd accept it.'

Despite the situation, Calfain had to secretly admire her. But now the game had changed. Now, he could get seriously injured or worse. Even if she offered him one hundred thousand crowns, the risks to him were too great - Look out for number one, Cal. That was his motto.

'I'm truly sorry, Peltene, the money isn't important any more. You should have been more honest with me right from the start. I can't see that I can do anything against these monks of Cipeus.'

'You can't just abandon my son and me. We had a deal.'

'That was before I discovered the truth, Pel and since you still have my payment, the deals off.'

'A hundred and fifty thousand.'

Calfain rapidly blinked at her. Did she just offer a hundred and fifty thousand gold crowns? His mind began to spin. That was more than his original asking price.

'That's more than my original asking price.' He glared at her.

She looked at him steadily, 'It will wipe out everything I have in the world, but I'm prepared to give it to you if you'll still help me get Dennel back.'

Calfain looked up at the sky; it was dull and threatening rain. He turned his attention back to her,

'I need to talk some more with Venden first. He seems to know an awful lot about that place.'

'Oh Cal,' she leapt at him, clasping her arms around his neck and kissing his cheek rapidly, 'Thank you thank you…'

He pulled her arms roughly from his neck,

'No! Look, he spent a few years there. If - and only if - he says there *could* be a possibility, then I'll *think* about it. I'm not promising anything until I hear more from him.'

He let go of her arms and turned back towards the cowshed. He was more than a little upset that he had allowed himself to be convinced she had no money and that he had been out-manoeuvred by her.

Calfain spent the next two hours talking with Venden. He was now fairly confident that he knew exactly what he and Peltene were up against. And he did not like it at all.

Even the lure of one hundred and fifty thousand gold crowns – a kings ransom – had somehow, now lost its attractiveness. Nonetheless, all that he had said to Peltene about aborting the rescue of her son did not sit well with him.

It was not that he felt obliged. It was the woman herself. He had begun to develop feelings for her. Feelings that he had told himself years before he would never allow to cloud his judgement again. He could not – would not, allow himself the luxury of falling in love once more. If he did, then, he knew from previous experiences what would be the outcome. He knew he did not need the pain again.

No! Under no circumstances must this decision to go or not to go be based on his fondness of a woman. It must be viewed objectively and in practical terms and his chances of success should be calculated on his abilities alone.

But, just how good were these people at controlling the minds of others? Calfain decided, based on everything Venden had told him that they probably were far superior to anything he could ever hope to achieve. After all, they had been practising for two thousand years. And, as the farm worker had said, there were at least two hundred of them on the island, perhaps more!

What possible chance would he have of sneaking onto an island in the middle of Tamlay bay, snatching a boy and placing a dream into the mind of the boy's father that would erase the memories of his son? And, what if the boy had already been shown the ways of Ciptransu and he liked them? How then, would Calfain deal with that? Was he powerful enough or even clever enough to cleanse the boy's mind of what had been placed in there? He doubted it.

And...even if he could do all of these things, they still had to get away from the island without being detected. Even if they did escape, it was very likely that he would spend the rest of his life being hunted down by these people. Religious fanatics had a habit of being extremely unforgiving. The promised fortune of gold crowns would not protect him forever. He may never live to enjoy it.

All things considered, it was simply not practical to do what he was being asked to do. The risks to him were far too great. The boy was probably one of them now anyway. The easiest way out was now to say no and if Peltene tried to convince him otherwise, then he could always plant a dream into her head, cleansing her memory of her son and of himself.
He took a deep breath and went in search of the Lady.

She was sitting at the kitchen table looking afraid and alone, waiting anxiously for his return. As he opened the door, she looked up expectantly. A wane smile crossed her lips and she held her breath.

Calfain moved straight to the table and slid onto a chair opposite her. This was not going to be easy he knew, but...she

68

had not told him everything at the outset and that, in itself, had made a huge difference, he told himself over and over.

'Cal...I really wanted to tell you the truth...' she blurted then suddenly stopped. She saw the expression set on his face and she already knew the answer.

He looked into her eyes and saw her fears, her desperation; He saw lost hope, her sadness and her love for her son. But mostly he saw his own reflection in those pale blue eyes and it glared angrily back at him.

'It's too late in the day to leave now. We'll leave at first light tomorrow.' He heard his voice saying the words and his brain was desperately trying to silence it, but could not.

Peltene could not believe what she had just heard either, she stared at him dumbfounded for several seconds, then yelped and launched herself across the table at him. Once again she grasped at his neck and began frantically kissing him with unbridled gratitude.

Calfain sat there wishing he could take his knife and cut out this cursed tongue that had a life and a will of its own.

After a light breakfast and attempting to pay the farmer for their food and lodgings and being told in no uncertain terms that payment was not required, Calfain and Peltene waved their goodbyes and headed west once again.

Within three miles Calfain was idly gazing around when he realised there was a rider behind and gaining on them. He watched the figure as it approached. Then, to his great surprise, he saw it was Venden, the ex-monk. He reined in his horse and waited. Peltene now saw the rider and did the same.

'Good Morning, Master Venden. What brings you this way at such speed? Did we forget something?'

Venden pulled up his horse and drew it close to Calfain's mount.

'Thou hath decided upon an attempt at rescue?' he asked pointedly, ignoring Calfain's greeting.

Calfain shrugged hopelessly, 'Yes, well, what do you do?'

Venden stared hard at the dreamweaver. 'Ye knoweth of course, that thine quest be a futile one?'

'When it comes to lost causes, I'm a hopeless romantic,' Calfain replied weakly.

Venden looked to Peltene and then back to Calfain,

'Wouldst it be of any great consequence to offer mine own knowledge and services to benefit thy noble quest?'

Peltene looked at Calfain, 'What did he just say?'

Calfain grinned, 'I think, My Lady, he just asked if he could join us.'

'Why would you wish to help, Master Venden?' Peltene asked.

'Because, My Lady, I hath mine own scores to settle with those evil one's and I hath naught, until this moment, had the true courage to fulfil them.'

'Venden,' Calfain protested, 'We are not on a revenge mission.'

'I dost realise that, Master Calfain, I seek naught revenge but a chance to right so many wrongs I hath performed in the name of Ciptransu.'

Calfain nodded. He did not really understand what Venden meant but he reasoned he would be a good ally to have along, if only for his knowledge of the geography.

'We would be grateful, Venden and honoured for you to accompany us.'

They fell into a line of three and started off again on their journey. Peltene leaned across her saddle and whispered to Calfain,

'He seems like a nice man, but we really must teach him everyday Yarlish. I can hardly understand him.'

The little group made good progress that day, eventually reaching a tiny village at the crossroads to either the west and Paland or northwest, to Bullta, the market town that had suffered terribly at the hands of Lord Grith in the early days that preceded his invasion.

Venden knew the innkeeper reasonably well and was able to secure a room for himself and Calfain to share and one for Peltene to herself. On hearing that, Peltene was more than a little upset.

Whilst the two men had talked as they rode, she had spent much of the time meticulously planning her thank you gift to Calfain for agreeing to continue on. It was to be a resumption of their encounter three nights earlier, when the mushroom addict, Twill, had interrupted them.

Although she told herself it was to be a 'thank you' gift, it was her polite way of coming to terms with the realisation that she wanted him. From the moment she had first seen him along the pathway to her cottage, she had felt that tight little knot of anticipation in her stomach every time he looked at her.

Peltene had never experienced that pleasure with her husband, indeed she had, in truth, never been able to bring herself to fully love the man. Yes, she had cared for him - eventually, after many years of being together, but he had never truly excited her. She had never been able, or willing to give herself completely to him. Their irregular lovemaking had been a dutiful thing, born out of an arranged marriage; it was what had been required of her. The only good thing she had ever received from her husband had been the son that she bore him.

Calfain was like no man she had ever met. She realised he was a bit of a rogue, or at least, he attempted to convey that impression but she had immediately seen through him. She sensed he was basically an honest man but there was another thing. She had known from the moment he had returned the day after she had told him that she could not afford his asking price and he had agreed to help her anyway, she knew in her heart that this was a man whom she could trust and respect.

During their journey of the last few days, when they had talked briefly of their lives, he had not told her in detail but she knew, as only a woman does, that another had hurt him, perhaps badly. He spoke, not with bitterness, but as one does when one has eventually come to terms with a failed relationship.

Throughout this journey she had found herself doing something she had only done as a young innocent girl, she had been daydreaming. Imagining herself spending the rest of her life with this mysterious man they called the dreamweaver.

Could she find happiness with him? Could she make him happy? Could they weave some dreams of their own together, in her cottage living a long love filled life? A life she had thus far and she suspected he also, had never known.

The other night, she had been ready and so willing for him to take her. Now, she was determined that they would take each other as far as physical passions would allow and if each of their tortured souls did not join together, then their bodies certainly would.

They ate their evening meal sitting around a cramped little table with barely enough room to hold three dishes of stodgy dumplings and two varieties of weeds disguised as vegetables.

Calfain and Venden made room on the table for Peltene's wineglass by placing their own tankards of ale on the floor next to their feet.

'Is this what they mean by "cosy and intimate"?' Calfain quipped through a mouthful of dumpling.

'It does have a certain air of closeness,' Peltene agreed.

She had nudged herself nearer to Calfain using the tightness of their surroundings as an excuse to allow her body to brush with his occasionally.

'I wouldst venture to suggest this structure was naught designed to accommodate such a sudden and numerous influx of patrons,' Venden offered.

'Excuse me?' Peltene asked trying to remember in the correct order, all the words he had just spoken.

'Venden agrees, it's a small place.' Calfain grinned at her.

Their meal over, Peltene suggested an early night.

Venden looked dubious,

'It hath been an interminably long period of abstinence from intoxicants for mine own self,' he said winking at Calfain and looking longingly at the ale casks lined up against the wall.

'What did he say?' Peltene whispered to Calfain.

'He says he wants to get reacquainted with the pleasures of old Yarlish ale, Pel.'

Peltene sighed, 'And I suppose you'll have to accompany him on this venture?'

Calfain laughed aloud, 'Well, if he truly has stayed away from it for so long, it's only prudent that one of us watches out for him.'

Defeated and deflated, Peltene had to accept that the two men were going to have a drink or two.

'Will you be long?' she asked, her voice barely a whisper.

'Oh! Only a couple, I should think. That'll be enough to start with.' He smiled at her reassuringly.

'Well,' she said softly brushing the back of his hand with hers, 'don't stay too long, there are much better things to do than drink the night away.' She could not have made herself more obvious and she felt her cheeks reddening as she spoke the words. Then, she quietly departed for her room.

'Come, my new friend, let me introduce you to something called Southern Yarlish Bite.' Calfain slapped Venden's back in a fatherly gesture, 'All the local innkeepers brew their own and some of it really does bite. Trust me - I'm an expert.'

'Pel! We really didn't do anything wrong. We *did* behave ourselves,' Calfain pleaded the next morning as they rode out of the village.

Peltene remained, as she had since breakfast, stony silent. She nudged her horse forward into a trot that clearly told him she was displeased with his previous night's behaviour and she wished not to converse with him.

Venden rode alongside the dreamweaver. He leaned closer and said quietly, 'Methinks the Lady is upset with our penchant for Southern Bite.'

'No, I think she had other plans for me last night, Ven and I messed it all up.' Calfain replied sadly.

'That the Lady Peltene is smitten is plainly obvious even to the blindest of beggars.'

Calfain turned his head to look directly at the ex-monk and he raised an eyebrow in question.
Venden smiled and nodded knowingly.

Calfain thought about her and their encounter on the night that Twill had interrupted them. He realised that things would have progressed way beyond a simple kiss had they not been disturbed. And last night, Peltene had - come to think of it, made her intentions abundantly clear. He smacked himself on his forehead so hard that the noise startled his horse.

'Thine remonstrations suggest the act of a foolish man who hath had a revelation given unto his own self.'

Calfain sighed heavily. 'Thou couldst sayeth that, Ven, but the truth is, I canst naught become entwined with her,' Calfain stopped mid-sentence, realising that he was slipping into Venden's archaic speech.

'Wouldst thou elucidate for one uneducated in the skills and arts of love?'

'She's a friend, no more than that. If I became too close to her, it would only result in heartbreak for at least one of us. Probably me.'

'Methinks thou hath dabbled in this thing called romance before and hath naught faired too well in the game.'

Calfain stiffened at the memories. 'You could say that, Ven. Yes.'

Venden grinned, 'Love is a truly wondrous and perplexing thing is it naught?'

Calfain glanced at him, 'It just gets in the way, Venden,' ending the conversation then and there.

They ate a small lunch of fruit and bread; all three remaining silent with their own thoughts. Eventually, Calfain could not hold back. He turned to Venden and asked,

'Isn't it about time you watered the horses?'

'They hath drunk their fill, Calfain.' Venden replied sombrely.

Calfain glanced heavenwards. Any normal person would have taken the obvious hint.

He tried again, 'Then, shouldn't they be fed?'

Venden looked at him curiously, 'I didst performed that task immediately after watering them.'

'Venden!'

'Yes, Calfain?'

'Go for a walk.'

Realisation of what Calfain wanted suddenly struck the man. Keeping his face perfectly straight, he stood and stretched his arms out wide.

'Nature prevails upon mine own self,' he said winking at Calfain, who openly groaned at the obvious excuse.

Peltene sat on the ground, nibbling at a dried biscuit, seemingly oblivious to the little charade that had just been played out by the two men.

Calfain stood and slowly walked to where she was sitting and casually sat himself down next to her.

'Peltene, about last night...' he began.

'Did you enjoy your drinking session?' she asked without looking up from her biscuit.

'Well, actually, no, I didn't. I...'

'Then why didn't you stop?'

'Pel, Venden hadn't had a good drinking session in the two years he'd worked at that farm. I was just trying to help him out...'

'Oh, you certainly did that all right.'

'Oh come on, Peltene...'

'Calfain you didn't see the amount I had to pay to the innkeeper this morning.'

'It was only a couple of tankards...'

'Only a couple of barrels more like.'

Calfain suddenly checked himself. He looked hard at her for a moment, then,

'You sound just like my mother, Pel.' Before she could answer him, he stood and marched off to find his erstwhile drinking companion.

Venden had his back to Calfain as he joined him in the bushes. They stood shoulder to shoulder staring at the ground as Calfain unfastened himself.

'Dost true love prevail?'

'Oh - shut up!'

Venden smiled to himself and persisted with the conversation, 'Whilst sorely lacking first hand knowledge of such matters, mine own self hath nonetheless witnessed such similar encounters twixt mine previous employer and his spouse.'

'And?' Calfain asked impatiently.

'Mine employer hath developed the art of remorse to such finesse, twas wondrous to behold.'

'Yes, well, that's well and good for him, but I don't need it, Ven. Between you and me, when I first met her I thought there might just be something different about her. I almost let myself become involved. I should have known better. *I do know better!* It's not going to happen!'

Venden smiled. 'We shallst see what the gods holdeth in store,' he looked casually down, 'Master Calfain?'

'What?'

'Why dost thou see fit to waterlog mine own boots with thine indiscriminate aim?'

Calfain was about to apologise when Peltene shouted from beyond the bushes.

They hurriedly rearranged themselves and tumbled from their privacy to see her talking with another man.

It was Twill!

'What the...' Calfain blurted.

'No!' Peltene stopped him, 'He's hurt. He needs our help.'

'He needs my boot up...'

'Calfain!' she snapped, 'that's enough!'

Twill was standing, but swaying gently from side to side. His eyes were glazed and flecks of spittle trickled from the corners of his mouth. He was attempting to speak but gibberish was all that he uttered.

'Who is this person?' Venden asked.

'He's someone we met at the beginning of our journey. I thought I'd taken care of him.' Calfain explained.

Venden glanced sternly at the dreamweaver, 'I beseech thee, Calfain, dost naught ever take mine own self into that kind of care.'

'*I didn't do that to him!*' Calfain snapped back, 'He's been sniffing those funny mushrooms again.'

'Mushrooms?'

'Will you two stop talking and help me?' Peltene snapped, taking hold of Twill and trying to make him sit or lay down. He would do neither, shaking his head and muttering something completely incomprehensible.

'What manner of language dost he speaketh?' Venden asked.

'To some, Ven, it sounds just like the way you talk.'

'Calfain, Venden - please!' Peltene implored.

Venden was the first to reach the addict. He took hold of his arm,

'Come friend, tarry with us at our fireside.' He gently pressed, forcing Twill down. Twill was like supple willow. As soon as he bent a little, he snapped back again to his full height and muttered something, grinning.

'Oh! Here. Let me!' Calfain said impatiently striding forward. He placed his hand on Twill's forehead. The addict dropped to the ground instantly.

Venden's eyes widened, he first looked down at the prone man, then up at Calfain.

'I'll explain later. Let's see to mushroom-head, here first.'

It was a full hour before Twill was capable of speaking in anything resembling a coherent manner. Peltene had gently bathed his face and neck, speaking soothingly all the while.

Calfain told Venden the full story of how they had met Twill on both occasions and what Calfain had inserted as dreams into the ragamuffin's head.

'Ye canst truly perform these feats, Calfain?'

'Yes I canst.' Calfain replied matter-of-factly.

'I doth see plainly now why the Lady Peltene hath chosen thee for this extraordinary mission.'

They sat watching Peltene minister to the sleeping Twill, who constantly twitched this way and that as his mind exorcised whatever demons the last intake of mushroom spores had imbued him with.

'Ye realise of course,' Venden said quietly after a while, 'The power vested within thineself is naught dissimilar to that of the Cipean brethren.'

'I didn't know until you told me about them yesterday. I still have my doubts that I'm anywhere as good or as skilled in its usage.' Calfain admitted.

Venden continued to stare at the sleeping man, his mind working on Calfain's problem. Then, he looked up,

'They dost insert images, naught words into the minds of their disciples.'

Calfain glanced up quickly, 'But - that's exactly what I do!' he now turned to the ex-monk, 'have you had first hand experience of this, Venden?'

'They invaded mine own head thrice times. Each wouldst be accompanied by a most peculiar sensation.'

'What type of sensation? Can you explain it?' Calfain was now definitely interested.

Venden thought dutifully about the feelings he had experienced, 'Twas as if the monk who so performed the feat was inside mine own head, standing there, searching through

79

mine own memories. I canst only liken it to flicking the pages of a great volume whenst thou art searching for something of particular interest.'

The dreamweaver listened to Venden intently, attempting to gauge if his own method of planting dreams into people's heads was the same or similar to the way in which the Cipean monks went about it. He decided after listening to Venden's explanation, that it was not.

His thoughts were jarred away from him by Twill. The would-be thief was waking and began to vomit profusely down the front of his already well-seasoned tunic.

'He is naught dissimilar to the volcanos of the far northwest I wouldst venture.' Venden remarked, watching the addict spew forth, great globs of foul smelling orange goop.

Calfain was about to turn Twill onto his side in a half-hearted attempt at saving him from choking on his own vomit. Instead, he turned back to Venden,

'You've been there?' he asked genuinely interested.

'Aye, many years ago. Tis a wondrous place, the high mountains. A man canst ride a full month long in any direction and see naught another soul.

'I'd like to go there one day,' said Calfain, warming to the subject, 'They say gold nuggets lay on the ground ripe for the picking.'

Venden chuckled, 'I fearest, mine friend, someone with a finer humour than yours hath been exaggerating.'

'Will someone help this poor man?' Peltene finally interrupted the two others.

Calfain and Venden glanced at her then at Twill, now his chest was completely soaked in an orange lumpy liquid, which was still issuing from his mouth in spasmodic bursts.

'After you, my friend,' Calfain out of sheer politeness offered Venden the chance to reach in there amongst the smelly vomit.

'Nay, Master Calfain, I wouldst relish the chance to observe a master lifesaver at his work.' Venden grinned broadly.

'Oh for goodness sake!' Peltene could stand it no longer.

She leapt from the rock she had been sitting on and bent over to roll Twill onto his side. The nauseating smell attacked her senses and she drew back to catch a breath of clean air. She turned her head back to Twill but could not bring herself to lean closer. Peltene suddenly stood up and rolled him with her booted foot until, grunting and with one last orange coloured heave, he turned, face down, with a little plop, into his own stinking mess.

'There!' she proclaimed, 'It wasn't that difficult - was it?'

'No,' answered Calfain, still sitting next to Venden on the ground, 'but then, we don't have the bother of washing that orange sticky mess off our boots now.'

Peltene looked down at her boots. One had vomit all over the sole and uppers. She uttered a curse and stomped off towards the little stream a few feet away.

'I think we won that one, Ven.'

'Nay, Calfain, tis only a temporary victory. Methinks we shallst suffer mightily for our un-helpfulness.'

Calfain nodded grimly, 'Verily! I thinkest, mine friend, thou couldst well be proven correct in thine assumption.' He turned his gaze on Twill.

'*Calfain!*' Peltene cried from the banks of the stream, 'don't you think he's had enough now?'

'Just a little more should do it.'

Calfain and Venden had lifted Twill and carried him to the stream where they stripped him naked and amidst voluble and protracted cursing and threats of all kind, they scrubbed the addict until he had some semblance of cleanliness. Twill was roughly the same height as Calfain and the dreamweaver had prepared a set of his older clothes for him.

Whilst Calfain fetched them, Venden stood guard over the man, placing a big foot firmly on his chest as he lay in the fast flowing waters.

Now, dry and almost glowing healthily, Twill sat by the little fire and drank a cup of warm broth that Peltene had made.

'Tell me, my friend,' Calfain asked amiably, 'is what you do to your mind and body really worth it?'

If Twill's eyes could have issued forth, razor sharp daggers at Calfain, they surely would have. Sulkily, he replied,

'Course it's not worth it. It never is, but it's a way of escaping.'

'From whom or what wouldst thou wish to escape, Master Twill?' Venden asked.

'Life of course.'

'If tis merely a question of naught wishing to live, then, I wouldst venture there be men a plenty who wouldst gladly help thee relieve thineself of these mortal shackles.'

Twill glared at Venden for a few seconds, then turned to Calfain,

'What did 'e just say?'

'He said...' Calfain began slowly, 'If you want a little help ending it all - we'd be only too glad to lend a hand.'

Twill moved his head, turning first from Calfain, then to Venden and back again, 'I don't much like 'im.'

Calfain smiled, 'Why? Because he cleaned you up or because he offered to kill you?'

'Both!' Twill mumbled grudgingly, 'But mostly 'cause of the bath.'

Peltene, who had remained silent throughout most of the conversation, glanced at the sky and remarked there was probably only three or four hours of daylight left.

'Yes,' Calfain agreed, 'we really should get going.'

As he stood, Twill also jumped to his feet.

'I'll get me 'orse!' he declared.

'You have a horse?' Peltene asked, surprised.

'Course I do, Lady, 'ow else would I 'ave kept up with you?'

'Er, You won't need the horse, friend,' Calfain said, 'We travel as three.'

Twill instantly saw his supply of whatever Calfain did to his mind, slipping away, 'But...but I can 'elp you people.'

Calfain grinned, 'I don't think so.'

'I can! I can 'elp yer!' Twill continued to protest.

'In which endeavours doth thou excel?'

'What did 'e just say?' Twill asked Calfain desperately.

'He said - what are you good at? What skills do you have? Apart from being able to select the best funny mushrooms.'

'Depends what ya need,' Twill said cautiously, not wishing to give too much wrong information out.

'We don't need any skills you may have,' Calfain said, 'we're going to Tapp City on business, that's all.'

'Ah!' Twill immediately latched onto that, 'I can gather information about yer competitors.'

'What competitors?' Calfain asked.

'If yer in business, then ya must 'ave competitors. I can get near to 'em an' learn what they know. Nobody takes too much notice of people like me.'

'Thank you, but...no,' Calfain replied in a tone of finality.

Twill, now desperate to stay with them, turned his attention to the woman of the group, in an effort to elicit her support.

'Mistress...please!'

Peltene smiled benevolently at him, I'm sorry, Twill, it's as Calfain says, we go to Tapp, but not to stay, we move on to the isle of Cipeus within a day or so.'

Calfain shot her a look of disgust at the revelation.

Twill was quick to pick up on her words, 'Ah! Cipeus Island, know it well. And you'll need a sailor...a good sailor. I'm yer man!'

Calfain glanced at Venden.

'If he speaks truthfully, then I doth know that naught any of the locals wouldst guide us there in their own crafts. We wouldst hath to purloin a boat and I fear, mine own sailing skills are woefully inadequate.'

Calfain looked back at Twill, debating with himself. Presently, he asked,

'Are you speaking the truth about being a sailor?'

'Of course I am, Master Calfain,' Twill oozed the words and puffed out his chest.

Calfain glanced at Peltene, who smiled back at him and nodded slightly.

'Where's your horse then?' he asked in a resigned tone.

Twill looked around, 'Oh! She'll be around someplace. She should be on 'er feet by now.'

'On her feet? What do you mean...on her feet? Don't tell me she takes the same mushrooms that you do?'

'Well, yer, course she does, 'ow else do yer think she runs so quick?'

Calfain shook his head in total despair.

Chapter Eight.

By the time they had located Twill's horse and allowed it to drink the best part of a gallon of water and then fed it, it was almost too late to continue on their way. They had travelled only four miles before Calfain decided they should stop for the night.

The next morning, well before daybreak, Calfain and Venden had risen, fed and watered the horses and were ready to leave as soon as Twill and Peltene had finished a small meal.

They now had only eight clear days before the Ensalintides celebrations, Calfain wanted to be on and off the island well before they started, so he now pushed hard to reach the city as soon as possible.

He and Venden rode a little way in front of the others, so as to be able to speak freely.

'Tis going to be a tight run thing…reaching Tapp City and organising our landing onto the island.'

'How much further to Tapp?'

'Perhaps, at this pace and running dawn till dusk, then four days I wouldst venture.'

Calfain fell silent on hearing that. His mind now turned to the challenge of pressing on and stopping for nothing, save to rest the horses.

That night they stopped riding only when it became impossible to safely continue. Venden located a little copse of trees and began to make camp. Calfain tended to the horses whilst Peltene set about preparing supper. Twill slunk off into the bushes, ostensibly to answer the call of his body.

'Where is he?' Calfain asked as they sat down to their meal.

'Who?' Peltene asked.

'Twill.'

'Oh! He, er, went into the bushes...nature.'

They ate their food in relative silence, each too tired from the days riding to be anything other than glad to simply rest.

'When did he go?' Calfain asked as he put his empty plate down.

'Just as we arrived here. Why?'

Calfain stood quickly, 'I don't think it was the call of nature. More like the call of wild fungi.' He stomped off in the rough direction Twill had taken.

'Although we hath barely just met, mine own senses detect that Master Calfain is truly a caring person toward his fellow man.' Venden said quietly as he drank the last of his tea.

Peltene smiled, 'Yes, Venden, he is, although he would deny it.'

'He cares greatly for thineself, Lady.'

'I thought there was a chance that there could be something that would develop between us, but,' she sighed, 'I'm not sure anymore.'

'Why wouldst thou now hath reservations, Lady Peltene? Hast he mistreated thineself in some way?'

Peltene laughed at the suggestion, 'No, no, of course not. I think I brought it on myself. I was annoyed with him the other day and chastised him for it. He said I sounded like his mother and he marched off. Perhaps I did, Venden, but I was acting out of concern for him.'

Venden nodded, 'Perhaps when one cares for another so, it canst seem to stifle the other.'

'Very true. And I think I stifled the relationship before it began.'

'Words canst either hath naught value or canst be priceless beyond compare. An action hath only one meaning.'

Peltene grinned at him, 'I'm sorry, Venden. I don't mean to be rude, but your dialect is hard enough to follow, when you talk in riddles also…'

Venden smiled un-offended, 'I understand, Lady. I confuse mine own self at times. What I say to thee is this. Words canst be cruel or be kind, or worst - mistaken for either. An action canst only be perceived one way. Therefore, if thy hath feelings for this man, then taketh action upon them.'

Peltene gazed steadily at the big man. 'You have words of wisdom for every occasion don't you, Venden?'

I surely try, My Lady.' He smiled back at her, 'But remember this, Calfain *seeks* to be a puzzle wrapped within a mystery. It suits him to appear so, for it perpetuates his allure as a dreamweaver. Yet, he is naught more than a man. A man, who hath great feelings of love within, but hath been wronged terribly. He seeks to hide his feelings for fear they wouldst surface and he wouldst be wronged and much hurt once again.'

'I would never hurt him, Venden.' She whispered solemnly.

'I am mine own self, truly convinced of that, Lady Peltene, It is he thou wouldst now seek to convince. By actions if necessary.'

Calfain stumbled across Twill in the near darkness, propped up against a tree stump. The addict was laughing quietly to himself, muttering incoherently, his eyes were seeing some far distant image not in this world. Spittle dribbled down his chin and his whole body convulsed spasmodically.

Calfain stood over him and shook his head resignedly.

Several minutes later, the dreamweaver had dragged the inert Twill by his collar, back to the camp. Venden saw him approaching and jumped up to help carry the still twitching form of Twill near to the fire.

The two wrapped him in a blanket and turned him on his side, just in case he decided to vomit.

'I fear our companion may cause us regular concern unless we canst encourage him to resist the delights of the flora.

'Hmmm,' Calfain stood looking down at the now sleeping form. 'Let's see what's in his saddlebags.'

After several minutes of searching every pocket and pouch in the bags and the saddle, Calfain and Venden had, spread on the ground before them, a selection of wild flowers, plants, dried leaves, twigs and some coloured powders they could not identify.

'Whilst, Master Twill related unto us his many talents, he seemingly forgot to mention his skill as an apothecary.'

Calfain smiled at Venden's observation. 'I don't recognise any of these,' he said, sifting through the piles with his finger.

'That rag plant there,' Peltene offered, 'is used sometimes to kill pain.'

'He probably takes that with the mushrooms, then, when he trips and falls, he won't feel anything,' Calfain replied ruefully.

'And that one,' Peltene continued, ignoring his remark and pointing at a little flower, 'is deadly nightshade. And that other is a foxglove.'

'Well, whatever all the others are, they'll all burn bright on the fire.'

Calfain scooped everything up and tossed it carelessly towards the flickering flames. The fire seized the opportunity to engulf the powders and dried twigs.

Bright, vivid colours sparkled in the flames and sweet, sickly smelling smoke billowed for an instant, then the fire returned to its original task of providing heat for the group.

'I wouldst venture our friend may naught sing thine praises whenst he returns to this mundane world and discovers his loss.'

Calfain continued to stare at the fire, 'I'll keep his mind occupied with nicer dreams. He'll thank me for it someday, Ven.'

'Truly, Calfain, thou art a considerate friend to have, but what proposal doth thou intend with which to wean his horse from these odious substances?'

Calfain chuckled, 'I have no idea, Ven. I'll think about that tomorrow. Right now, I'm going to bed.' He stood and glanced around, 'Goodnight, Ven. Goodnight, Pel.'

Then, he stepped lightly over the snoring body of Twill and walked towards his bedroll, which was a few feet from the fire, under the low hanging branches of a small tree.

Peltene sat by the fire, quietly watching him as he lay down and made himself comfortable.

'Methinks I shall partake of a stroll before mine own self retires,' Venden said softly, 'upon mine return, the heat of this fire wouldst dictate that I shallst sleep many feet distant. Many feet distant.' He glanced at Peltene and raised an eyebrow, waiting for her to acknowledge his meaning.

Peltene looked at him steadily, 'Thank you, Venden,' she whispered, understanding his implications, 'have a good night.'

'I pray thee will too, My Lady,' he smiled.

As the tall, one time monk slipped quietly away from the camp, Peltene stood. She took one deep breath and headed silently towards the prone bundle of bedding that hid the dreamweaver within.

'Cal!' she whispered his name as she knelt by the side of his bedroll.

'Hmm?'

'Cal, I'm cold and I'm tired and I'm sorry.'

Calfain's head emerged from under the blanket; he looked at her for several seconds,

'Pel, you have nothing to be sorry about. I was the fool. It should be me who is apologising.'

'No, you were right. I had no right to say what I did. It was me being selfish.'

'It's over. Done! Mention it no more. Agreed?'

'Agreed,' she smiled, 'I'm still cold though.'

Calfain unravelled the blanket and opened it allowing her access. She climbed in and lay on her side with her body facing his, their faces inches apart. He wrapped the blanket around her shoulders and drew her even closer to him.

Their kiss was long and tender. A kiss without urgency - with no need of an ending. It was a meeting of two people, two souls who had been searching all of their lives for each other. That kiss told of their past, their present and the anticipation of their future.

Calfain and Peltene awoke to the smell and sound of bacon sizzling over the fire. Venden squatted across the other side of the flames and looked up at their movement.

He smiled, 'Good day, breakfast is almost ready.'

Twill sat groggily, coughing the last of the phlegm from his throat and sipping from his mug of hot tea.

'Where did you get this? It's delicious.' Peltene asked through a mouthful of hot, crisp bacon, 'and the eggs too?'

Venden grinned, 'The boar offered itself unto our cause this very morning. I came across it on mine early morning stroll. The eggs, were less of a challenge, but nonetheless still high in the trees.'

'Venden, you can be my personal cook anytime.' Calfain laughed and swallowed another helping of egg.

Venden offered a plate of food to Twill who was still recovering from his previous evenings self inflicted nightmare. He shook his head moodily, refusing the offered plate.

'T'wouldst be prudent if thou introduced thine body to proper nourishment, mine far away friend.'

'What?' Twill asked, snidely.

'Eat the damned food, you oaf!' Venden bellowed. His face perfectly straight and a menacing look in his eye.

Twill was so shocked by the outburst; he snatched the plate from Venden's still outstretched hand and scooped a handful of bacon into his mouth.

Calfain still held a slice of bacon halfway to his open mouth, unable to believe what had just happened. He glanced at Peltene; she sat in the same shocked manner.

Venden turned to them and smiled self-consciously, 'Sometimes only a forthright manner canst prevail.'

Both Calfain and Peltene vigorously nodded their agreement. 'Oh, absolutely, Venden,' they both said together.

The four rode hard that morning, the horses eating up the miles. Calfain was beginning to think they might just get to Tapp City with a few days margin left to them.

Around midday, the heavens decided otherwise. A prolonged torrential downpour slowed their progress to that of a plodding slog. The road transformed itself into a quagmire and sucked at the horse's legs with such intensity that the animals fast became drained of their stamina.

A weathered little wooden signpost proclaimed the village or town of Gind was no more than a mile distant. Calfain decided that even though it was only mid-afternoon, this weather would make it virtually impossible for them to gain any distance this day.

He voiced his opinion and the others readily agreed. It took them almost an hour to plod into the cattle town a mile down the road.

Bathed and shaved, Venden sat with Calfain at the rectangular table in the only tavern in the town.

'Where's our flora expert?' Calfain asked casually taking a sip of ale.

'I didst leave him contemplating the complexities of time and heat upon the fabric of his only clothing.'

'Ah!' Calfain nodded, he and Venden carried more than one set of clothes, unfortunately for Twill, the clothes Calfain had given him were the only ones he now possessed.

Peltene walked into the room and several heads belonging to local people turned to watch her.

She had bathed and dressed in a long, plum coloured thin dress. The sleeves were cut at three-quarter length and the neck tapered in a vee down to the swell of her breasts. Her blonde hair was piled and tied in a loose bob at the back, thin ringlets tumbled down at the sides and her complexion had a glow about it. She looked beautiful.

'You look beautiful, Peltene,' Calfain gasped as he stood to allow her access to the seat next to him.

'Why, thank you, Cal, I try,' she answered modestly as she sat down.

'Master Calfain hath summed up precisely the thought that runeth through mine own feeble mind, Lady. Thou art indeed a treasure of such wholesomeness for mine own eyes to gaze upon.'

Calfain leaned close to her and whispered, 'He say's you look nice too.'

The dreamweaver moved from his seat to fetch a glass of wine. Venden took the opportunity to lean across the table, 'Dist thine actions of the previous night have the desired effect?' he whispered.

'I think so, Ven,' she whispered, as Calfain returned.

'What are you two whispering about?' he asked as he sat down.

'Lady Peltene was concerned for the whereabouts of our travelling companion.' Venden replied smoothly.

'He's here now,' Calfain nodded towards the door as Twill entered looking slightly dazed at the number of people and the noise from the general conversation in the room. Calfain held up his arm in an effort to catch the addict's attention.

Eventually, Twill spotted him and threaded his way through the throng towards the table. As he sat, Venden asked,

'Wouldst thou care to slake thine thirst and partake in a bevy of Southern Bite?'

Twill stared at him, nonplussed.

'Do you want a tankard of ale?' Calfain asked.

Twill nodded dumbly and Venden went to collect one for him and also to replenish his own and Calfain's empty tankards.

'How are you feeling now, Twill?' Peltene asked.

Twill shrugged his shoulders and gazed around the room for a moment. Then, he turned to her and smiled lopsidedly.

'Ungry.'

'Well, that's a good sign,' she replied, 'why don't we all eat? Calfain's paying.'

'I suppose I asked for that one,' Calfain grumbled, recalling the bar bill that he and Venden had run up and Peltene had paid.

They ate a reasonably good meal and drank a reasonably fine wine, given that this was a cattle town in the middle of nowhere and the cuisine was not perhaps what could be expected of grander places such as Yarlis or Peane City.

Peltene asked for and received a selection of cheeses and small biscuits to complete her meal. Venden had, in his customary long-winded fashion, said that they looked nice and she ordered some for him also.

Twill, having wolfed down an extremely large steak, looked on enviously. He too was rewarded with some cheeses.

Then she ordered another bottle of wine. Calfain sat, calculating the additional costs in his head.

Peltene had taken her revenge.

Twill, his belly full of food for possibly the first time in years, slept soundly. Venden, sharing the same room also slept, snoring gently as he lay on his back.

In the next room, two eager lovers consummated their first night in a soft bed of duck down that was as yielding and compliant as the persons lying upon it.

Chapter Nine

Calfain the dreamweaver pushed even harder now, in an effort to make up for the lost time of yesterday. The weather had cleared and it was bright and sunny once again, although the ground remained soft and cloying, the horses, now fully rested, pounded their way along the westbound road.

The day was uneventful and the little band rested the horses only twice. By nightfall, Calfain was happier than he had expected himself to be with their progress.

They camped in the woods and ate the remains of the boar that Venden had killed. Twill had begun to twitch again and was fast becoming irritable. Calfain surreptitiously administered to his needs by placing a dream of uncompromising beauty into his head. The scenes he conjured up were of waterfalls and woodland glades with dewdrops sparkling from the dancing rays of the sun, frolicking deer and rabbits that hopped as high as the imaginary grass. Calfain rounded off the illusion by having Twill happily running naked through the grass trying to catch butterflies with his bare hands.

Later, as he lay under his blanket with Peltene snuggled into his arms, Calfain told her of the dream.

'That's nice,' she said softly, 'where did you get that idea from?'

'Oh, it's something to do with the way I'm feeling at the moment, I suppose.'

She gazed up at him, smiling, 'I'm having a feeling at the moment too.'

He turned his head towards her and they kissed passionately.

Another day and another hard ride saw them pass through a small hamlet. As they stopped to water the horses, Venden asked a local where exactly they were and how far was it to Tapp City.

'Five leagues more,' Venden informed the others as he returned to the watering trough.

'Fifteen miles...less than half a days ride.' Calfain calculated aloud. He looked up at the sky assessing the time to nightfall. 'I don't think we'll manage it today. And even if we did, it would mean finding lodgings in a strange city in the dark.'

'I doth know people in the city, Calfain, but none of whom wouldst I trust to accommodate us.' Venden said apologetically.

Calfain smiled. 'That's all right Ven, It'll be as well if we keep ourselves to ourselves and not give anyone the chance to become suspicious.'

'Truly a wise decision, mine friend.'

With no available lodgings in the little hamlet, the group moved out along the road for a couple of miles. There, they camped.

Calfain having spoken to Twill that morning had discovered the addict was relatively happy with running naked through the grass. He showed no ill effects or signs that it had done him any harm. Which of course, Calfain had known it would not. Calfain decided that, after supper, he would alter the dream slightly so as to gradually wean Twill away from his addiction.

'What exactly are you planning when we reach Tapp tomorrow?' Peltene asked as they sat around the campfire, sipping their evening drinks of tea.

'First, find some obscure lodgings in a fairly smart quarter of the city, then...'

'Why a smart part?' Twill asked, joining the conversation for the first time.

'Mostly because if we lodged in a run down part, the inhabitants there almost always know everybody and would more than likely steal our possessions, or kill us and then steal them but in either case, word would spread far and fast that strangers were afoot. And *that*...would attract attention.'

'Makes sense I suppose,' Twill agreed.

Calfain nodded and then continued. 'Then, we split up. Ven, you and Twill locate some sort of boat that's capable of taking us to the island and big enough to hold the four of us and Peltene's son on the return journey.'

'Venden glanced at Twill, 'Methinks, Master Twill here wilst no doubt, avail us of a suitable craft in the twinkle of a mariners eye.'

Twill stared at the big man dumbly.

Calfain interpreted, 'Venden said...with your experience of sailing, finding a boat will be easy for you.'

'*Me?*' Twill spluttered. '*Why me?*'

Calfain watched him closely. 'Because, my nautical friend, you were the one who convinced us you could handle a boat.'

Twill grinned, his cheeks flushing scarlet, 'Ah! Right! Yer! I was er, forgetting. Course! Not a problem.'

Calfain continued to gaze steadily at him for a few seconds longer,

'Good,' he finally said.

Then, he turned to Peltene, 'Pel, I want you to buy two more horses one extra saddle and provisions for the other, so you'll need to buy sacks and bags to carry the food in. We need to be out of the city as fast as possible and we may not have much time to go shopping afterwards. It's possible we'll have to eat and sleep on the hoof for a few days.'

'Do you think we'll be followed?' she asked.

'From what Venden has told me, these people don't take kindly to having their new recruits stolen from them.'

She nodded slowly, now the full realisation and possible dangers of what she was about to attempt were at last sinking in.

'I'll get the horses,' she said softly.

'What challenges doth thou set for thineself, Calfain?' Venden asked.

'I'm going shopping too. Just in case my powers of the mind let me down, then I want to provide some more, mundane attention grabbers for our holy friends.'

After Calfain had put Twill to sleep and Venden bedded himself down, Peltene came to the dreamweaver's bed.

Without a word, she climbed in and snuggled down into his arms. They lay quietly for several minutes, holding each other tightly.

'Do you think we will succeed?' she asked presently.

'Do you want an honest answer or one that will just make you feel better?'

'Both.'

Then, to make you feel better, of course we will. But in all honesty,' he sighed, letting go of his breath slowly, 'it'll be tight. I really don't know if I can pull it all off, Pel.'

She looked up at him, 'Will we get to Dennel?'

He thought for a moment. 'My plan is to grab the boy at all costs. Even if I fail to find your husband and fix his mind so that he forgets everything, your son comes first. As for the monks, well, we'll deal with them as and when.'

'You're a good man, Cal,' she whispered reaching up to gently kiss his cheek.

'If we're all still alive in a week's time, then tell me again and I'll believe you.'

Peltene snuggled closer to him, content just to be near this puzzle, wrapped in a mystery, as Venden had called him.

Just after midday, Tapp City loomed large and ornate on the horizon. Bristling spires of granite, hewn from the feet of the Atan Mountains pointed high into the afternoon sky. Smaller buildings made of the same material stood everywhere.

Tapp was the largest city anywhere on the western side of the continent. Its teeming population numbered some three million and its boundaries sprawled out in all directions. Had it not been for the overriding influence of the church, Tapp could easily have slipped into total corruption and decadence. Such was its size and divergence of inhabitants.

'That place looks nice,' Peltene said, pointing to a large, stone building with a sign hanging from one of its walls proclaiming vacant rooms inside.

Too expensive!' Calfain muttered and rode on past.

'What about that one then?' she offered, again pointing.

'Too bright!'

'Cal!' she blurted exasperated, 'that's the eighth or ninth one you've refused. What exactly are you looking for?'

Calfain reined in his horse and stared across the wide avenue at a single storied building made of wood.

'That one, Pel!' He answered her with finality.

It was a modest looking hotel. Not too big and grand, but not shabby and run-down either. Just right! Insignificant and in a reasonable part of town.

After depositing their belongings in their rooms, the four took a walk around the area.

Venden had visited Tapp on several occasions but did not recognise this part of the city.

Eventually, after more than an hour, they located the docks where hundreds of ships, boats and assorted sailing craft were moored. Even in the late afternoon, it bustled with activity.

'Shouldn't be any problem finding a suitable boat here.' Calfain remarked, gazing around at the myriad shapes gently bobbing up and down on the swell of the tide.

'Sail or oars?' the dreamweaver glanced at Twill, who was trying to make himself insignificant behind Venden.

'Er…what?' he mumbled, raising both eyebrows innocently.

'Which do you think will be best suited for us? A sail boat or a rowing boat?'

'Erm…' Twill anxiously gazed around the harbour. 'Whichever!'

Calfain's jaw began to set in a look of irritation.

'Tis thine own maritime skills which we doth now prevail upon.' Venden said, turning to look at the addict hiding behind him.

'Twill!' Calfain snapped.

'What?'

'Which type of boat?'

Twill came out from behind the shadow of Venden's broad back. He glanced around again at the harbour.

'Er…where is this island then?' He asked, squinting into the distance out to sea.

Venden pointed vaguely over the horizon. 'T'wouldst be ten, perhaps twelve miles distant out there.'

Twill peered across the distance, as if the island would be visible to him.

'So…which is it to be?' Calfain pressed.

'So, there won't be a rope then?' Twill asked no one in particular.

'A rope? A rope for what?' Calfain asked.

'To pull us along…like on the ferry.'

'What are you talking about?' Calfain was becoming exasperated.

Twill looked down at the ground; a guilty expression began to spread across his face.

'I…I…er…well, I really only ever sailed on a ferryboat.'

He looked up, turning to Peltene, hopefully attempting to elicit some sort of female understanding, 'when I stole one…to chase after yerselves, Lady.'

'*I knew it!*' Calfain said, throwing his hands up and turning his back on the man.

Peltene looked intently at Twill, 'Do you mean you've only ever been on a ferryboat on the river?'

Twill nodded quickly, 'Yes, Lady Peltene…but I 'andled it all by meself.'

Calfain spun around, his eyes narrow slits. 'What's there to handle, you oaf? All you have to do is pull on a rope! Which is what I'm going to do when I put one around your stupid lying neck!'

Twill looked desperately at Peltene. She would understand, he reasoned, 'Lady, I…'

Peltene shook her head slowly, 'No! I'm sorry, Twill, if Calfain doesn't kill you, then I will.'

Twill's eyes widened in panic. His last chance, his last line of help stood behind him now. He turned to the big one-time monk,

'Ven! We're friends! Tell 'em 'ow easy it is to use a boat. Tell 'em we'll get across the water. *Tell 'em, Ven!*'

The big man stood impassively staring down at the desperate Twill as he attempted to extricate himself from the problem.

Venden remained silent for several seconds, and then he looked up and at Calfain.

'If the waters are calm and mine own feelings are that they wouldst be so, at this time of year, then, tis conceivable that we couldst possibly undertake the excursion by means of a rowing boat.'

Twill spun around, triumph in his voice, 'There y'are, whatever 'e just said sounds good doesn't it?

Calfain ignored him and addressed himself to Venden,

'Are you sure, Ven?'

'I hath some moderate knowledge of the crossing. On the occasions I traversed the water, each was a relatively uncomplicated procedure.'

'Yer see! Yer see!' Twill danced about jubilantly.

'Shut up Twill! You don't even know what he just said.' Calfain snapped.

Peltene now spoke, 'Let's go back to our rooms and work this out, gentlemen,'

On the way back to their lodgings, Venden had detoured to a shop that he had seen earlier. Now, back in Calfain and Peltene's room, he displayed the purchase he had made.

Spread across the bed was a large hand drawn parchment map of Tapp City, and the northern end of Tamlay bay.

Venden had told the shopkeeper than he wished to purchase an island in the bay, where he might build a home. The seller had assured him that the distances and compass bearings were accurate. Venden had given half a gold crown for the map.

'Yer were robbed!' Twill piped up, his confidence now returning.

'Twas, I believe, a prudent investment, Master Twill. Given that our only other source of navigational competence hath evaporated as dramatically as water in a sun baked desert.'

Twill stared at him, 'I *know* yer insulting me. I just don't know 'ow...yet.'

'Shut up, Twill!' Calfain said softly and, ignoring him began to scrutinise the map.

'It certainly is a fair way off shore,' the dreamweaver mused after several seconds of pondering, 'was your estimate of the distance correct, Ven?'

'Indeed, Calfain, tis naught more than ten miles in a straight line.'

'How will we keep the boat headed towards the island?' Peltene had asked a valid question.

'Cipeus is due south of Tapp harbour,' Venden explained, 'given a clear and cloudless night; we must endeavour to keep the Great Northern Star to our own backs at all times.'

'*Night?*' Twill protested, 'we're sailing at night? In the dark?'

'Shut up, Twill!' Calfain said once again.

'He has a point, Cal,' Peltene put in, 'none of us can handle a boat in broad daylight, let alone on the high seas in the dark.'

'Fearest naught the night-time, Lady. These next days see us blessed with a high bright moon to guide our way.'

Calfain looked with some concern at Peltene. She had a dubious frown on her face.

'It's the only way, Pel,' he said as reassuringly as possible, 'there would be no way we could land in daylight. They'd see us coming for miles. It has to be in the dark, if only to give us enough time to hide the boat and ourselves.'

She smiled self-consciously, 'I'd never actually thought of that. I just sort of had a vision of arriving at the front gate and knocking on it.'

Calfain glanced at Venden. Venden looked at him curiously, then, they both blurted the word 'Rope,' at the same time.

'Best get a grapple, as well,' Calfain added.

'Ha!' Twill chirped, 'you forgot the rope! I can't believe yer both forgot the rope.'

'*Shut up, Twill!*' Both Calfain and Venden snapped.

'Was she pretty?' Peltene asked softly as they lay together in the darkness.

'Who?'

'The woman you once loved.'

Calfain had at some point always expected this question arising. Women always did this sort of thing. They just could not help themselves.

'Yes,' he replied simply.

'Did you truly love her?'

'I thought I did.'

'What happened to make you believe otherwise?'

'Pel,' he began to protest, 'it's in the past. A long, long time ago.'

She truly hurt you didn't she?' Peltene persisted with her questions.

Calfain shuffled uncomfortably on the bed, 'I deserved it, I suppose.'

'What did she do?'

'She took a lover, I eventually found out. She left, then she came back a few months later and I forgave her.'

Peltene shifted her body to lay on her side with her head propped on an arm, 'Then what happened?'

'We were fine for a while, then it started again, with a different fellow, only this time, she took everything I had. Money, clothes, even sold the house I'd bought and I didn't even know it until the new owner came knocking on the door.'

'Why? Why would someone do such a horrible thing?'

'Nature of the beast I suppose, Pel.'

'That's not fair! I would never do such a thing.'

Calfain smiled to himself in the darkness, 'No, I'm sorry, Pel, I didn't mean that you would. But, so far in my life, it's happened twice with the same woman and again with a different one. It just sort of makes a man wary, that's all.'

Peltene brushed a hand down the side of his cheek,

'Cal,' she whispered, 'when we get my son back, I want you to come and stay with us...in my cottage.'

Calfain lay motionless; this was what he had envisioned when they had first met. He had daydreamed about it, but now, that thought, only a week old, seemed like a lifetime ago. It had, he forced himself to admit, been no more than idle speculation. He knew deep within that he could not afford to allow himself the luxury of another woman to love. If he failed again...

'We'll see, Pel,' he said softly. 'We'll see.'

Peltene suddenly raised herself up. 'What do I have to do to convince you I'm serious, Master Dreamweaver?' she asked lightly.

'I know you are,'

'Do I have to do...this!' her hand moved across his body and he jerked violently.

'Pel, no, of course not, I...' he involuntary jerked again as her hand moved once more.

Suddenly, she moved across his body into a sitting position. 'This then, perhaps?'

'Mmm, yes...that'll do it, Pel.'

Venden and Twill left their lodgings immediately after eating a light breakfast. They were on their way to locate a vessel big enough to carry five people comfortably.

Peltene and Calfain ate a more leisurely meal; Peltene was to purchase two extra horses and equipment. Calfain had other plans.

She kissed him lightly as they stood outside their lodging house, then she was gone, instantly becoming swept along with the throng of people hurrying about their daily lives.

The dreamweaver sauntered along the street in the opposite direction, setting his bearings, memorising landmarks and generally getting a feel for the bustling metropolis. It always paid to make oneself familiar with the landscape. That was his motto!

Two hours later and he was wandering around an obviously less affluent part of the city. People here eyed him warily, as they would any stranger who happened into their close little community.

Calfain eventually found the kind of shop that he was looking for. He knew from past experience, whichever town or city one found oneself in, there was always an outlet which supplied one's requirements – whatever they may be - for a price.

Calfain entered the bedroom of his lodgings sometime around mid-afternoon, he was surprised to find Peltene and Venden quietly talking.

The dreamweaver glanced around, 'Where is he?' he asked, resignation already creeping into his voice.

'I was relating the tale unto Lady Peltene, Calfain,' Venden said somewhat guiltily.

'What tale? What's he done now?'

'Fearest naught, Calfain, Naught harm - as such, hath befallen him, thine heart whilst be lifted to hear…'

'Oh I don't know,' Calfain interrupted.

Venden smiled and continued, 'Whilst we surveyed all and sundry of the many splendid marine vessels on offer, Master Twill didst begin to succumb to his weakness for self-indulgent stimulation.'

Calfain pointedly stared at the big man. 'What did he find? Fish oil? Dried octopus intestines?'

Venden shook his head, 'Nay, Calfain, naught so exotic as those articles. Twas indeed, another form of stimulation. Our own friend was propositioned by er,' he glanced at Peltene, trying to vocalise a delicate way of structuring his next sentence, 'one of the, er, friendlier inhabitants of the harbour.'

'Oh!' Peltene gushed, 'you mean a street lady?'

Venden's face reddened, 'Er, yes, ma'am, indeed, that wouldst be an accurate interpretation'

'Did you let him go with her?' Peltene leaned forward in her seat, perversely enjoying Venden's obvious discomfort.

Venden blinked and sat upright, 'Lady Peltene, I am mine own keeper, as Twill is his own. I twas naught cast adrift into this world with the preconceived notion of becoming his mother.'

'So you let him go with her, then?' Peltene pressed, a wicked little grin appearing at the corners of her mouth.

'I didst mine own best to avail him of the obvious perils of such a liaison. Alas, mine own words fell to the ground, unwanted and unheeded.

Calfain shrugged his shoulders, 'Well, if he did, he did. He's a big boy.'

Venden looked up at the dreamweaver, 'Nay, Calfain, t'worst is yet to be revealed,' he said in a sad voice, 'our eminent lady of the street didst naught only sell him her body, she also didst make a tidy profit supplying unto him, certain unidentified substances.'

Calfain groaned aloud.

'How do you mean...unidentified, does he have any left?' Peltene asked.

'Nay, Lady, Everything she provided, he didst consume, before emerging from her bed. So much, didst he engorge himself, forced twas I to return him here atop mine own shoulders. Such twas his consumption, it rendered him unable to place one foot in front of t'other.'

'We'll leave him here.' Calfain made an instant decision, 'we don't need him. We'll probably be better off without him anyway.'

'He'll try and follow, Cal,' Peltene suggested, 'you know what he's like. He may well cause more trouble here trying to follow, than if he's with us.'

Calfain stared at the floor, she was right, he reluctantly had to admit.

'If I mayest offer a suggestion?' Venden spoke.

Calfain and Peltene looked at him.

'I shouldst pray for mine own soul for even suggesting such wickedness, but we couldst leave the man mid-point twixt the mainland and Cipeus.'

'You mean...throw him overboard?' Peltene gasped. A look of horror crossed her face.

'Yes!' Calfain hissed jubilantly, 'Brilliant, Ven, absolutely brilliant!'

'Calfain!' Peltene shouted.

Calfain and Venden saw the look in Peltene's eyes and knew they could push this one a little further, but time was now of the essence. Getting back to the subject in hand, Calfain asked Venden,

'So, after all that, did you find us a boat?'

Venden nodded, 'Tis a fifteen or sixteen footer. Well capable of transporting our party I wouldst think. Two sets of oars and it hath been placed carelessly within our reach.'

'Excellent, Ven. We'll go and have a look shortly.' He turned his attention to Peltene, 'Pel, did you acquire the horses?'

Peltene smiled and nodded affirmatively. 'Of course, dear and the saddle and the provisions. I didn't become sidetracked like our budding sailors,' she replied smugly.

'Are the animals stabled with the others?'

'Yes and the saddle is there also and the provisions are under the bed.'

'Wonderful,' he congratulated her. Then, standing, he looked down at her, 'Pel, Ven and I are going to look over this boat. Would you keep an eye on our sleeping friend? If and only if, he wakes, give him this to eat. Nothing more and just a tiny sip of water. Enough to send it down and no more.'

He handed her a small round green coloured tablet, not much bigger than a mouse dropping.

'It looks like a mouse dropping,' she remarked, turning it in her fingers, 'what is it?'

'A mouse dropping,' he replied.

'Euww,' Peltene pulled a face and held the pill at arms length

'No, seriously, it's just a little something to revive him very quickly, that's all.'

The two men stood gazing down at the water lapping gently against the stonework of the harbour. Bobbing around ten feet below them on the low tide was a beautifully constructed and well-maintained rowing boat of traditional design. Neatly placed within the hull were two sets of polished oars. The rudder had been lifted and laid under the stern seat.

'It certainly looks in good condition,' Calfain remarked.

'I hath always greatly admired the craftsmen whose skills and devotion canst produce articles of such outstanding quality and beauty.'

Calfain glanced out of the corner of his eye at him,

'I said it looked all right, I wasn't falling in love with it.'

They wandered around the harbour for a short while, seeing who was around and doing what.

'How long will it take to reach the island?' Calfain asked.

'I wouldst allow five, perhaps six hours for our inexperience. If we endeavour to row as the light deserts us, then we hath more than enough time before daybreak.'

Calfain studied his face. 'You sure?'

'Naught at all, mine friend.'

They turned and made their way back to the lodging house.

Twill had begun to return to the ordinary world and as instructed, Peltene gave him the tablet as Calfain had prescribed. Within ten minutes, Twill was up and about, if still a touch groggy. When she had convinced herself his brain was working properly, Peltene set about giving him a tongue lashing that would have made Calfain and a battalion of soldiers blush with embarrassment on hearing.

'Is he awake?' Calfain asked her on their return.

'Yes.'

'Did you give him the pill?'

'Yes.'

'That should keep him awake for the next twelve hours then.'

They set about packing their equipment and clothes, leaving everything in neat piles around the room. Next, Calfain went downstairs to pay for two extra nights, advising the owner that they were going on an expedition for a couple of days, seeking out land to purchase and that he should leave the rooms undisturbed.

They left the lodging house shortly after supper, carrying a small sack of food, the rope and grapple, Venden's map and little else.

The boat was just as they had left it, save for being a little higher up the harbour wall due to the tide. The group sauntered passed it and carried on around the harbour as if taking a late evening stroll.

The place was fairly deserted except for a few others presumably taking the air also.

Satisfied that they would not be stopped or questioned about their actions, they made their way back to the boat. Venden was the first aboard, followed by Peltene then Twill and finally after checking the area one more time, Calfain lightly tripped aboard.

Twill sat in the forward seat, Peltene took the stern. Calfain sat facing her with a pair of oars and Venden behind him, towards the bows also with a pair of oars. It took them several minutes of splashing and cursing before they managed to place the oars in the water at the right time and at the proper angle to make the blades cut the water cleanly, but soon the two oarsmen were like old hands and beginning to – almost - enjoy themselves.

Chapter Ten.

Two hours out into the bay and the swell had subsided to almost the texture of a pond. Venden remarked that this was because the tide was turning now and very soon, they would struggle to keep the boat on course.

Twill remained silent in the bows, his sallow complexion now tinged with a hint of green. Peltene had, as instructed by Venden, positioned the tiller into its metal socket and was happily steering them along a true course.

'I think I could enjoy life on a boat,' she remarked, 'there's really nothing to it.'

'That's because you're not rowing, my sweet,' Calfain replied through his exertions of pulling on the oars.

She chose to ignore his comment and continued, 'Yes, a nice little boat on Tansa Bay, a spot of fishing and…'

'I hate fishing,' Calfain snapped through gritted teeth.

'Since when?'

'Since I started rowing…two hours ago.'

'Boat!' Twill broke his silence by announcing what he had seen clearly and vocally.

'Sshh,' Venden hissed, 'Belay thine oars, Calfain,'

'What?'

'Cease rowing!'

Calfain pulled in the oars and whispered to Peltene,

'Why does everyone start talking in a strange language as soon as they get on a boat?'

Peltene shrugged, 'Venden doesn't need to be on a boat to speak strangely.'

'Sshh,' Venden hissed again, 'The tinniest of sounds wilst traverse great distances over still water.'

The little craft drifted on under its own momentum for several more yards, then, gradually began to wallow as its occupants sat perfectly still and quiet.

Somewhere out in front of them a large sailing boat sliced through the water. The wind was light and it did not seem to make great headway, just enough to move it on.

Lanterns in the high rigging allowed them to determine how tall the masts were and how many. To the aft of the ship, other lanterns burned brightly in a cabin. None appeared to be on deck, but Venden was aware that there would be a lookout somewhere, even if he were dozing.

It took a full ten minutes for the ship to open the distance between them to a point where Venden was satisfied they could continue their journey.

'A close thing,' Venden remarked.

'Close? He was a half-mile away!' Calfain snapped.

'Nay, Calfain, sailors have the keenest of eyes, especially when the moon burns as bright as this. I wouldst venture the lookout was sleeping or we wouldst now be attempting to convince the captain that his assistance was naught required.'

They lowered the oars into the water and within a few strokes, had regained their previous rhythm.

'I think that's it!' Twill announced, some time later.

Calfain's back was covered in sweat, but more, the pain from this previously unheard of hard work was excruciating.

Thankfully, he took the opportunity to stop rowing and turned his head as much as the stiffened muscles in his neck would allow.

'Is that it, Ven? Is that Cipeus?' he asked, trying to loosen his hands from the oars where they had clamped tight and set solidly.

'From this distance, I wouldst venture…yes. But I cannot be certain until we sight the lantern tower on the north shore.'

'Lantern tower?' Twill repeated.

'Aye, tis a visible warning to all who sail too close to the island. Seemingly it speaketh two words…Go away!'

'Not overly hospitable of them,' Calfain muttered, returning to his position.

They rowed for another fifteen minutes, then, as if from nowhere, a distant light became visible just as they rounded a tiny headland. Within a few minutes more, they all saw it clearly. A lantern burned steadily, high on a foreboding wooden tower. It did indeed seem to menacingly whisper, 'Go away!'

They rowed on, keeping the island to their right and a quarter-mile distance between them and it. As the little boat made its way along the western shoreline, Calfain kept a sharp eye out for likely landing places. It was difficult with only, moonlight to see by, but not impossible.

It was Peltene who pointed to what seemed to be a beach, at least that was, she thought, what the noise was – waves, gently crashing on a beach. She was correct. A tiny cove came into view and Venden made an instant decision to land.

They beached the boat with a struggle, and then sought to hide as much of it as possible from prying eyes. Bracken was the obvious choice and there was plenty.

Satisfied the disguise would stand up to a cursory inspection, Calfain and the others cautiously made their way up a gentle, sandy slope of a hill and stood for a moment assessing their position.

'Mine own assumption wouldst be that we hath travelled almost half the length of the island, along its westerly shore, therefore the monastery wouldst be sited thataway.' He pointed southwards towards what seemed like a forest of trees.

'What lies to the east?' Calfain asked casually.

'Rice fields as I recall. The centre of the island is almost at sea level and thus waterlogged a goodly part of the year. I doth think it wise to travel under the cover of the green canopy rather thanst out in the openness of a rice bog.'

'Agreed!' Calfain replied, immediately seeing the logic of Venden's words.

They walked along, silently for the best part of half a mile. Peltene gently placed her hand in Calfain's own. He squeezed it for reassurance and smiled at her. Venden, who was several yards in front, stopped and turned, putting his fingers to his lips, indicating silence. The other three came and stood alongside, waiting.

'The rice fields art now behind us. In front, layeth the monastery.' He pointed.

Calfain could barely make out in the moonlight, the shape of a huge building.

'I never expected it to be that big,' he whispered.

'Lest ye forget, it doth house several hundred persons,' Venden reminded him.

Calfain nodded silently. His mind calculating the odds of getting in and even more importantly, getting out again. He doubted it was going to be straight forward, but...he had come this far...

'Ven,' he said quietly, pulling the big man a short distance from the others, I have no right to ask this of you, but I'm going to ask anyway.' He took a long deep breath. Venden simply watched him, saying nothing. 'If it all goes wrong and something happens to me...like getting killed...or worse...then promise me you'll get Peltene out of that monastery and away from this wretched island. Even if it means not rescuing her son.'

Venden stiffened and stood up straight. He looked Calfain squarely in his eyes

'Calfain, ye have mine solemn oath that it shall be so. I shallst naught rest until I hath returned the Lady safely to her home.'

'No!' Calfain said quickly, 'No, whatever you do...don't take her home.'

'Then to what destination wouldst thee have us travel?'

'Take her to the queen. Queen Aramella, in Yarlis City. Peltene knows her and she may be able to help.'

'In what way couldst the queen be of assistance to the Lady, Calfain?'

'I don't really know, Ven. But if you don't get the boy out, then as night follows day, Peltene will want to return to collect him...one way or another. I'm thinking Queen Aramella might be persuaded to put Pel under her protection and send a few Nayal knights down here and tear down this whole place.'

The moon was sinking fast now. The sky was gathering a pink, pre dawn glow that suggested it would be a fair day. Venden scanned the horizon once more and then spoke again.

'I wouldst suggest we secrete ourselves a tad deeper into the trees and take our turns in resting and observing.'

Calfain nodded, 'I'll take first watch. You find us somewhere to settle for the day.'

Venden led the way back into the trees, easily finding a place to sit and rest perhaps even sleep for a few hours.

Peltene opened the little bag of food she had brought and the three ate a meagre meal, then, they settled to wait.

Twill sat on a fallen log, surveying the ground. Venden saw him and watched silently for a few moments.

116

'Master Twill,' he called in a low voice, 'I wouldst resist the temptation, twere I thee.'

Twill glanced up scowling, 'Well, yer not me... are yer?' he snapped.

'*Twill!*' Peltene hissed, 'If you touch anything, then you're no good to us and if you're no good to us...then we leave you here.'

Twill stared hard at her, working out in his mind whether she was serious or not. Peltene stared back. He decided that she was serious.

'I was only looking, Mistress, I wouldn't 'ave... 'Onest!'

'I mean it!' she said in a hard tone.

He slid from the log and sat on the grass, his arms folded looking suitably chastised.

Calfain found a comfortable branch, high in an oak tree. He settled in and began to survey the surroundings.

From the height above ground level, he could easily see the monastery, or at least part of it. Several uneventful hours passed without incident, then, suddenly, a bell tolled in the distance.

Almost immediately, black and brown robed monks began to file from a door that was hidden from the dreamweaver's view.

The line of holy men snaked its way along a path towards the general direction of the rice fields. Some, Calfain could see, were carrying farm implements, others, what appeared to be wicker baskets, slung over their shoulders.

Calfain counted forty men. He smiled ruefully, that left only one hundred and sixty, or there abouts, in the monastery itself. On a whim and with another smile to himself, he decided not to attack the building...just yet.

Calfain had been perched in the tree for more than five hours, when he heard a gentle whistle from somewhere below. He glanced down and spotted the sandy mop of hair that belonged to Venden. Silently, Calfain climbed down threading his way through the branches.

'The Lady hath concerns for thine stomach, Calfain,' the big man whispered.

'Me too, Ven. I thought you'd forgotten about me.'

Venden shook his head and smiled, 'Nay, I for mine own part, hath been active elsewhere. I thinkest I hath determined our entry point into the brethren's lair.'

Briefly, Venden described what he had discovered and how they should tackle breaking into the monastery after dark. Calfain listened, nodding occasionally and adding one or two points of his own. Then, he returned to where Peltene and Twill were waiting.

As late evening approached, the daytime birds that inhabited Cipeus Island began to call it a day and said their goodnights to each other. The night flyers took over the eternal vigil and hooted out their greetings to the rising moon.

Venden crept silently back into the camp, so quiet was he that he was standing behind Twill before any of the other three knew he was there.

Twill jumped in alarm. *'Don't do that!'* he hissed over his shoulder.

Venden smiled down on the addict 'Twas a wake up call, mine befuddled friend,' Venden replied softly, 'I venture to suggest, Calfain, it wouldst be prudent to break camp and make our way to the brethren's house.'

Calfain glanced up at the rapidly fading light, 'I agree, Ven.'

'Did 'e just say we were leaving?' Twill put the question to anyone.

'Exactly that, Twill,' Peltene answered him.

'Ha!' he retorted, pleased with himself, 'I'm getting the 'ang of 'is funny talk, now. It's not that difficult.'

Venden looked down at the little figure hunched before him. 'Thine own perceptiveness is at long last becoming exposed to the real world now that thine addiction be on the wane. It doth indeed, lighten mine own heart.'

Twill turned slightly and gave him a questioning look.

'He said,' Calfain spoke up, 'get your backside off that log…we're moving out.'

The three intruders to the island took a little over an hour to walk the distance from their hiding place to within a hundred yards of the monastery.

Venden had led them on a roundabout route, keeping to whatever cover he could find. On several occasions, even Calfain lost sight of him as he moved silently and swiftly along. When Venden disappeared, all they could do was to halt and wait quietly for his return.

On one occasion, Venden remarked, 'I canst perceive that our two companions are naught truly versed in the arts of subterfuge and cunning, Calfain, but, I chanced to thinkest that thine own self wouldst be partially conversant.'

Calfain had stared at him sourly, about to reluctantly admit that the ex-monk was a superb woodsman,

'Oh…shut up, Ven.' He changed his mind.

They lingered in a clump of shrubbery, Venden watching the dark ominous building for several minutes.

Twill began to fidget, scratching noisily and slapping away midges and flies, which were looking for a ready meal of sweat.

Calfain, standing next to him, clipped him on his ear and continued to watch Venden.

Peltene rolled her eyes.

Eventually, Venden glanced over his shoulder and nodded for them to follow him. He moved forward out of the security of the bushes.

The moon was shining brightly, as it had for the last two nights. As they walked swiftly in a straight line towards the huge stone building, their shadows danced on the ground that they passed over.

An owl screeched in the distance and Venden immediately stood still. Calfain and Peltene instantly did the same. Twill crashed into Peltene's back, causing her to catapult into Calfain. The dreamweaver instinctively spun to catch her. She smiled apologetically up at him. He realised what had happened and shot a withering look at the addict.

Twill mouthed a silent sorry and began to study the ground more closely than of late.

Venden, without a word, was off again.

The perimeter around the monastery buildings was a fifty-yard wide, immaculately maintained lawn. A few shrubs were dotted here and there and several stone benches had been carved from the local material and placed randomly. Gravel paths intersected in all directions across the lawn, but the four intruders kept well clear of them.

As they approached the main door, itself a magnificent structure, Calfain tapped Venden's shoulder lightly and nodded towards their left. Some twenty feet from the big oaken door, a smaller entrance was just visible. This door was also made of wood, but was less than half the height and width of the main entrance. Immediately in front of it, two stone steps led down to its base.

Venden lightly stepped down and Calfain could see now that the door was almost as tall as the ex-monk. Venden pressed an ear to the wood and held his breath.

Presently, he turned to the dreamweaver and shook his head, indicating that there was no sound from the other side.

Calfain stepped down into the tiny space at the front of the door and extracted something from one of his pockets. Venden watched him curiously. Peltene watched with an innocent fascination. Twill smirked to himself. He knew a burglar when he saw one.

The dreamweaver placed the thin metal rod into the keyhole and twisted the tool expertly. After several seconds of probing, a faint click signified that he had successfully unlocked the door.

Calfain glanced at Venden and winked. The ex-monk smiled thinly back and took hold of the latch. Pressing it gently until it was free of the stirrup; he placed his other hand on the door and pushed.

Calfain was impressed by the attention the monks gave to the state of the door's hinges. They moved with absolute silence.

Venden's head was around the door. He peered into the darkness, then, in an instant, he was inside. Calfain was next through, followed by Twill, who, in an un-gentlemanly manner, pushed past the Lady Peltene.

Calfain half-turned just in time to see the manoeuvre and unhesitatingly, smacked Twill across the back of his head and glared at him, defying the addict to make a sound. Twill remained silent and scowled.

The group of four stood in the darkness, Venden struck the flint in his tinderbox and for an instant they saw their surroundings. Venden struck the flint again this time lighting a few strands of tiny wood shavings he carried in the box. It was all he needed to locate a lantern hanging from a hook on a nearby wall. Quietly and expertly, he removed the lantern from the hook and lifting the old, soot covered glass; he flicked his tinderbox once again. The lantern flickered into life and as the dull glow from the wick grew brighter the whole room came into view.

Calfain glanced around. He could now see that the room was, in essence, a tool shed. Garden implements were stacked neatly against a wall. An ancient wooden wheelbarrow was upturned onto its wheel and leaned against a pile of cloth sacks. A small wooden bench stood in the middle of the room, obviously used to repair the tools. Potted plants were stacked in one corner.

Twill had seen the plants and moved shiftily across the room to give them a closer inspection. Peltene saw him and watched guardedly.

Meanwhile, Calfain and Venden were eyeing another door. This one was an internal structure and would obviously lead them deeper into the building. Venden reached out a hand and gripped the handle firmly. The door was not locked and moved freely under the big man's pressure.

'Let's go,' Calfain whispered as he turned in the general direction of where Peltene and Twill should have been standing. They were not there and for a brief instant, Calfain panicked. He glanced around again and saw them huddled together, bent over the potted plants.

'*Let's go!*' he hissed again, this time with urgency.

Peltene stood up and beckoned him to come to her.
The dreamweaver narrowed his brow in a look of consternation but did what was asked of him and tapping Venden on his shoulder held up a finger, signalling the big man to wait a minute.

As he approached her, Calfain raised an eyebrow in question. She placed a hand on his shoulder and gently drew him near so as to whisper into his ear.

'Twill has found something interesting here.' She said softly.

'What?' He whispered back.

'Plants.'

Calfain snorted. 'Any plant is interesting to him. So what?'

'No, no,' she replied hurriedly, 'he recognised these plants as particularly potent...and dangerous. They are grown only for the stems. Crushed and boiled, the liquid has the power to alter a person's mind...forever'

Calfain looked into her eyes and then glanced at the harmless looking, plants with their short thick brown stems, stacked in pots against the wall. Twill was squatting on his haunches, rubbing a leaf between his thumb and forefinger and sniffing at it with the expertise of a connoisseur.

'Stop that!' Calfain hissed at the addict.

Twill glanced up, still rubbing the leaf, 'It won't 'arm me, Calfain,' he said softly, 'they only releases the mind benders from the stems when they're boiled. Don't worry, I could eat them right now and nothing would 'appen.'

'Well...don't,' Calfain snapped. 'Just put them down and leave them alone.'

Peltene's mouth was back, close to his ear again, 'It must be what the monks use to alter the minds of their new members. It means they really don't have the same powers as you, Cal.'

Calfain glanced at her again and thought about what she had said. This had been his overriding concern that the monks were more powerful - more adept at invading minds than he was. If they were indeed using an inducer of some kind, then he had the advantage. He did not require boiled vegetables to get into a person's mind.

Calfain smiled ruefully, 'I'll bear it in mind, Pel.'

He gently took hold of her hand and said. 'Now come along...we have to get moving.'

As Calfain tugged at Peltene's hand, he failed to notice that Twill was stuffing a fistful of plant leaves into his trousers pocket.

Venden was waiting patiently at the door. As the three stood before him, he shot a questioning look at them all.

Calfain whispered to him, 'Twill has found some plants and Peltene thinks the monks use them in their mind altering ceremony.'

'Interesting,' the big man mouthed.

'Hmm, perhaps,' Calfain replied, 'Right! Let's go.'

Venden tugged on the door and it opened as silently as the outer door had done.

As it did, they could see stone steps immediately in front of them, leading upward to the next level. As the steps were the only point of exit, they mounted them in single file, Venden leading the way, the dreamweaver next and then Peltene and Twill behind her.

Twenty-two steps later, another door confronted them. Once again, Venden cautiously listened for any sounds from beyond before opening it.

The area beyond the door was large and empty. It was perhaps thirty feet square with dimly lit torches hanging from the walls. At mid-point along each wall, there were other doors. All closed.

'Which one, Ven?' Calfain asked softly.

'Whichever thine heart desires, Calfain,' Venden replied.

'Are you telling me you don't know?'

'Correct.'

Calfain threw his arms up in despair, 'Pick a door, Pel,' he whispered, turning to face her.

Peltene studied the three identical doors intently.

'Pel, they're all the same,' Calfain hissed desperately.

'Sshh!' she replied, as she continued to gaze at them one after the other and back again.

'Oh...*for goodness sake!*' Calfain hissed again

'That one,' she said finally, determined not to be rushed when faced with such an important decision.

Calfain followed her pointing finger with his gaze,

'May I ask what drew you to that particular door?'

'I rather liked the colour of its aura,' she answered him smugly.

'So be it,' he sighed, wishing he had not asked.

Venden and Calfain moved towards the chosen door. Once again Venden opened it cautiously,

'More steps, Calfain,' he turned his head back to the dreamweaver as he spoke. 'They doth lead back downward.'

Calfain turned to Peltene, waiting for her agreement to proceed or not. She nodded eagerly and motioned him to move forward.

'Then we go down, Ven,' he replied.

'How far have we come?' Peltene whispered in the near darkness of the stairwell.

'I've counted ninety-seven steps so far,' Calfain whispered back over his shoulder, 'so that means we're four times deeper than when we first entered the building.'

They continued on in silence, Calfain mentally ticking off the steps as they descended.

Without warning, Venden who was leading them down suddenly stopped.

'Another door,' he announced

'One hundred and sixty steps.' Calfain confirmed the final number.

'I reckon ya got the wrong door, My Lady,' Twill spoke from behind and above her.

'No. No I didn't,' Peltene replied, 'I trust my instincts.'

'The only places that are this deep in the ground is dungeons,' Twill insisted.

'Shut up, Twill,' Calfain's voice drifted up from a few steps below.

Venden had by now opened the door. A dozen or more torches brightly illuminated the room beyond. Placed against the far opposite wall and the adjacent right one were high backed wooden benches with elaborate carvings of winged serpents. In the centre of the room were two low tables; each one was about three feet square. To the left, on the plain wall, another door seemed to beckon them.

'No choice this time, Pel,' Calfain whispered as he moved in its direction.

Venden lifted the latch and just as he pulled, he felt a resistance that instinctively made him pull harder.

Unbeknown to him, on the other side, one of the brethren was just about to push on the door. Venden tugged and the monk came wheeling through and bounced into the big farm workers muscular chest.

The monk cried out, more from the shock and surprise than from alarm at seeing the intruders. In that split second, Venden recovered first and with his free left hand, punched the man squarely on his nose.

The monk dropped to the floor with a muffled thud.

'Well done, Ven,' Calfain said softly, 'only one hundred and ninety-nine to go.'

'What shall we do with him?' Peltene asked nervously.

Calfain was already through the door and inspecting the room beyond for more of the brethren. There were none.

'Put him in here. It looks like a dining room of some kind. Long tables and benches everywhere.'

Venden gathered up the unconscious monk and slung him over his shoulder with ease. As he passed through the door, he glanced around and saw a large wicker basket that was big enough to take a body. He walked over to it and glanced inside. Napkins, towels and other laundry were piled within. Venden heaved the man from his shoulder and allowed him to fall into the basket.

Calfain stood beside Venden and looked at the inert form.

'I doth thinkest he will awaken shortly,'

'Not after he's had a smell of this, he won't,' Calfain replied, taking a small metal phial from his jacket pocket. He leaned into the basket and pulled a napkin from beside the monk. Next he removed the stopper from the phial and poured a small amount of a clear liquid onto the fabric. Then, he placed the napkin tight against the monk's nose and mouth allowing him to breathe in the vapours.

'A sleeping draught?' Venden inquired.

'Smells like the juice of the Fostic plant,' Twill observed from a few feet away and stared longingly at the metal phial that Calfain still held.

'Well spotted, Twill,' Calfain said, 'and if you don't behave…you'll be the next to sniff it.'

'I can 'andle that,' Twill answered nonchalantly.

Calfain glanced disgustedly at the addict, refusing to be drawn further into a futile argument at this point. Instead, he turned to Venden,

'Let's go, before we attract any more late night wanderers.'

The four intruders made their way across the dining room towards a door at the opposite end of the room. Once through the door the only way was to turn left. They did so and immediately felt the upward incline of the corridor.

'Are we going back to where we came from?' Peltene asked quietly.

'Perhaps so, if we carried on straight ahead,' Calfain replied, 'but I think this would be a better way.'

He indicated to turn right, into another corridor.

''Ope you're remembering all this,' Twill grumbled from behind Peltene.

'Shut up, Twill,' Calfain hissed.

Another thirty or so feet and another decision was required.

'Left or right, Pel?' Calfain asked over his shoulder.

'Right,' she answered without hesitation.

Venden had heard her whisper and began to proceed along the corridor.

Within ten paces, steps appeared before them, leading down. Venden began the descent cautiously, aware again that should someone be coming upward, then, there was nowhere to hide.

Exactly one hundred steps later, the group arrived at another door. This time, Venden hesitated as he withdrew his ear from the wooden barrier.

'Several persons are asleep within, Calfain,' he whispered very quietly.

Calfain took a deep breath before answering,

'Let's have a quick peek,'

Gently, the big farm worker squeezed his powerful hand over the metal door latch and lifted it silently. The door opened smoothly, much to Calfain's relief. Now, with no obstruction to speak of, the sounds of regular snoring could be heard clearly.

'It's...' Twill was about to speak when Peltene's hand flashed up from her side and smothered his mouth. She glared at him in the gloomy light, defying him to speak further.

Calfain turned his head and shot him an angry glance, and then he put a finger to his lips to signify complete silence.

Venden opened the door a little more. As the dim light filtered into the room, Venden with Calfain standing on tiptoes close to his shoulder could see several rows of beds stretching away into the dark distance. Each bed clearly had a monk laying on it. All appeared to be sound asleep.

Venden closed the door again and turning to the dreamweaver raised a questioning eyebrow.

Calfain shrugged his shoulders in a manner, which suggested, that having come this far, they may as well continue.

Venden nodded silently, understanding the gesture. He re-opened the door and stepped into the room full of sleeping bodies.

Calfain slipped in behind him, followed by Peltene and then Twill. Venden stole a quick glance around and immediately saw another exit in the middle of the left adjacent wall. He closed the door behind him and started out in the general direction of the exit. Calfain reached for Peltene's hand and grasping it gently tugged at her to follow on.

Venden successfully navigated his way around the beds without incident and stood by the exit door waiting for the others to catch up. Just as Calfain and Peltene reached him, Twill let out a loud, clear curse. He had tripped over something and had fallen to his knees, scraping his leg on the side of one of the wooden bed-frames as he fell.

The room erupted almost immediately. Sleeping monks came instantly awake on hearing the commotion. Venden grabbed wildly in the darkness and grasped Calfain's shirt, dragging him forcefully towards the exit door. Peltene was still holding onto the dreamweaver's hand and she too was dragged along with him.

Venden tugged at the door and was through it in an instant, Calfain was alongside him and then Peltene.

'Leave him,' snapped Venden as he continued to haul his two accomplices behind him.

Venden moved quickly forward, totally unsure of where he was headed. Calfain and Peltene followed him along the straight corridor, which, unlike the monks sleeping quarters was dimly lit with torches. They could see yet another door awaiting them. This time, Venden opened it almost without halting his stride. He was immediately surprised to see that this room was more than that. This was a chapel of some sort. As he glanced around, searching for firstly, any of the monks and secondly, their next exit, he noticed how high the curved ceiling was.

'Can we hide here?' Peltene asked anxiously.

'No, Pel,' Calfain replied firmly, 'we need distance between us and the monks. It gives us a better chance of escape.'

'This way,' Venden said. He had located their next way out. It was a wooden spiral staircase, leading yet again still further down into the ground.

Calfain glanced down the curved stairway and then at Venden,

'I'm not keen, Ven,' he said, looking back down into the darkness.

'Tis either this way, or back along the way we hath just travelled and I fearest our fanatical friends wouldst require an explanation as to why we hath encroached into their domicile without firstly knocking on their door.'

Calfain glanced back towards the dormitory, then quickly at Peltene. She looked anxiously back at him, waiting for his decision.

'Your argument is sound, my friend.'

Without further preamble, Venden led the way down the spiral stairway.

Less than a minute later, they found themselves in what appeared to be another chapel. This one was less than half the size of the one above their heads and much darker.

'Let's hold on here awhile and see what happens,' Calfain said to the others.

Some fifty feet above their heads, forty or so naked or semi-naked monks had surrounded Twill. They stared at him impassively. He stood, nervously glancing, first at the floor and then at each of their expressionless faces. None spoke, or made

130

any attempt to touch him or take him into their custody. They simply waited, tightly gathered about him, forming an inescapable circle of flesh.

'Do you think they will torture him?' Peltene whispered as the three of them sat hiding behind a stone Diaz.

'Probably,' Calfain replied, flatly.

Venden was a little more optimistic, 'I wouldst doubt it, My Lady,' he answered slowly, 'I thinkest however that after they doth question him, they mayest invade his mind in order to determine the truthfulness of his answers.'

'Then they're in for a nasty shock when they get inside *his* head,' Calfain snorted.

'Calfain!' Peltene dug him in his ribs.

'What?' he asked, innocently.

'That's awful of you.'

'But it's true, Pel. His mind is so tangled and messed up with drugs; it'll take them a week to work it out.'

'Stop it!' she remonstrated again.

'Calfain doth hold a valid point, My Lady,' Venden cut in, ''tis unlikely Twill wouldst give us up to the brethren. That in itself gives us more time to continue our search for thine son and make good our escape.'

'But, but we can't just leave Twill here, they'll turn him into one of them.'

'Yes we can, Pel,' Calfain said coldly, 'He's well aware of the risks. He came with us with his eyes wide open. But I agree with Ven, Twill knows that if he keeps quiet about us, then there's always a chance we could rescue him. If he tells them we're here in the monastery and they catch us, then his chances of escape are nil.'

Chapter Eleven

'There was me and three others. 'Ow many more times?'

'So, that would make four of you, where are the others?'

The abbot who asked the question stood before Twill with his hands tucked away inside his white robes of office. His manner was quiet, but firm. He spoke with a soft regional accent that Twill did not recognise.

The cowl of his robes was laid back, revealing his shaved head. He reminded Twill of a skeleton. His skin was taut across his face and in the glow of the many lanterns; his colour was pale, very pale. Twill could almost see the veins under the surface.

Twill could not help but stare into the abbot's eyes as he spoke. They were hypnotic, demanding Twill's complete attention. Each time the addict tried to look away, he was mysteriously forced to return his gaze to the man's eyes.

'Where are your three accomplices now?'

'I don't know,' Twill replied softly, 'they were with me in the bedchamber, when I fell. Then, they just disappeared.'

The abbot turned his attention to one of the two monks standing at either side of Twill. His eyes flicked to the monk and they stared at each other for several seconds, then, the monk nodded his understanding at the unspoken message and turned, quietly leaving the room.

'They will be found,' the abbot spoke directly to Twill, 'Now, what is thy reason for trespassing into our home?'

'Let's move,' Calfain said gruffly, 'we've been here long enough.'

'Where?' Peltene asked.

'Anywhere, Pel. The longer we stay here, the more chance they have of working out which way we came.'

'But you said Twill wouldn't tell them about us, so they don't know we're here in the monastery, do they?'

The dreamweaver sighed and glanced at Venden, 'Let's not take the chance, shall we? From now on…we assume nothing.'

Calfain stood from his crouching position. Venden slowly uncoiled his bulk, flexing his cramped muscles, when the door they had closed behind them slowly opened. Calfain stood stock still, placing a hand on Peltene's shoulder, forcing her to stay crouched. Fortunately, they were hidden in shadows as the lanterns flickered from distant corners of the room.

Calfain held his breath, waiting. The door closed presently and he could hear small shuffling sounds. It sounded to him like the footfalls of someone who was barefoot. There was more than one set of footfalls.

'I bid ye - show thineselves.' The voice was dark, deep and commanding.

Calfain and his companions remained still and silent. With luck, he thought, the owner of the voice may just be attempting a ruse, neither knowing if they really were in the monastery or even here, in this room.

Suddenly, the dreamweaver experienced a blinding flash of pain in his head. It was as if a needle sharp knife had been passed through his right eyeball and on into his brain. His head shot backwards and he stifled a grunt of surprise.

Peltene screamed out. The same searing flash of pain had invaded her head. Venden grunted in alarm, as the pain seemed to pass from Peltene and on to him.

'Ah! There be ye all!' the voice spoke softly from somewhere near the door. 'Step forward and declare thineselves.'

Several seconds passed, although it seemed to Calfain like an interminably long time. He knew the only thing now was to surrender, but his mind raced, trying to weigh his already limited and rapidly diminishing options.

Once again Peltene's scream snapped him back to the present. Whatever it was had been directed at her and only her this time. She slumped from her crouching position onto the floor and sobbed loudly.

'Alright!' Calfain shouted, 'Enough!' He bent and gently grasped her shoulders, lifting her upright.

'Are you alright?' he whispered close to her ear.

She nodded and rubbed her eyes, leaning heavily against him for support.

'Step forward,' the voice persisted.

Faced with no other options, Calfain began to manoeuvre himself and Peltene out from behind the tables they had hidden behind. Venden followed closely. Once out into the relative openness of the room, the three stood awaiting their fate.

'Search them!' commanded the voice. Immediately, five figures moved forward. Three moved behind the captives and began to secure their hands behind their backs with thin, biting cords. The two others stood in front of Calfain and Venden, running their hands up and down the men's bodies, searching for weapons. One quickly located the knife that Calfain carried in his belt. The search was quick and thorough although, the robed figure did not search the dreamweaver's boots…much to his relief.

Venden's body search proved fruitless and the man doing it moved towards Peltene.

As he placed his hands on her shoulders, Calfain struggled against his restraints and snarled,

'Leave her alone. She carries no weapons.'

The man ignored him and continued to roam his hands down her arms and then onto her body.

'I said…' Calfain's outburst was cut short by the leader's voice.

'Allay thine fears, Mine brethren shalst taketh naught pleasure from the touch of her body. We harbour naught desires of the flesh.'

Peltene stood defiant as the robed figure moved his hands over her body. She stared back at him with a seemingly detached curiosity.

The man bent slightly to search the insides of her legs. As he placed a hand on her inner thigh, Peltene snapped her other leg upwards, connecting her knee with his jawbone. The crack was loud and resounded throughout the room. He staggered backwards, yelping and collapsed onto the floor.

The three monks standing behind their captives quickly responded, tugging at the rope bindings and restraining their prisoners from further movement.

'Nice move, Pel. Really nice.' Calfain said admiringly in spite of their predicament.

Just as she turned her head towards him, her body collapsed against the guard holding her from behind. Calfain made to move to her aid, but was held firm.

'She hath been restrained,' the voice in front of Calfain spoke again, 'it appears she be the greater danger to mine brethren at this time.'

The voice turned and faced the door. Without looking back, it said, 'Come, thine interrogation awaits.'

Calfain could see little point in resisting now. He glanced at Venden. The big man shrugged resignedly. Peltene's inert body was hoisted over the shoulder of one of the monks who moved off towards the exit. The two captives followed on behind.

Along dark corridors, up stairs, more turns left and right yet more stairs, a slope or two and a few doors later; Calfain was hopelessly confused and lost. He had absolutely no idea where he was. He was ordered to halt before a robust looking wooden door. It was opened for him and the robed figure pointed, indicating that the dreamweaver should enter.

Calfain dutifully did so and the door was slammed shut behind him.

He stood, struggling with the bindings on his hands. They would not come loose and bit deeper into his flesh. Presently, he gave up trying and glanced around the room. It was no more than a prison cell. Ten feet by ten feet and completely bare of any furniture or decoration. Four stonewalls stared back at him.

He had seen similar cells before and he knew there was little if no chance of escaping from them. He moved to the farthest corner away from the door and, slumping against the hard, cold wall, he slithered down it until he reached the floor. He sat worried for the safety of the others…especially Peltene.

The sound of the latch being lifted from outside brought the dreamweaver instantly awake. He had been lost in his thoughts of escape.

The heavy wooden door opened inwards and framed in the glow of lanterns from outside, the figure of a man stood, watching.

Calfain stared back, waiting. He sat perfectly still, offering no threat to the visitor; he assumed was to be his interrogator.

'Good day, Master Calfain,' the visitor said in modern-day Yarlish. 'Or would you prefer, "Dreamweaver?"'

Calfain stared hard at the man, trying to see his features through the bad light.

'Do I know you?' Calfain asked, squinting at the figure.

The man stepped forward, into the cell. Calfain could now see that he was not wearing the robes of a monk, but well tailored and expensive looking clothes. He stood, Calfain estimated, at a little over six feet tall and was lean with an athletic build. His hair was black and combed tight over his head; a small tail of it was tied at his nape. He was clean-shaven with alert eyes and a long, thin nose. A row of even white teeth showed through a thin smile from even thinner lips that Calfain thought could easily contort into a cruel grin.

This man, Calfain realised, was Peltene's estranged husband.

'No, Master Calfain, you don't know me personally, but I know of you. You are the one whom my wife has brought here to steal my son from me. Are you not?'

Calfain took a deep breath and hid his surprise at the man's knowledge, as best he could.

'I know nothing of what you speak,' Calfain said slowly.

The tall man's lips curled into a grim smile, 'We'll see, Dreamweaver…we'll see.' He replied coldly.

The flash of pain took the dreamweaver completely off guard. It invaded his head like a bolt of lightening, searing into every corner of his brain. Calfain let out a yelp of alarm, his head shooting back, banging on the hard stone wall behind him.

As his eyes cleared of the red mist that had drawn across them, Calfain could hear the man's voice, not through his ears, but inside his head.

'Now,' it said coldly from within, 'let's have a look around and see what you really do know.'

To Calfain, it felt like someone was in there, stamping their boots on the inside of his skull. The pain was excruciating. He yelled out aloud and violently shook his head to rid himself of the intruder.

'Do not fight it, Dreamweaver,' the voice said almost soothingly, 'let me see your memories, let me see what you know and it will be over quickly. Fight it and it will drive you insane.'

For that single instant, Calfain felt relief from the invasion. His mind suddenly became clear and sharp. Clear enough to gather his wits about him and realise he could indeed fight it if he so wished.

'No!' he shouted inside his head and concentrated on blanking out the voice. He concentrated hard on the first thing that came to mind - his knife. He pictured himself holding it menacingly, crouching and spinning around in an effort to confront the invasive voice that was inside him. Then he saw his foe clearly. Peltene's husband was standing in front of him, in nothingness, smiling knowingly. His thin lips curled at the corners.

'This won't do you any good at all, my friend.' He sneered.

Inside Calfain's mind, the dreamweaver lunged with the knife. The intruder simply sidestepped the attack easily out-manoeuvring Calfain's clumsy attempt to rid himself of the manifestation.

'Told you,' Tennay mocked.

Calfain lunged again and again. Each time his thrusts missed by a considerable distance. He was becoming frustrated, but strangely, he felt that he had to keep attempting to drive this thing from his head. He had to attack again and again. Calfain began to feel a certain comfort in the knowledge that whilst he was doing this, the intruder was not able to search out his memories and discover the truth.

'Just what, exactly, are you attempting to achieve by all this dancing around, Dreamweaver?' Lord Tennay asked, seemingly amused by Calfain's wild lunging with his knife.

Calfain knew that he had caused little or no concern to the man with his thrusting weapon, but it had proved a point that needed to be cleared up. Each time Calfain lunged with his knife, Tennay moved out of harms way. This, Calfain reasoned, should Tennay be struck, would cause him damage, physical damage, even though this battle was taking place inside the dreamweaver's head.

This brought some comfort to Calfain. Now he knew two things, the other being that Peltene's husband could not search his memory whilst occupied with avoiding Calfain's weapon.

With this knowledge, Calfain grew bolder and more confident. He was sure his abilities were evenly matched with the Lord Tennay's own

Without thinking too much about it, Calfain tried to create a dream inside his head - in the nothingness that the intruder had settled in.

* * *

Fifty feet above Calfain's cell, Twill lay naked on a hard table. His hands and feet were not bound, but a broad leather strap spanned his chest, holding him flat to the wooden top. His eyes were closed and his breathing was ragged. He had been force fed a mixture of plants and herbs. They now began to take effect on his mind.

'What is thine given name?'

'Twill.'

'Twill of where?'

'Twill of anywhere I choose.'

'Try hard, mine friend, naught to become flippant, lest thee suffer accordingly.'

'I'm not, I have no 'ome. My 'ome is where I lay for the night.'

'Very well,' Twill's inquisitor sighed, 'how many travelled with ye to this sacred island?'

'Three others.'

'What are thine accomplice's names?'

'Calfain, the Lady Peltene and Venden.'

'Which of them is their leader?'

'That would be Calfain.'

The inquisitor sighed heavily again, he looked at Twill closely, then, on a whim said, 'Stay calm, Twill. I shalst attempt to enter thine own mind and ascertain whether ye speak truthfully.'

'I *do* speak the truth,' Twill replied with an edge of desperation in his mumbling voice.

'We shalst see.' The inquisitor closed his own eyes and taking a long deep breath, he relaxed himself for his journey into the mind of Twill.

Twill felt a sudden flash of pain behind his eyes and then, there he was. The face of his inquisitor stared back at him from inside his head.

'Relax thine own mind, Twill. Let me explore the reaches of thine memories.'

Twill watched him through his minds eye with detached focus. Then, suddenly, something snapped inside Twill's head. He decided to himself that intruders were not allowed in here after all. It was his own private place. He had to do something about it. He would fight this man if need be, in order to recapture his mind.

'I want you to leave here,' Twill spoke in a commanding voice inside his own head.

The monk seemed to stare across the dark reaches. He could clearly see the shining figure of Twill who was standing, dressed in full battle armour polished to perfection and at least ten feet tall. He carried in one hand, a mighty two-handed sword and in the other, a heavily decorated and ornate leather shield.

'Ye canst naught intimidate mine own self, Master Twill. I dost knowest this to be a mere figment of thine mind. Banish it afore it does ye harm.'

'Get out of my head, monk, or face the consequences,' Twill amazed himself with his strong voice.

The monk laughed mockingly and took several steps towards the armoured mushroom addict. 'Enough of this, boy,' the monks voice became harsh, 'Place down these silly dreams and I wilst naught harm ye. Resist and ye will be driven insane within a heartbeat.'

'I will not permit you into my memories.' Twill persisted.

'Ye hath little choice, I wilst look, whether or not.'

Twill took a deep breath and made his decision, 'Then, monk, come with me on a journey through my memories. I will show you personally what it is like to be me. Come!'

Twill dropped the shield and lunged forwards, grasping the monk around his waist and launching the two of them into the black void of Twill's mind.

'Release me!' the monk screamed, 'Let go of me.'

Twill smiled to himself as he watched his own likeness grasp the intruder even more tightly as they seemed to fall into nothingness.

'Here,' said Twill to the monk, 'I will give you some memories of your own. Welcome to my world.'

Suddenly, Twill held the shining two-handed sword aloft and pointed it towards some far off speck of light. Within an instant, the two figures were there, floating before the pulsing, shimmering light.

'Come my nosy friend, come into my world. The insanity you thought you could give me is already here. I live with it every day. Come and see.'

Twill burst through the light and into a world that only people who constantly feed on the intoxicants of plants and herbs can ever understand.

Twill and the monk were almost horizontal, as they seemed to fly through a sea of swirling yellow mist and red clouds. The monk screamed harshly now, demanding to be returned to his own body. Twill ignored him and grinned fiendishly.

Suddenly, a loud, screeching bellow rang out and there before the two floating men stood a dragon of immense proportions. Its large, long snout belched a plume of hot steam,

'This is Tracca,' Twill letting go of the monk and explaining almost casually continued, 'we have been fighting each other for years. Sometimes he wins, sometimes, I win. Today, he will kill you.'

'Let me go back to mine own body!' the desperate monk pleaded, 'Let me go, I beseech thee.'

Again Twill smiled, an evil glint in his eyes, 'Not today, friend. Tracca is hungry and you are to be his dinner.'

Before the monk could recoil, Twill reached out, his arm seeming to extend five times its normal length to grasp the terrified monk around his neck. Twill snapped his arm back and suddenly; the monk's face was an inch in front of Twill's own.

'Stop squirming!' Twill commanded, 'Tracca likes his food in one gulp. If you thrash about, he might bite chunks off of you and that would hurt. Trust me, I know.'

Twill manoeuvred his body around in the nothingness and gazing one last time at the terrified holy man, nonchalantly pushed him away from his own body. The monk seemed to gently float across the void into the already salivating mouth of Twills old adversary.

The thrashing monk failed to heed Twills advice to remain still and sure enough, an arm and a leg were bitten from his torso to spin off into the swirling void.

Tracca swallowed hungrily and flicking his head towards the disappearing limbs, the beast saw them moving away from him. With a flap of his inadequately sized dragon's wings, he leaped off in greedy pursuit of them.

Outside of Twill's head, the monk lay prostrate on the floor. His body occasionally twitched with the last throes of death. His heart had stopped beating from the sheer fright of Twill's dream world.

Presently, Twill's eyes flickered open. The headache he now experienced was like none he had ever had. He groaned loudly as he tried to swallow. His mouth felt as if someone had poured a handful of gravel into it.

Several minutes passed before the addict dare to try moving his limbs.

Eventually, Twill plucked up enough courage to lift his arms and untie the leather belt that restrained him. Swinging his legs from the table, he gingerly sat upright and, leaning forward slowly placed his head in his hands and involuntarily vomited over the body of the monk. Twill stared at the mess before him, then, placing one foot carefully beside the body and stepping over it he muttered, 'Don't remember eating that.'

Chapter Twelve.

Venden's body jerked with the shock of the ice-cold water as it splashed over his nakedness. The two monks who were administering the harsh treatment each threw another bucket-full over him bringing him fully awake. He stood slumped against a wall. His manacled wrists reaching to a metal ring suspended somewhere from the ceiling.

The big farm hand had been recognised by the abbot as being the one who had deserted their cause some five years earlier. Now the abbot was taking his revenge.

'Thou wilst confess thine sins, brother,' one of the monks snapped as Venden's eyes opened.

'I hath naught to confess,' Venden drawled through the congealed blood that encrusted his lips.

The monk pressed on, ignoring Venden's rebuttal,

'Thou must confess before our holy one that thee didst bring into disrepute the sacrosanct name of our beloved holy order of Cipeus. *Confess now!* And be spared the humiliation of an ignominious death.'

'I didst naught bring disrepute onto thine order,' Venden protested, 'Thee and thine fellow brethren didst that of thine own volition.'

The second monk viscously lashed out at Venden's ribs with a thin piece of cane.
Venden grunted and winced at the sharp stinging pain.

'We the brethren charge thee with bringing outsiders to our sanctuary. Dost thou deny this charge?'

Venden looked up at the man, 'I didst naught bring them. Their decision to come hadst already been taken.'

It was a technicality, but one that Venden saw fit to pursue, if only to antagonise these people.

Venden flinched once more as the cane whip came down on his ribs again and again.

'Traitor! Traitor!' the first monk bellowed as the second one beat repeatedly at Venden's body.

Venden could feel himself slipping into blessed oblivion again, when the door to the cell burst open.

'Oi!' Twill cried and the two monks turned their heads in surprise, 'Leave my friend alone,' he growled.

The second monk recognised Twill instantly and lifted the cane to swipe it at the intruder.

The addict, fuelled with the assortment of herbs and plants that were still coursing around his body showed no fear of the monks. He took a deep breath as the whip-like cane slashed across his chest. Twill barely winced at the stinging pain it caused, but looked down to see a rapidly growing angry red wheal forming on his naked chest.

The second monk made to take another swipe at Twill, but as he drew back his arm and then brought it forward to hit the addict once more, Twill raised his own hand and in a surprise move, snatched the cane whip from the monks grasp.

Before the monks could react, Twill moved in close and with his left hand, seized the monk behind his neck. With the cane still grasped in his right, Twill savagely yanked the monk's head back and forced the cane up under his chin.

The man let out a stifled scream and died almost instantly as the hard fibrous material pierced his brain.

Twill yanked the cane from the monk's throat and turned murderously towards the first monk who was staring dumbfounded at the event.

'Where would *you* like it?' Twill queried through clenched teeth.

The startled man did the only thing he was trained to do under such circumstances. He dropped to his knees and clasped his hands together pleadingly,

'I beseech thee, brother, spare mine own miserable life that I mayest live to repent for mine wickedness and learn the goodly ways. I ask for thine own magnificent forgiveness.'

Twill looked down at him with crazed eyes,

'*What?*' he said frowning, 'Listen – *brother* - I 'ave trouble enough understanding *'im,*' he said, cocking a thumb at the still shackled Venden, 'never mind *your* babble.'

The monk began to visibly shake at his impending demise; Twill continued staring at him as if still deciding on which part of his body to lance with the cane. Then, on a whim, he lifted his bare foot and placed it squarely in the monks face, kicking hard.

Venden watched the scene through half closed eyes and finally raised a glimmer of a smile

'I wouldst be eternally grateful, mine friend if thou canst see thine way to freeing mine own self from this predicament.'

'What?' Twill asked. Half of his attention still focused on the two bodies.

'I said,' Venden began, 'unhook me from this contraption.'

'Ya see? Ya see? Yer can talk proper – when yer wants to.'

'Just do it!'

Twill reached up as far as his arms would stretch and jumped to catch the iron ring that held the chains to the hook secured into the ceiling.

Venden's arms slumped down to his midsection and he fell heavily against the wall for support. He took a deep breath to clear his head.

'Thank you,' he said softly.

'Should we go and find the others now?' Twill asked, ignoring the big farmhand's gratitude.

'T'wouldst be a reasonable idea.'

Twill searched the robes of the monks and eventually discovered the key that unlocked the chains from Venden's wrists. Once free and on an impulse, Venden began to strip the men of their robes.

* * *

Calfain held a mighty two-handed battleaxe above his head

Tennay stood impassive, watching the dreamweaver from a distance, still inside his head.

'And, pray tell, what are you about to tear apart with that fearsome instrument?' he asked scathingly.

'The insides of your head,' Calfain replied easily.

His idea now was to confuse his opponent as much as possible. He knew Tennay, however nonchalant he appeared, would keep out of the way of any weapon. Now, all he had to do was create the dream that would make Peltene's husband think his mind was being invaded as he had invaded Calfain's own.

'I know what you're doing, Dreamweaver, and it won't work,' Tennay said aloud.

None the less, there was a distinct edginess in his voice, which Calfain immediately realised. The dreamweaver allowed a whisker of a smile to cross his lips. Now he had him!

Calfain assumed the scene inside Tennay's mind to be much the same as his own, so his dream consisted of swirling tendrils of mist in a vast dark place. No point in elaborating too much – that was his motto.

'Dreamweaver,' Tennay said again, 'this will not work. You cannot turn my own mind against me.'

Calfain ignored the man and tried to imagine what his own face would look like if it were turned inside out.

Calfain suddenly heard a gasp of surprise and again, smiled, inadvertently causing his now reversed features to produce a horribly deformed gaping hole where his mouth was. The tendons and flesh parted leaving blood dripping from the lip-less orifice and his blood covered eyes stared out menacingly.

Calfain used the fraction of a second in which Tennay had gasped, to launch his attack with the battleaxe. He flew across the space that divided them and with the axe high above his head, brought it crashing down.

Tennay moved to side step the rapidly descending weapon, but was caught a glancing blow to his left shoulder. The contact was enough to knock him sideways and as he turned his head yelping in pain, he could see blood gushing freely from a three-inch long gash.

Tennay's shock at the damage caused by Calfain's battleaxe reverberated through his head. Calfain felt the shudder and for an instant thought that he would be shaken free of the grip he had on his advisory's mind.

A murderous glare crossed Tennay's face. Calfain reasoned that Lord Tennay might just now make the mistake that the dreamweaver had been awaiting. The one that would allow Calfain his freedom from these mind games.

Calfain took another swipe with the axe, forcing Tennay to retreat still further into the blackness of the dreamweaver's illusion. Then, unexpectedly, Tennay turned and seemed to disappear momentarily, only to reappear moments later on Calfain's right side.

Tennay stood immobile, his head hung down. He seemed exhausted – drained from the wound he had received, however slight.

Without any thought of mercy, Calfain swung again, this time he held the axe at the end of its shaft attempting to gain maximum leverage as he aimed a sideways swipe intending to sever Tennay's head.

The initial resistance of Tennay's exposed neck to the axe blade transmitted itself along the wooden shaft almost catching Calfain unaware. Not ever having taken someone's head before, it surprised him. Then, the axe blade was through, the momentum allowing it to continue its arc. With no earthly support to speak of, Calfain's body was obliged to follow the heavy weapon and he spun almost a full circle.

As the dreamweaver came to rest, he saw Tennay's body, still in an upright position, but minus its head. Calfain fleetingly thought it strange that the torso should remain standing, then, he realised that here, in this dream world, there was no up or down. He took a deep breath and began to relax.

'Now look what you've done, Dreamweaver.' It was Tennay's voice echoing all around. Calfain snapped his head around, searching for the lord, expecting him to appear any second. As he glanced around, the severed head came into his view and then as if of its own volition, rolled towards him.

Calfain stared, then blinked, and then stared hard again. He shook his head unbelievingly,

'*No!*' he cried 'No, don't do this, Tennay,' he yelled, 'this isn't right. Keep her out of this!'

The severed head continued to roll towards him and stopped only when it collided with his foot. Calfain stared in horror at the face of Peltene, her sightless eyes returning his gaze.

Chapter Thirteen

'*Calfain*' The harsh voice crashed into Calfain's head. 'Dreamweaver! Wake up! You're not dead! I won't allow you to die - yet!' the voice snapped.

Calfain opened an eye and saw the ceiling stones of the cell as they arched away to his left and right.

Curious, he thought, how just those small centre stones keyed the whole structure together to stop them from falling. Indeed a tribute to the stonemason's art – no – craft – no – art. Yes, it was surely a work of art, created by a true artist....

'*Calfain!*' His name bellowed in his ear, 'Wake up!'

The dreamweaver turned his head sluggishly toward the voice, screwing up his eyes and re-opening them to stare at Twill's unwashed, unshaven and to Calfain, his unwelcome face.

'Go away, Twill,' Calfain mumbled and turned back to contemplate the keystones.

Twill ignored the request and continued, 'Calfain, Venden is 'ere wi' me, I freed 'im. Come on, we 'ave to go, quickly.'

'Then go, leave me alone.' Calfain took a deep breath, exhaling slowly.

Venden had been watching at the door, now, seeing that something had obviously happened to his friend, strode quickly to the bedside.

Calfain, tis mine own self, Venden, Doth something trouble thee deeply?'

Calfain again turned his head and looked into the eyes of the big farmhand.

'She's dead, Ven. She's dead! I killed her!' The words tumbled from his mouth.

Venden straightened and looked shocked, *'Peltene?* The Lady Peltene, *dead?'* How, Calfain? And why doth thee taketh responsibility?'

'I murdered her, Ven. I cut off her head.' Calfain slumped back onto the bed, staring once more at the ceiling.

Venden sat heavily on the edge of the bed, his mind refusing to accept this shocking news.

'Calfain, tis mine own contention thou art delirious. The mad monks hath fed thee a potion of some sort...'

'No potion, Ven, Tennay, her husband was in my mind and I fought with him. He tricked me into killing him, but I killed her instead and if you kill someone in one of *those* dreams, the shock can kill them in the real world. She's dead, believe me.'

Venden shook his head violently, 'I refuse to believe thee, Calfain. I refuse until I hath seen her body with mine own eyes,' he said adamantly.

'I know it's true,' Calfain mumbled, 'I was there.'

Venden turned to Twill who had by now taken up guard at the door.

'Twill,' he commanded, 'Go and seek out the Lady Peltene. I wilst remain here, with Calfain.'

Twill nodded and disappeared silently around the edge of the door.

Venden turned back to the dreamweaver,

'Dead or nought, tis a grim truth that we still hath to leave this evil place.'

'I'll not leave without her body; Ven. I can't leave her here. She needs a proper resting-place.'

'Calfain!' Venden pleaded with him.

'I'm not arguing, Ven. I'll do it with or without you.'

Venden's shoulders slumped and he stared blankly down at the floor, assessing the situation,

151

'Then, surely we wilst *all* die this day.'

Calfain swung his legs gingerly from the bed,

'Then so be it. It's as good a day as any other.'

'Where do yer want me to put 'er?' Twill stood in the doorway, carrying the limp body of Peltene in his arms.

Calfain looked up from where he was sitting on the edge of the bed. His first sight was of her golden hair tumbling down over Twill's arm and one of her own arms, hanging lose from the addict's grasp.

'Here,' Calfain said gruffly, 'Give her to me.' He jumped from the bed and swayed a little, still suffering from the effects of his dream-battle with Tennay.

Venden reached out to steady his friend, but Calfain shrugged away the offered help and moved to Twill, holding out his arms to take the Lady from him.

Calfain settled her body on the bed and smoothed down her tunic, then, he gently placed a hand on her hair and smoothed that also and whispered,

'I'm sorry, Pel, I'm truly sorry for having failed you.'

Venden was back at the door, snatching quick glimpses all around,

'Calfain,' he said over his shoulder, 'Instinct doth tell me we are stretching our fortune by remaining here.'

Calfain ignored the advice and continued to gaze down on Peltene's tranquil features, all the while stroking her hair. In his mind, he saw them both – together – he, splashing the water from the little stream where they had dallied, she, laughing like a little girl and doing her best to avoid a soaking. He recalled the conversations they had had as they rode toward Paland. He could hear his own voice remonstrating with her for giving the ferryman far too much money for the trip across the river.

Then, he saw her face, smiling up at him as they lay on the soft feather bed at the inn, locked in an embrace that would lead them to consummate forever, their desires for one another.

Calfain's memory leapt back to their first meeting, the touch of her hand on his. The sun glinting in her blonde hair, her eyes sparkling as she looked into his, assessing perhaps, if she could trust him, or perhaps, she had felt the same jolt as he, the first time that he had caught sight of her.

He remembered his argument with himself on that first night as he paced the room he had rented, determined to convince himself that it was purely a business transaction and that under no circumstances should he become emotionally involved with her.

Once again, despite all his efforts not to, Calfain had fallen in love, but this time the woman he desired had made the ultimate sacrifice and now she was dead, killed by his own hand.

'*Calfain!*' The urgency in Venden's voice jolted him back to the present.

'I love you, Pel. I always will,' Calfain whispered for the last time.

The dreamweaver glanced around the cell, searching for his shirt. Twill handed it to him from the floor where it had been thrown. Calfain dressed hastily and then reached to lift Peltene's body from the bed.

'I'll take 'er,' Twill offered.

Venden glanced around, 'Nay, I whilst carry the Lady, Mine own strength is greater.'

'Not at the moment it ain't,' Twill replied, 'right now, I could lift a mountain.' He gently pushed past Calfain and bent to scoop the body up into his arms.

Whatever the monks had fed to the addict in order to release his mind to them, had not only sharpened his senses ten fold, but also inadvertently endowed him with the strength of two men.

The three men assembled on the inside of the cell door, Venden took a long glance around its edge and turned,

'Ready?' he asked.

'Wait!' Calfain suddenly said, 'we need to find the boy.'

'What boy?' Twill asked.

Calfain glanced over his shoulder at him and said harshly, 'Peltene's son, Dennel.'

Twill looked astonished, '*Calfain!* The three of us probably won't make it out of 'ere alive, why risk the boy's life too?'

The dreamweaver cast Twill a withering look, 'Twill, I'll not leave him. He's the reason we came here, remember? And I owe it to Peltene.'

Venden sighed, 'I understand thine concern, Calfain, but needles and haystacks doth run through mine own thoughts.'

'I'll not leave him.' Calfain said with finality.

Venden studied his face closely, assessing Calfain's determination, finally he said,

'These cells are at the lowest level of the monastery, tis mine own assumption that the Lady's son wilst reside on a higher one.'

'I agree, Ven,' Calfain said, placing a hand on the big mans shoulder, 'his father wouldn't have made him live down here. He has to be above – with the other monks, or possibly in quarters of his own.'

'Or shared with his father,' Venden speculated.

As they spoke, the latch of a door less than ten feet away clicked loudly and the door creaked open. The three companions moved back into the cell, into the shadows. Two pairs of sandal covered feet slapped along the stone floor toward the cell. Venden pressed himself further into the wall, body tensed.

The two monks entered the cell and immediately saw the empty bed. They faltered, unsure as to what to do, Venden's fist crashed down on one of the monks heads with such force that his skull fractured. The other spun around just in time to see the big farmhand's fist two inches from his nose. The crunch of bone was sickeningly loud and the monk staggered backward adding to the noise by shrieking at the top of his voice. Calfain came out of the shadows behind the man and grabbed him around his neck. With a vicious twist, the dreamweaver snapped the monk's neck, saving him from further pain and suffering.

Venden looked at the body, and then up at Calfain's face, he saw in the dreamweaver's eyes a hardness he had never seen before. It was the hardness of a man bent on revenge.

Quickly Calfain and Venden stripped the robes from the two monks, then Calfain instructed Twill to place Peltene's body on the bed. He carefully pulled one of the robes over her body and tied the waist thong. Next, he covered his own clothes with the second robe. Now, they were all dressed alike.

Chapter Fourteen.

Calfain stood at the foot of the spiral staircase, nervously glancing upward and shaking his head,

'This is too easy. Where are they all?' he whispered

Venden was at his side,

'As I recall, the brother's taketh prayers at four-hour intervals, regardless of night or day. I doth assume that is the reason for their absence.'

'Would Tennay go too?' Calfain asked.

Venden nodded,

'The Lord Tennay hath been proved to be of their religion, Calfain, therefore undoubtedly he wilst attend also.'

Calfain shrugged, 'Well, it keeps him off our backs, I suppose. How long does the prayer meeting last?'

'A full half-hour,' Venden replied, then, remembering the two monks they had left in Calfain's cell, he spoke again, 'I wouldst think they are no more than five minutes into their worship.'

'I hope you're right, Ven, let's go.'

'Er…' Twill broke in, 'the boy?'

Calfain looked at the addict, 'That's where we're going now…to find him.'

'But won't 'e be at the prayer meeting – with the others?' Twill asked simply.

Calfain's shoulders slumped, he mentally kicked himself, 'Yes, you're right, Twill, he probably will be.' He glanced at Venden for confirmation.

Venden shrugged, 'It maketh a good deal of sense.'

Calfain grasped the cold iron railing of the spiral staircase,

'So all we have to do is locate the chapel, wait for him to come out and either grab him or follow him back to his quarters.'

Twill coughed, the others looked at him, waiting,

'Another question, Calfain…'

'Yes, Twill?' the dreamweaver asked impatiently,

'Do yer know what the boy looks like? After all, only Lady Peltene did and she's…er.' he left his sentence unfinished as he glanced down at the body in his arms.

Calfain glanced at Venden, who raised a querying eyebrow.

'It's obvious,' Calfain snapped, refusing to be undermined, 'he either looks like Peltene, or his father – or both. Now let's go.' Without waiting for another interruption, the dreamweaver began climbing the circular stone steps.

As Calfain neared the top of the steps, he could here the sounds of voices chanting. Inadvertently, they had stumbled onto the chapel almost immediately. Below him Venden was holding out a hand to assist Twill who was struggling to carry the body of Peltene,

'I can manage, Venden,' he said softly.

'Let me taketh her weight,'

'I can do it; she's my responsibility, alright?' He added with a thickening voice, 'and she was my friend. I owe 'er.'

'Sshh!' Calfain admonished from above. 'They're right above us.'

Almost at the same time as Calfain spoke, the chanting from above came to an abrupt end. For an instant, the dreamweaver thought the monks had heard them climbing the stairs.

'Perhaps I hath miscalculated the length of worship,' Venden whispered worriedly.

Calfain took the risk and glimpsed above the level of the floor. All was still quiet on what appeared to be a landing at the top of the stairwell. He signalled the two men below to follow him up and went on ahead cautiously.

The area above was quite large and square in shape, perhaps twenty feet square with wooden flooring and two long wooden benches placed either side of the door to the chapel.

'Twill,' He hissed through clenched teeth, 'Put Pel's body under the bench.'

As he said the words, he felt a terrible feeling of betrayal towards her and horror that he could even think of such a thing, but, he reasoned, if they were caught again, he would not let them have the pleasure of knowing where she was.

Twill was about to argue the point, he felt the same as Calfain, but Venden snapped,

'Do it!'

Twill reluctantly complied, gently placing the body down and pushing it carefully under the long bench well out of sight. At the same moment he stood, the door opened and brown robed monks began to file out of the chapel.

Calfain and Venden stood to the left of the door, Twill to the right; all three had their hoods pulled down low over their faces. None of the brethren turned to look at them. Calfain watched carefully, waiting for the last monk to emerge. It was the abbot and on his left, was Tennay himself, whispering into the old man's ear as they walked.

The dreamweaver allowed them to walk on a few paces before he nudged Venden and began following at a discreet distance.

Lord Tennay and the abbot were so engrossed in their discussions that they failed to notice the three other monks following several paces behind. Tennay was quite animated in his gestures as he spoke into the eager ear of the older man. The pair climbed a spiral staircase and entered the abbot's private chapel, Tennay closing the door noisily behind him.

'Right!' Calfain sighed, 'Now we know where those two are, we can go on and search for the boy.'

'Tis still a dangerous exercise, Calfain,' Venden whispered, 'even as we knowest the whereabouts of Tennay and the abbot, the brethren we overcame wilst eventually be found and the alarm raised.'

'I know that, Ven. That's why we have to stick together this time and do this quickly and methodically.'

'Calfain?' Twill spoke up questioningly.

'Yes?'

'What's methodically mean?'

The dreamweaver sighed again, 'It means, Twill that we have to search every corner of this place and find Peltene's son.'

'Ah!' Twill said, comprehension in his voice, 'then wouldn't it make sense for us to start our search at the lowest levels and work our way up?'

Calfain blinked and stared at the addict blankly,

Twill glanced at Venden, 'Won't the boy be, er, what you call 'em, er....'

'A novice?' Venden offered.

'Yer, that's it, a novice. If 'e's a novice, won't 'e be down at the bottom of the pile, so to speak?'

'No, Twill, this is Tennay's son, he'll have quarters of his own. That's why we came up...'

'Sshh!' Venden interrupted the flow of words. Almost before Calfain stopped speaking, a group of men turned the corner in front of the three and without a glance, continued past them.

Venden touched Calfain's sleeve and leaned close to whisper,

'Didst thee observe that?'

'I could hardly have failed to, Ven, they walked straight past us.' Calfain replied scathingly.

'Nay, Calfain, thou misunderstands, didst thee taketh account of the attire worn by the two in the midst of the other four?'

Calfain momentarily closed his eyes, attempting to recall the appearance of the six men as they had walked past.

'Grey robes! The two were wearing grey robes,' he whispered.

'So what?' Twill asked.

'So the grey robes are novices, Twill, that's what. Come on!' Calfain turned on his heels and began to follow the six monks. Twill glanced at Venden, who held out a hand, offering Twill the right to follow the dreamweaver.

In his private quarters, the abbot poured Tennay a glass of mead and offered it to him.

'Tis quite startling that ye wife be here amongst us, My Lord'

Lord Tennay placed his own goblet of mead down on a table, glancing at the abbot.

Tennay nodded sombrely, 'Yes, it has come as a surprise, but one that I somehow expected would happen sooner or later. My marriage was one of convenience. Our families were wealthy, but not wealthy enough singularly. The two had to be joined in order that I could continue to finance this little project,' Tennay smiled thinly and waved his arms about expansively, 'The boy was something I had not planned for, but, nonetheless, he's here now and he is my gift to the brethren. Use him as you see fit, she will not take him away. In fact, if you have use for her, then take her too.'

The abbot took another sip of his mead, 'We hath little use for females here, My Lord, as ye are aware.'

'Then put her to work in the mine, or kill her. Whichever you think is best. I have no further use for her except to be sure that she and her three companions are the only ones on the island.'

At the mention of the three men, the abbot stiffened, placing his goblet on the table next to Tennay's own.

'Those intruders causeth mine own self much concern, My Lord,' he said anxiously, 'I hath a strange perception of remembrance for one of them. The tall, muscular one speaks with the ancient twist in his words, much as mine own.'

'He is of no consequence – a hired hand – nothing more No, the one who was a danger to us, but is no more – is the one named Calfain. He has the power of the dreammaker in him. I tried to find the reason for his helping my wife, but his mind was stronger than I thought. However, I did give him a taste of his own medicine and gave him a nasty shock. He'll live his extremely short life now thinking that he killed the Lady Peltene.'

The abbot nodded, relieved that the disturbance to his routine was now almost at an end.

'Willst thou taketh the emeralds to Paland after the ordination of thine son?'

Tennay grinned, 'Of course dear man, I wouldn't miss my son's ordination for the world.'

The old abbot nodded again and glanced around his private study.

Tennay saw the look and smiled, 'Are you ready to return to your birthplace?'

With barely a flicker of emotion, the old man said, 'I hath lived on Cipeus Island these last sixty-three years and naught a day hath passed that I hath prayed that this time wouldst come.'

Tennay reached for his goblet, 'Then here's to a successful completion of our agreement. I get the throne of Paland and you get the souls of its people.'

'Whilst there be sufficient emeralds for payment to the dissidents?'

Tennay snorted. 'Of course! Anyway, there has to be. The mine is almost dry. We've been mining it for twenty years, after all. And if there isn't, then I'll kill whoever stands in our way.'

The dreamweaver and his companions had followed the group of six to their destination, which was only a short distance from the abbot's private quarters. It was indeed some sort of dormitory and as Calfain, Twill and Venden almost cheekily followed the others inside, they saw several rows of cot beds all with grey robed student monks either sitting and reading or kneeling beside the cots, praying silently.

The four guard monks halted in unison beside a bed, allowing one of the novices in their group to move out and stand by his allotted bed space. Then, they moved on a little way and the same procedure happened again. After the novice had been deposited, the monks moved off again and exited through another door at the far end of the dormitory. Never having turned, they did not notice Calfain and the others behind them.

The three intruders stood silently waiting for the door to close, then, looking around, Calfain said quietly,

'Take a row apiece and ask each novice his name.'

It was Venden who waved his hand in the air and beckoned the dreamweaver over to the middle row of beds.

'This young fellow readily admits to having a given name of Dennel, Calfain.'

Calfain studied the boy's features closely. Even in the gloomy light from the four lanterns that hung at the corners of the room, Calfain could not mistake his mother's features and her eyes. This was Peltene's son, no question about it.

'Dennel,' Calfain whispered gently as he placed a hand on the boys shoulder, 'my name is Calfain. I have come to take you away from here.'

The boy looked him squarely in the eye and asked. 'To where, sir? Where will you take me? This is my home.'

For an instant, Calfain was lost for words. Strictly speaking, that may well have been true. Peltene was dead; the boy's father was here. Where indeed, the dreamweaver thought, would he take him?

'Back to your mother's cottage, Dennel. Back to where you belong.' Calfain answered feebly.

'My mother?' Dennel asked simply, 'I have no mother, she died many years ago. This is my home.'

'I fearest his mind hath been tampered with, Calfain,' Venden said gravely.

'Yes, well, let's tamper a little more shall we?' the dreamweaver said, placing a hand on the boys head.

Suddenly, Dennel's eyes grew distant and unfocused. He sat on his cot, staring blindly at Calfain.

'What instruction hath thou given unto him?' Venden inquired.

'I simply instructed him to watch me at all times and follow me wherever I go.'

'Like a puppy?' Twill asked grinning.

'Like a puppy, Twill. Now let's get out of here and collect his mother's body.'

Calfain and Venden, along with the boy, Dennel, stood guard whilst Twill retrieved Peltene's body from underneath the bench outside the chapel.

'Come on, Twill!' Calfain hissed under his breath, 'what's taking him so long?'
Venden risked a quick peek around the corner of the corridor in order to see what the addict was doing.

'Our fumbling friend stands and stares, and naught at the Lady's body I fear.'

'What?' Calfain hissed the word, 'What's he up to now?'

Calfain leaned around the wall and hissed again, 'Twill! Twill, get on with it!'

Dennel was leaning also, almost along the length of the dreamweaver's back. As Calfain straightened, he bumped into the boy and was about to admonish him for being clumsy when he realised that Dennel was merely doing as instructed – staying close at all times. Calfain mentally decided to re-issue his instruction in a more precise manner just as soon as was practicable.

Twill returned to the others, his face ashen.

'*What?*' Calfain snapped.

'She's er, gone,' Twill stumbled over his words.

'Gone? Gone where?' Calfain gasped as he tried to push past the addict and see for himself.

''Er body, it's not where I left it.'

'Are you looking under the right bench?' Calfain asked scathingly.

'I know where I put 'er, Calfain,' Twill said, his voice rising angrily.

'You can't remember what you did two minutes ago, let alone a half hour ago,'

'*I know where I put 'er,*' Twill snapped back.

'Tis an obvious and simple answer,' Venden cut in, 'Someone hath discovered the Lady and removed her body.'

As the truth dawned, Calfain groaned,

'You're right, Ven, but where would they take her?'

'Perhaps into the chapel,' Venden nodded his head in the general direction of it, 'or, more likely, back from whence she came.'

'The cells?' Twill gasped, 'I ain't going back there.'

'*Shut up, Twill,*' Calfain snapped, 'Ven, wait here. I'll take a quick peek inside the chapel before we go back downstairs.'

Calfain made to move forward, Dennel immediately did the same as if tugged along by some unseen force. The dreamweaver stopped and turned, aware of the boy's presence,

'No!' he held up his hand, 'You wait here with the others, Dennel.'

Calfain turned again and took a step forward. So too did the boy. Calfain halted again and sighed, cursing his mental instruction to Dennel.

'Dennel,' he said patiently.

'Methinks, Calfain, thine instructions to the novice were a tad over emphatic.'

Calfain glanced at Venden and nodded glumly,

'I wilst be the one to reconnoitre the chapel,'

Relieved, the dreamweaver stood to one side and let the big farmhand pass. Dennel did the same.

Within minutes, Venden was back, shaking his head as he rounded the corner,

'Nay, the Lady is naught at rest within the chapel.'

'Then she must be downstairs,' Calfain said, turning as he did so. He led the way back down the spiral staircase. Closely followed by Dennel, then Twill and finally, Venden.

Everything in the cells was as they had left. The two bodies of the monks that Twill had killed were still in the same positions. And the ones in Calfain's cell were still there also. Peltene's body was not however in her cell.

'Where? *Where?*' Calfain asked desperately, 'Where have they put her?'

'Wherever it be, Calfain, I fearest time is naught on our side for an extended search,' Venden observed.

The dreamweaver's shoulders began to slump. He knew that Venden was right. He knew also that the longer he made his companions stay, the greater the possibility became of them being recaptured.

Calfain glanced at the low vaulted ceiling, defeat seemed to loom large. This had all started out as a pleasant trip with a beautiful, charming woman. A bit of a distraction from his normal work. And now? Now, that woman was dead, killed by his own hand.

'Pel,' he whispered as he continued to stare at the ceiling, 'Pel, I'm so sorry. I truly am.'

Venden put a hand on the dreamweaver's shoulder, 'She wouldst understand, Calfain and she wouldst also want thee to taketh her son to safety.'

Calfain nodded sadly, finally accepting that he would never get the chance of giving her a proper burial.

'You're right, Ven, as always.' He slowly turned to climb the spiral stairs. Dennel turning as if glued to him.

'*Listen!*' Twill suddenly snapped. His senses still heightened by the drugs that had been forced into him.

Venden halted immediately, as did Calfain. Dennel crashed into the dreamweaver's back and they both stumbled forward two steps.

'Someone moaned,' Twill whispered.

'One of the guards coming round, that's all. Let's get out of here before he wakes properly,' Calfain said.

'*No!*' Twill insisted, 'we killed them all.'

'Well, we obviously didn't kill them enough, let's go.'

'It's coming from that cell,' Twill was insistent now. He pointed to another cell none of them had previously occupied.

'None of our business,' Calfain retorted continuing toward the stairs.

Twill however stepped up to the cell door and peered through the slatted bars in the door.

'It's 'er!' This time he shouted, 'It's Lady Peltene – she's alive!'

166

Chapter Fifteen

With little regard for the noise he was making, Calfain charged again at the cell door, connecting violently with his shoulder. The door did not give an inch. After several unsuccessful attempts, Twill grabbed the dreamweaver's robe,

''Ere, let me,' he said with authority.

Twill glanced at Venden and nodded toward the door. Venden understood the significance of it and silently returned the nod.

'On three,' Venden said, flexing his body, ready to pound the door.

'One, two, three!' Venden counted and the two men charged at the heavy wooden door. Twill, still fuelled with the drugs was equal to Venden in strength and their combined force splintered the metal lock in its housing. The door burst inward revealing Peltene lying on the single cot, moaning and holding her head in her hands.

Calfain rushed in and glanced around the room. Peltene was the only one there. He went straight across to her, 'Pel! Pel! Are you all right?'

Dennel was one step behind him, even though it was his mother lying there, he gave no sign of recognition and continued to stare blankly at Calfain's back.

'I, I don't really know – yet,' Peltene mumbled rubbing her eyes with the backs of her hands.

Calfain still could not quite comprehend that she was alive, his mind racing to find an answer; he took another step toward her and bent over her embracing her gently.

'Pel, I thought you were dead.'

She pulled away slightly and looked into his eyes, 'Dead? Why would you think that, Cal?'

'Because I killed yo…' his words were broken off by the yelp in his ear as Peltene saw her son standing behind the dreamweaver. She immediately let go of Calfain and swung her legs from the cot.

'*Dennel!*' she yelled, pushing past Calfain to embrace the boy.

Dennel did not respond, instead he simply stared past his mother searching out the dreamweaver's back as he had been instructed.

'Dennel!' Peltene exclaimed, holding him at arms length to observe his face, 'Whatever's wrong? It's me. Don't you recognise me?'

'Er, Pel,' Calfain said weakly, 'I had to, erm, give him an instruction…'

'*An instruction?*' she asked, staring hard at Calfain but still holding onto her son.

'I had to, well, sort of – plant a suggestion into his mind – no, not a suggestion – an order…'

'*An order?* What sort of an order?' Peltene's voice was beginning to harden.

'Well, not exactly an order as such – more a command…'

'*A command?*'

'Oh – Pel – *look,* he wasn't exactly willing to come with us, so I had to persuade him.'

'Well, un-persuade him please, Calfain. I'll look after him now.'

Calfain glanced at Venden, then back to Peltene,

'Perhaps it's better that we leave him as he is – for the time being.'

'*Calfain!*'

'No, Pel – *listen.*' The dreamweaver's words were broken off as Venden interrupted him.

'Calfain, I fearest the worst if we shouldst stay here whilst ye argue the point.'

'You're right, Ven,' Calfain said thankful for the timely intervention, 'Come on, Pel, we can discuss this later.' He grabbed her hand and pulled her toward the door. Dennel followed as always, one step behind.

As the group approached the door at the foot of the spiral stairs hoping to retrace their steps, Twill, who was now leading the way, halted suddenly and signalled for complete silence.

'They're coming this way,' he whispered.

'Are we trapped?' Peltene asked anxiously.

Just as Calfain was about to reassure her that they were not, although he knew in his heart that they surely were, Venden hissed his name,

'Calfain, come hither.'

The dreamweaver glanced around, seeking out his friend. Venden was nowhere to be seen.

'Where are you, Ven?' Calfain asked quietly.

'Here, follow thine nose fifteen paces.'

Calfain stared hard into the darkness. He could just make out the almost invisible shape of the big farmhand standing further along the dark passage.

As Calfain and the others drew nearer, Venden whispered,

'It doth seem like yet another stairwell.'

'Up or down?' Calfain asked.

'Down.'

'Then that's the wrong way, we have to go back.'

'T'wouldst seem, Calfain, we dost naught have a choice,' Venden mused, glancing over his friends shoulder in the direction of the other stairwell from where the monks were about to appear.

Calfain stamped a foot in frustration, *'I don't need this!* If I'd have wanted to keep going deeper into the ground, then I'd have become a miner.'

'We can stand and fight,' Twill, encouraged from the back of the group. His bravery knew no bounds due to the effects of the drugs.

Calfain glanced at him disdainfully, then, turning back to Venden, he said,

'Lead on, Ven. we don't have any choice.'

It took a full five minutes to descend the stair. Firstly because Venden proceeded with extreme caution in the darkness and secondly because the steps went down for more than a hundred and fifty feet.

At last and to Calfain's relief, they bottomed out onto a dry earthen floor.

'Here must lay the old mine workings,' Venden said peering as far as he could into the gloom.

'Mine workings?' Calfain enquired, 'Mine workings for what?'

Venden turned to face the dreamweaver. 'Tis only a rumour, but the stories doth tell that the monks mined emeralds from this very ground.'

'Emeralds?' Twill's head snapped up, 'You mean – emeralds as in – I could be rich if I find one – emeralds?'

Venden smiled in the darkness, 'Tis only stories and rumours, young Twill. Gossip from idle minds.'

Twill shuffled and glanced down at the black floor, kicking the earth with his foot as if hoping he would stumble upon one, or several, of the precious green stones.

'Tis more than likely these workings were here long before the brethren arrived on this island.' Venden offered.

Twill continued to study the ground.

'*Cal!*' It was Peltene. The urgency in her voice made him peer over his shoulder at her, 'I can hear them coming down the stairs.'

Venden moved on quickly, reaching out as he did so, touching the rough wall of the passageway with his fingertips for reassurance.

'Here me, Dreamweaver,' Tennay's voice reverberated through the stillness of the passage, 'this is as far as you and your friends go. I do not have the time, nor the patience to pursue you and this is as good a place as any for you to die.'

Suddenly, a loud bang resounded as one of the monks under instructions from Tennay, crashed a sledgehammer against the wooden shoring that supported the ceiling of the passage.

The wood began to creak and groan as the monk repeatedly hit it again and again.

'They're sealing us in,' Twill shrieked.

'Tennay!' Calfain shouted, 'Your wife and son are here. Stop this madness. Let them come out.'

From somewhere further back along the now dusty passage, Tennay's disembowelled voice came through,

'Then send out the boy, my wife you can keep. She birthed my son; I have no further use for her.'

'*No!*' Peltene screamed, '*Dennel stays with me!* I'd rather let him die here than let you twist his mind more than you already have.'

'Have it you're own way, Peltene. I don't have the time to argue,' Tennay shouted back resignedly.

Peltene shook with rage,

'He's...he's...' She stamped her foot with sheer frustration.

The hammer blows began again and after four strikes a loud sickening crack split the air. Wood groaned and shrieked as it tore and twisted in on itself, the timbers no longer able to support the weight of rock above them, crashed to the floor. The roof followed with boulders the size of oxen tumbling down to entomb the dreamweaver and his companions in the dark, airless passage.

The group moved further back along the passageway, coughing and spluttering with the dense choking dust cloud that sprang up to envelop them.

For more than an hour, they huddled together in the far reaches of the passage, waiting for the cloud to settle. As they did so, Calfain spoke with Venden in hushed tones, all the while; his arm was around Peltene's shoulders, comforting her.

'What's our chances, Ven?'

The big farmhand considered the question for a while before making his pronouncement,

'I wouldst say, after careful consideration, bleak to fairly grim, Calfain.'

'I could've told ya that!' Twill put in disgustedly.

'It may taketh a year to dig our own way out.'

Peltene, who had been holding on tight to her son, asked,

'Don't mines have escape routes?'

'Possibly, My Lady,' Venden answered her, 'but if this truly be a mine and naught just a tunnel or cellar, then we couldst wander its labyrinths forever.'

Calfain had been listening carefully,

'If it's a tunnel, Ven, then it stands to reason that it should lead somewhere.'

'Tis a reasonable assumption, Calfain, but I fearest that in this total blackness, we couldst find our own selves plummeting down an unseen shaft.'

'Not if we let Twill go first,' Calfain replied, half jokingly.

'*Calfain!*' Peltene cried and jabbed him in his ribs.

'I wasn't serious, Pel.'

'Well, it's about time you got serious and got us out of here.'

'You're right, of course,' Calfain replied and began fiddling with one of his boots.

'What are you doing?' she asked, not being able to see, she could feel he was up to something.

'Just a little something I purchased back in Tapp City. It might just help.'

From within a special pocket, Calfain had personally sewn into the top of his left boot; he produced a thin packet, no larger than the palm of his hand. Then from his right boot, he pulled out another, along with a tiny single-sided knife, no longer than his index finger.

The dreamweaver next shuffled free of the monk's robe he was still wearing and cut a strip of material from the robe.

Working carefully in the darkness and mostly by touch, he unwrapped first one package, spreading a little of its paste like contents onto the robe material. Then, after re-wrapping the first, he opened the second package and did the same with it.

Once the two different pastes were mixed together, the material burst into a vivid blue-white glow that illuminated the immediate surroundings.

'What the…' Peltene gasped,

'Good isn't it?' Calfain smiled back at her now visible features.

'Calfain,' Venden said admiringly, 'Thou art truly a genius.'

'I know.'

'A miracle worker naught less.'

'I know.'

'It's not *that* amazing,' Twill remarked in a surly voice, 'I've seen that stuff before. Thieves use it sometimes to see by while they're stealing from rich peoples 'ouses in the dead of night.'

'I know.' Calfain said again, still smiling to himself.

'How do you know, Cal?' Peltene asked, shocked by his easy admission.

'I just do, Pel.'

'You told me you weren't a thief,' she said accusingly.

'I'm not!' he replied defensively.

'Then how do you know?'

'I just do, Pel.'

'How?'

'Peltene!' he said desperately.

'How, Calfain?'

'*Look!* I can build a wooden bench if I have to but that doesn't make me a carpenter.

Peltene considered his argument, 'Well, I suppose so,' she said grudgingly.

'Right. Now can we concentrate on finding a way out of here, please, before this "burglars light" burns out?'

Although the fiercely glowing mixture was cool to the touch, Calfain knew the dangers of it coming into contact with his skin and carefully twisted the strip of material around the blade of his knife before lifting it above his head and standing up.

'Shall we go?' He looked directly at the one, who had caused Peltene to ask awkward questions, 'Lead on, Twill,' he said menacingly.

Twill took a step backward, 'Not me, friend, you 'ave the light. You first.'

Calfain, Dennel, Peltene and Twill cautiously made their way along the dust filled tunnel. Venden followed a couple of paces behind, quietly counting his own footsteps.

* * *

'Art thou ready to forfeit thine own son to a lingering death by suffocation?' the abbot asked Tennay, a little surprised by the lord's unexpected decision.

'Needs must, my friend,' Tennay replied non-committally, 'I didn't want to lose him, he would have made a good addition

174

toward our cause and I have spent a lot of time and effort with him – but – the cause is above all mortals, is it not?'

'Indeed, My Lord,' the abbot replied blandly.

'Very well, Andarno,' Tennay smiled at the abbot, changing the subject, 'tomorrow is the feast of Ensalintides and then the ordinations. I will sail immediately afterward for Paland and spread the word of our cause. By year's end, the entire Palandian government will belong to us.'

* * *

'The water's getting deeper,' Twill needlessly observed.

In response, Calfain could not help but add a touch of sarcasm to his words, 'A moment ago, it was at my ankles, now, it's at my knees. I thought I was just getting smaller.'

Twill snapped back, 'Calfain, I…'

'Oh hush, the pair of you!' Peltene put a stop to their bickering, 'let's just use our strength to concentrate on where we're going.'

'Calfain!' Venden's voice drifted in from the back of the little line, 'Taste the water.'

The dreamweaver bent his knees and scooped up a handful of the freezing water, touching it to his lips.

'Saltwater,' he exclaimed, 'that means we're either at tides edge – or…' he shuddered at his next thought, 'under the sea.'

'What?' Twill burst out, *'but I can't swim!'*

Calfain stopped walking and turned to the addict,

'Twill, if we *are* under the sea and it breaks in, trust me, you won't need to know how to swim.' Then he continued on his way, Dennel and Peltene following closely.

'What? What does 'e mean?' Twill turned to Venden, standing just behind.

'He meaneth, mine friend, that shouldst the sea come crashing through the walls, to where wouldst thou chose to swim?'

Twill groaned loudly and took a cautious step after the others.

Up ahead, Calfain was by now rounding a bend in the passageway, where, as he completed the bend, he could swear he heard the crash of waves. He stopped walking and stood perfectly still.

'What is it, Cal?' Peltene asked from behind her son, who was standing, staring blankly at the dreamweaver's shoulders.

'Listen,' he said softly,

Lady Peltene cocked her head, trying to catch the sound.

'Sounds like the sea. Waves, perhaps?'

Calfain was glancing all around trying to understand where the noise was coming from. Then, as the burglar's light caught a twinkle of metal, he saw it. An old iron stair-ladder secured to the wall of the passageway.

Calfain stood next to the ladder and tested its grip on the slimy wet wall by tugging on one of the rungs at waist height.

Twill and Venden had by now, caught up with the rest of them and stood watching as Calfain began to stand on the rungs.

'Perhaps I mine own self shouldst make the first climb?' Venden asked.

Twill glanced at the farmhand and sneered,

'Why? Just so ya can be the first out of this stink- pit? I don't think so. I'll climb the ladder.'

Calfain was still peering upward and holding the light aloft. He could see nothing beyond the glow from the lighted material wrapped around his knife.

'All right, Ven. But be careful.' He said, still staring upward.

'Why 'im?' Twill demanded. I can climb just as well. Probably better. I don't weigh as much.' He sneered again.

'That's exactly why, Twill,' Calfain explained jumping lightly down from the iron rungs, 'If this ladder will support Ven's weight, then it'll certainly hold the rest of us.'

Just then, a flood of seawater came rushing down the wall, crashing onto Calfain's head. He gasped with the sudden shock of it and almost choked. The blue – white glow from the burglar's light was instantly extinguished, plunging everything into total darkness.

Peltene involuntarily jumped backward and crashed into Twill. He in turn stumbled back into the big callused hands of Venden who stood firm.

'Tis only a drop of water, mine friend. Methinks the tide turns and if we remain down here, we will surely float to the top of this black hole.'

'And be drowned in the process,' Calfain added still wiping the salty water from his eyes.

'Indeed, Calfain. Mine own thought exactly. Perhaps I shouldst now test the ladder?'

'Yes, but be careful.'

Venden waded through the swirling water to where he had last seen the iron ladder. He groped his way along the wall, feeling as he did so, the cold wet irregular surface.

Seconds later, Venden was standing next to the dreamweaver. He reached out again and blindly located the ladder, steadied himself and then hauled his weight up onto the first rung. Then the second and then the third. Up and up, hand over hand, until his face was suddenly blasted with a rush of cold sea air. He had reached the top.

'I counteth sixty-eight rungs,' He bellowed down the shaft.

Calfain stared up the shaft after him, but was unable to see anything. He tried to visualise the height.

'That's pretty high,' Peltene interrupted his mental picture.

'Oh, it's not so bad, Pel.' He replied as reassuringly as he could.

'It's the height of a good oak tree,' she said confidently.

'Don't worry,' he said gallantly, 'I'll be right there with you.'

'Oh, I'm not worried for me. I was thinking of you my love.'

Just as she finished her words, Calfain heard the rush of water.

'Hold on!' he cried and grabbed Peltene, pulling her close to his body.

The water crashed down with a vicious thud and swirled angrily around the passage. Calfain, Peltene, Twill and even Dennel were left gasping for breath and shivering with the shock of the freezing cold.

'Ven! Venden!' Calfain shouted upward, 'Are you all right?'

'Aye,' Venden's voice floated down from above. 'I didst see it coming but had little time to warn thee.'

'What else can you see?' Calfain shouted back.

'Tis indeed a cave-mouth and the sea approaches rapidly. I wouldst suggest a hasty climb mine friends.'

On hearing Venden's words, Calfain bodily spun Peltene around to face the iron ladder and gently pushed her toward it.

'Come on, let's get climbing.'

Peltene led the way, Calfain was close behind. He knew Dennel would follow.

Somewhere, almost halfway up, Venden bellowed down the shaft,

'Hold tight below!'

Almost immediately a whooshing sound followed his voice. Calfain gripped the iron rungs harder and leaned into Peltene's lower body, attempting to pin her to the rails.

Hundreds of gallons of seawater roared out its anger as it gushed past them, on its way to the floor of the passage, thirty-odd feet below.

Peltene was once again chocking and spluttering, gasping for air and hanging on tightly.

Calfain glanced below his feet. He could make out the head of Dennel just below, but he could not see Twill.

'Twill! Are you still with us?' he shouted.

'Only just!' Twill spat water from his mouth and shook his head.

'Keep going, Pel,' Calfain nudged her rear gently.

Peltene started off again, one foot up above the last, hand over hand.

'You're doing fine,' Calfain reassured her.

'Of course I am,' she spluttered, her face still wet, 'just look out for, Dennel.'

'He's right behind me.'

'Another wave!' Venden alerted them again.

They were buffeted twice more before they finally reached the top exhausted, not from the climb, but from the effort of clinging on as the water tried relentlessly to wrench them free.

At the top, the edge where the ladder ceased, Venden was there, reaching out to haul first Peltene to safety, then one by one, the other three.

Calfain rushed to the cave-mouth, several feet away and glanced out. At first, all he saw was water, then, after looking around, he noted a small strip of shingle beach. He turned to speak to Venden and bumped into Dennel who was standing dumbly behind him. Calfain placed his hands on the boy's shoulders and looked over his head, seeking out the big farmhand.

'Do you know where we are, Ven?'

Venden came towards him,

'Mine own guess wouldst be that we are right under the monastery.'

'Hmm, that's what I thought,' Calfain mused. Then, he asked, 'is there a jetty or landing point of some sort here?'

Venden nodded, 'Aye, tis where the brethren allow the new recruits,' he nodded towards Dennel, 'to land.'

'Let's hope there's a boat of some sort out there.' Calfain said just as another huge wave burst into the cave, drenching them all.

It was, Calfain reasoned, mid afternoon, Venden confirmed the dreamweaver's assumption of the time by the incoming tide. They emerged from the cave quickly and made their way east along the narrow shingle beach. Seagulls screeched overhead, whilst smaller seabirds, none of which Calfain recognised, fought noisily amongst themselves for tenuous positions on the cliff-face above the group's heads.

They kept close to the cliff wall and walked in single-file, alert for any stray monk who may have decided to wander the beach.

Within a relatively short distance, Venden was the first to spot the little wooden jetty, protruding into the sea, some fifty yards from them, seemingly defying the constant waves to wash it away. A single sailing boat of some forty feet in length was moored to it.

'Can we handle that size of boat?' Calfain wondered aloud.

'I can 'andle a rotting log if it means getting away from 'ere,' Twill said bravely.

Calfain looked disgustedly at the addict and was about to answer him when Peltene put her hand on his arm.

'Cal, not now.'

Calfain glanced at her and then shrugged. She smiled back at him, pleased with his self-restraint. Calfain turned to Venden,

'What do you think, Ven?'

The big man considered their options, then spoke,

'I thinkest our best option at this time wouldst be the secondment of yonder sailing vessel. Naught only tis it a huge beast, but tis our only lifeline to the mainland, excepting our own craft which lies berthed across the island.'

'What did 'e just say?' Twill asked, shaking his head and blinking rapidly.

'He said,' Calfain snapped, 'we're going to steal that boat and you can go and find a rotting log.'

'Calfain!' Peltene dug her elbow hard into the dreamweaver's ribs.

'Well…'

'Hush, let's get on with it.' She chided him.

Venden was already thirty or forty feet out in front, searching again the area between him and the sailboat. He turned and signalled for the others to join him.

The jetty was deserted, as was the path leading to the steep stone steps that were cut into the cliff and led to the monastery above.

Venden was off again, not waiting for the others; he ran quickly along the wooden decking of the jetty and lightly hopped aboard the long craft. Calfain, almost dragging Peltene along followed not far behind, Dennel blindly ran, desperately trying to keep his unfocused eyes fixed on the dreamweaver's back. Twill, the effects of the drugs now waning in his body, nervously followed.

Even as the addict was clambering over the rails of the boat, Venden was releasing the mainsail from its rolled up position.

'I thought ya told me ya couldn't sail?' Twill asked breathlessly as he came alongside the farmhand.

'Indeed, I cannot,' Venden cheerily confessed.

'Then why don't we just row this thing away?'

'Because, mine flummoxed friend, a craft of this size and weight wouldst be neigh on impossible for the five of us to propel with oars alone.'

Twill's eyes widened, 'So, yer taking us out to sea with almost no 'ope of getting us back to where we came from?'

'Correct.' Venden replied almost gleefully as he continued to administer to the sails and ropes.

Twill stood and watched him momentarily, attempting to work out whether Venden was telling the truth or not.

'Well, ya look as though ya know what yer doing, Venden,' he said hopefully.

'I hath had many occasions to watch and learn. I wouldst suggest ye do the same.'

'Me? Why? Believe me; I'm never getting into a boat ever again.'

'*Twill!*' Calfain shouted at him from somewhere at the rear of the sailboat, 'untie the ropes.'

'*What ropes?*' Twill shouted back, glancing about at the same time.

'The ropes that hold us to the jetty.'

The addict made his way to the rear of the boat and started picking at the knots.

'No, not that one,' Calfain shouted again, 'the front one first.'

'Does it matter?' Twill asked desperately.

'Yes!'

'Why?'

'*Twill, just do it.*'

Chapter Sixteen.

While Venden tended and trimmed the sails, Twill held the tiller tightly. Calfain was now with Peltene and her son in one of the two small cabins below deck.

Calfain concentrated his will and touched Dennel's forehead, instantly releasing him from the instructions to follow the dreamweaver at all times.

Dennel blinked several times as if awakening from a deep sleep. He stifled a yawn and then saw Peltene standing in front of him, a smile on her lips.

'Mother?' he asked, 'what are you doing here?'

'Dennel, oh, Dennel,' she said softly and grabbed him in her arms, hugging him tightly.

'Where are we?' the boy asked, 'Where's father?'

Calfain stood silently watching the reunion. Satisfied the boy had not suffered any undue effects from being swept into one of his dreams; Calfain quietly left the cabin.

They had been under sail no more than half an hour, hardly moving across the calm water. The Isle of Cipeus still loomed large and was clearly visible.

'Why can I still see that wretched place?' Calfain mumbled as he appeared above the deck.

Venden was tugging on a rope. He looked up at Calfain,

'I fearest mostly because I am naught an accomplished enough sailor to facilitate a speedy retreat. Naught are the tides fully in our favour yet.'

'Well, whichever god you pray to, Ven, I hope he's in charge of the wind and tide.' Calfain nodded toward the island.

Venden stopped pulling on the rope and stared hard across the water. Along the headland several hundred monks stood in a line, watching the slow progress of the boat.

'Word gets around fast in a small community,' Calfain observed ruefully.

'Tis welcome knowledge that this is the only craft available on the island.' Venden smiled.

'Well, we did leave ours there if you recall,' Calfain corrected him.

'Aye, but t'wouldst be a tight fit for them all to attempt to give chase in it.'

'That it wouldst, Ven,' Calfain laughed, 'that it wouldst.'

Gradually, the wind picked up as the tide turned and the sails filled sufficiently to propel them on their way. The figures grew smaller, as did Cipeus itself, until it disappeared from view altogether. The evening wore on and Calfain took the tiller from Twill, telling the addict to go below and get some rest.

Venden stood with the dreamweaver in the rear of the sailboat.

'Can we make it in one night?' Calfain asked in a serious voice.

Venden sniffed the air,

'I thinkest one night wouldst be sufficient for the journey, though I canst naught guarantee our exact landing point.'

'We got to the island in one night; we should be able to return in the same time.'

'In the rowboat perhaps, Calfain and if mine own self were properly experienced in this sailing boat, then I couldst assure ye of an accurate destination, but zigzagging as we appear to be, I fearest the best I canst do is merely to collide with the mainland – at some point.'

184

Calfain smiled,

'That's good enough for me, Ven.'

Just before dawn, Peltene wandered onto the deck. She looked around and saw Venden, propped up against a gunwale, snoozing quietly. Then, she caught sight of Calfain, still standing at the tiller. He saw her and smiled warmly.

'How's Dennel?' he asked softly as she approached.

'Sleeping soundly,' she replied slipping her arm through his and smiling up into his eyes.

'Have you explained what's going on?'

'Mmm,' she said, 'I think I may still need your help to put him straight though. He is still convinced his father acted with the best of intentions.'

'Alter his memories you mean?'

'If that's what it takes. Cal, then yes.'

'It may not be altogether the best thing, Pel.'

'It may be the only way. Otherwise, what Tennay did to him will scar him forever.'

The dreamweaver shifted his weight uncomfortably and sighed, 'Pel, sometimes - most times - we all have to live with the truth. It's all part of life. No matter how unpleasant it seems, we learn – or we should learn – from our experiences.'

Peltene studied his face closely, 'But you alter people's minds every day. You earn your living from it.'

'No, you're wrong; I don't *alter* their minds, or their memories. I add to them. I give them a pleasant interlude. Nothing more! What you're asking is for me to take away the boys memories of his father and replace them with something else.'

'Are you saying you won't do it?' she asked, looking into his eyes.

'I'm saying,' he sighed, 'we should be very careful. If it can be done, then I'll take away only the bad things Tennay put into Dennel's mind, but I don't think I should erase completely the memories he has of his father. Dennel should form his own opinions of him.'

'Then I'll settle for that.' She said and snuggled down against his body.

'Pel, I also think you shouldn't go home for a while.'

She looked up quickly, surprised at his tone,

'Why ever not?'

'Well, because your husband is still alive and well and more than likely, out for revenge.'

'What are you suggesting, Cal, that we wander the country until he dies of old age?'

Calfain laughed at that,

'No, hardly. I was thinking it might be a good idea to put your case to the queen and let her deal with it.'

'I don't think Queen Aramella would be able to do anything. If he stays on the island or even in Paland, then she has no jurisdiction. He could only be arrested if he set foot in Yarland and she couldn't have the militia sitting around waiting for him to pop up this year or next.'

'She could send the knights to the island and drag him back to Yarland to stand trial.'

Peltene laughed,

'Calfain, that isn't going to happen, you worry too much. Besides, I'm perfectly safe. You're here to protect me.'

Calfain stared out into the blackness of the night. He wished he shared the same confidence that she had in him.

'Land!' Venden cried sometime around midmorning. Calfain awoke with a start. He had been relieved by the farmhand as dawn broke. Peltene had gone back below decks to her son. Calfain had dozed in the bows of the sailboat. Now he stretched and yawned. This had been the first real sleep he had had in two days and he decided it was not enough.

'Do you recognise anywhere?' he shouted to Venden.

Venden turned and grinned at him,

'Indeed, Calfain, Tis most definitely Paland.'

'Wonderful,' Calfain snorted scathingly at Venden's attempt at humour, 'I meant, do you see anything that gives us a bearing on where in Paland we are?'

'I wouldst venture a guess at no more than five leagues south of Tapp City.'

'Fifteen miles,' Calfain mused, 'less than a day's march, that's not bad.'

'Personally, I thinkest it merits the status of a miracle.' Venden smiled.

'Don't get idea's above your station, friend.'

Peltene poked her head out above the decks. She looked tired and drawn.

'Have you slept at all?' Calfain asked her gently

'No,' she smiled weakly, 'Dennel was awake when I came down here, so we talked some more.'

'And?'

'Well, in his heart he knows his father was wrong to bring him here and he knows too that a lot of the things he was being taught are wrong, but he questions every argument I put forward.'

'Then that's a good sign, Pel. If he's asking you to justify your point of view it means he won't accept any old thing that's put to him.'

Peltene scowled, 'Calfain, I'm his mother. He should listen to me and do as I say without question.'

The dreamweaver laughed. Peltene glared at him.

'Pel, his father could also use that argument and then where does that leave you, hmm?'

Peltene looked down at the deck, thinking about Calfain's words. She looked up at him,

'You're right. I never thought of it that way.'

'I rest my case, My Lady,' Calfain smiled and walked over to Venden, leaving her to her own thoughts

'Shall we try and sail along the coast a ways?' He asked Venden.

The big man shook his head,

'Nay, Calfain, let us naught tempt providence, less it turns to bite us. We shouldst run the boat aground and take to our own legs.'

'Are you thinking we might snag a hidden reef or something?'

'Aye, that too, as well as we mayest be seen landing this vessel in Tapp harbour by a brethren spy. If we land here, who's to know which way we went?'

'I see your logic, Ven. Let's add to their confusion by casting this thing adrift after we land.'

Venden grinned, 'Thou art indeed a wiley man, Calfain.'

'Wiley is one of my middle names.'

Venden went below to wake Twill and tell Peltene and her son to ready themselves to jump ship. Twill was awake and huddled in a corner of the tiny cabin space. His back was toward Venden as he entered and the addict looked decidedly suspicious.

'What's afoot, young Twill?' Venden asked cheerily, watching the addict carefully.

Twill's head snapped up as he half turned, clutching something to his chest,

'Nothing, nothing at all. Why?' he asked a little too quickly and a lot too innocently.

'We abandon ship in a short time. Tis best ye cometh out on deck.'

'Er, yer, all right Venden. I'm on me way.' He turned back to continue whatever it was he had been doing.

Venden shrugged and closed the door, turning to knock politely on the cabin in which Peltene and her son were.

'Twill is posturing a tad suspiciously this morn,' Venden informed Calfain as he returned to the upper deck.

Calfain groaned aloud. 'Now what? Has he found some more plants or flowers - or something stronger?'

'I knoweth naught, Calfain; he keepeth whatever, close to his own chest.'

'I'll kill him!' Calfain launched into a blistering attack on the absent addict, *'I swear*, as I stand here, *I swear*, I'll throw him over the side if I find him unconscious.'

'Oh, he is lucid still, Calfain,'

Calfain was making his way to the hatchway in order to summon Twill up on deck. Peltene's head popped up before he opened his mouth,

'Whatever is all the noise about?' she asked alarmed at the murderous look on Calfain's face.

'Twill has found something, or brought something, to shove up his nose again.'

'Oh no!' she gasped.

'Oh yes, *Pel* and before I throw him over the side, I'm going to shove it up his...'

'Calfain! That's enough!' Peltene cut in quickly, 'How bad is he?'

189

'I don't know – yet. Venden saw him acting suspiciously in his cabin.'

Peltene climbed all the way onto the deck and said to Venden, 'Did you actually see him with something?'

'Nay, My Lady I only caught a glimpse of him hiding something,' Venden admitted sheepishly.

Peltene thrust out her chin and sniffed,

'Well then, gentlemen, give him the benefit of the doubt.'

'Pel!' Calfain wailed.

'Hush. Let's see what he has to say for himself and then – if he has taken something, I'll help you dispose of the body.'

Throughout this distraction, Venden had been constantly glancing at the rapidly approaching shoreline.

'I fearest the trial whilst hath to wait a while, our good ship is about to be beached.'

Calfain glanced up and over the bow. Less than a hundred yards away, was the beach and in-between that and the boat, the waves began to show their white topped caps as they prepared to break onto the shore.

'Hold on everyone!' Calfain shouted needlessly.

Perhaps a little belatedly, Venden thought to cut the sails. His lapse in the art of seamanship had the effect of driving the boat hard onto the beach. With a loud, sickening crunch, the craft came to rest truly and firmly wedged in the sand. The mighty jolt caused the four passengers to be thrown forward and left them sprawling on the deck.

Venden was the first to raise his head above the rails and peer over the side. The boat remained upright, but with a slight tilt to one side.

'Naught as difficult as I hath first anticipated.' He grinned to himself.

'I thought yer could sail?' Twill demanded; his body halfway up the stairwell from the cabins below.

'On open water I canst mimic a fair impression. Tis solid ground ahead I hath trouble navigating,' he joked.

Twill ignored him and grumbling under his breath, quietly rubbed his head.

Peltene now stood looking at the sandy beach.

'Well, Venden, at least I won't get my feet wet.'

'Twas my intention that ye never wouldst, My Lady,' he smiled at her and bowed theatrically.

'What a gentleman,' she beamed.

'Let's get moving,' Calfain interrupted the light-hearted banter, 'I want off this thing and as far away as possible before nightfall.'

'I shalst release the cocks,' Venden said.

'What?' Calfain asked dumbly.

'The sea-cocks, Calfain,' Venden explained, 'I shalst open them.'

Calfain continued to stare at his friend.

Venden sighed heavily,

'The plugs in the hull. I shalst open them and scupper the boat.'

'Cocks? Plugs? Scupper? Why *are* you talking all nautical again, Ven? It happens every time you set foot on a boat.'

'I'm going to sink the boat, Calfain,' Venden said, impersonating the dreamweaver's own voice.

For once, Twill understood Venden's plain speaking,

'Wait till I get off. I can't swim, remember?'

Calfain glanced at the addict with the sour expression he saved especially for him,

'Twill, we're stuck halfway up the beach. It won't sink until the tide comes in. Even then, all that'll happen is it will fill with seawater.' He turned to Venden, 'Am I right, Captain?'

'An accurate assumption, I wouldst say.'

Calfain and the others clambered over the side and sat on the sand, waiting for Venden to complete his self-appointed task.

'Twill!' Calfain snapped, making the addict jump visibly, 'What have you been taking again?'

'What? What do ya mean Calfain? I 'aven't taken anything.'

'Then what were you doing in the cabin?'

'Sleeping of course.' His reply was a little too quick for the dreamweaver's liking.

Calfain looked at him with a cold stare, 'If I catch you with anything in your mouth or up your nose that I don't recognise as food, I'll rip your head off.'

'Calfain, believe me, those monks convinced me I don't want any more of that stuff. I promise.'

'Fine.'

'A pity to lose such a fine vessel that way,' Venden remarked as he strode up the beach toward the others.

Calfain stood and brushed the sand from his clothes,

'What was never yours you never miss, Ven and doing that stops the brethren from ever using it again.'

Chapter Sixteen.

On the march to Tapp City, Calfain took the opportunity to try and get to know Peltene's son a little better. The dreamweaver began chatting innocently enough by asking him whether or not he had ever been to Tapp. As Dennel answered, Calfain slowed his stride a little, forcing the boy to match the pace and in doing so, allowing the others to move slightly ahead. Presently, the two were a good ten paces behind and alone.

'Your mother thinks the world of you,' Calfain observed.

'I know, sir and I love her too.' Dennel answered politely.

'What she's had to do to rescue you was at great personal risk to her.'

'I know that too, sir.'

'But…?'

Dennel looked quizzically at Calfain, 'But what, sir?'

Calfain smiled ruefully. 'You sounded as if you were going to say…but,'

Dennel shrugged his shoulders and stared at his boots as he walked.

'But…' Calfain coaxed him gently.

'But…I love my father also.' The boy replied, simply.

'Of course you do, Dennel. The thing you have to remember is…you were taken away by your father without your mothers consent or approval of what your father wanted of you.'

'I don't understand. All he wanted was for me to join the brethren. What can be wrong with that?'

'Joining a monastery is a big step in anyone's life and when someone takes that decision, they should take it having heard all the facts. Unfortunately, Dennel, you were only told one side of the story of the Cipean monks. At the very least, you should give your mother the benefit of explaining her side.'

'That's what she said on the sailing boat.'

'And did you let her tell you?'

Dennel studied his boots again, 'No sir, not all of it.'

'Why not?'

'Because I suppose I was angry at being taken away.'

'Were you angry when your father took you from your home and brought you to the island?'

'I, I can't remember, I might have been. It was a long time ago.'

Calfain blinked at that, 'It was only a little over a year ago, perhaps a year and a half at the most, Dennel.'

'I was only a child. I can't really remember.' The boy was adamant.

Just then, Peltene drifted alongside Dennel and gently squeezed his shoulder.

'How much further, Calfain?' she asked over the boy's head.

Calfain squinted up at the bright sun and considered how far they had come,'

Maybe another ten miles or so. We'll probably reach Tapp after nightfall.'

'Shall we rest a little?' she asked, clearly tiring.

Calfain nodded and called to Venden to wait for them. Venden and Twill halted and turned, waiting for the others to catch up.

'Let's take a rest for a while shall we?' Calfain said as he glanced around to locate a suitable spot in the shade.

Everyone sat, Peltene and Calfain together, Venden leaned against a convenient tree some distance away. Twill made his excuses and went to answer the call of nature. Dennel remained standing, not quite sure where to sit. He was obviously nervous about sitting next to the dreamweaver who was already in earnest conversation with his mother. Venden saw his plight and called to him,

'Dost thou wish to tarry awhile?'

'I beg your pardon?' Dennel was clearly uneasy with the situation.

Venden patted the grass next to him, 'Mine given name is Venden. Tis mine understanding ye have been a scholar at the monastery for some time.'

Dennel took a step closer. 'Indeed, sir, for many years. I was to be ordained er, today…'

Whilst Venden asked the boy vague questions, Calfain was speaking quietly with Peltene,

'Pel, it seems to me, Tennay has removed, clouded, altered - call it whatever – a huge piece of Dennel's memory.'

Peltene stared at the dreamweaver, speechless.

Calfain continued, 'When I asked him about his feelings at being taken away from you and his home, he said it was a long time ago, but you said it was no more than a year and a half ago.'

'It was only that, Cal. Honestly, I have no reason to lie.

Calfain pulled a face, 'I reckon your husband has obliterated at least five years of the boys memories.'

Peltene took a sharp breath and her hand shot to her lips, 'Oh, Cal, that's terrible. Can you do anything?'

He shrugged, unsure, 'I doubt it, Pel. What's gone is gone. I may do more damage by rummaging around inside his head. I just don't know.'

Peltene began to sob silently. Calfain gently placed an arm around her shoulders and drew her close,

'I'll take a look. I can't promise anything, but I'll look.'

'Through her sobs, Peltene managed to ask. 'And if you can't, then what happens?'

'Then time, patience and a lot of love from you will help Dennel to adjust. He's young, he'll be fine.'

Peltene hid her face in Calfain's tunic and wept. The dreamweaver glanced across at Venden as he engaged the boy in easy conversation.

Chapter Seventeen.

'We'll stay the night here and set out at first light,' Calfain instructed as they approached the boarding house at which they had reserved their rooms a few days earlier.

It was getting late and all of them were tired and hungry.

'I wilst check our horses, Calfain,' Venden said and slipped away in the general direction of the stable without waiting for a reply.

The house owner was sitting behind a small desk as the dreamweaver approached him. He looked up from his papers and smiled, then as he recognised who was standing before him; he began to sweat profusely,

'Ah! Er, Master Calfain. I er, I – hello!' he stammered.

'Hello, my friend,' Calfain smiled wearily, 'you look surprised to see us.'

'No! I er, um, no, not at all. That is – I'm honoured you er, are here. Yes, you're here!'

'Yes. I'm here. We all are.' Calfain replied, studying the man more closely. The hairs on the back of Calfain's neck began to twitch.

'Is there a problem?'

'Ah, no! No, not at all. Good to see you again.'

'Master Rendin, is there anything wrong?'

'Wrong, Master Calfain? Why, no, not at all. Your rooms are all ready - just as you left them. Everything's fine.'

'Good,' Calfain smiled, 'can we get some food perhaps?'

'Food?'

'Yes, food. You know, the stuff that goes into your mouth,' Calfain made a play of putting food into his mouth and chewing.

'Ah! Food! Yes, of course.' The house owner glanced around nervously then back at Calfain, although not into his eyes, 'I'll see what I can do.'

'Thank you so much,' Calfain replied smoothly.

As they climbed the stairs to their rooms, Peltene whispered, 'Something is wrong, Cal.'

'Most definitely,' he replied softly, 'I get the impression our host was not expecting to see us again.'

Barely had Calfain and Peltene entered their room, having left Dennel with Twill, when Venden knocked at their door and entered without awaiting a reply.

'Calfain!' he hissed the name in a low tone, 'something is afoot.'

Calfain glanced at Peltene; she returned a nervous look of her own. 'We were having the same feelings, Ven,' the dreamweaver slowly replied.

'The stable-hand let slip that five men were gazing upon our horses, asking questions as to their ownership.'

'Well, that in itself isn't so bad; a lot of people get interested in...'

'I fearest them to be agents of Cipeus.' Venden broke in.

'No!' Calfain said unconvincingly, 'how could Tennay have warned them to search for us? He didn't have a boat. He couldn't have made the journey. He...'

'Calfain,' Venden interrupted again, 'much as I hath come to enjoy a good debate with thee, prudence doth dictate we shouldst abandon Tapp City this very night.'

'Agreed,' Calfain said immediately. He turned to Peltene, 'Pel, gather your things.'

After hurried instructions from the dreamweaver, Twill had scurried off to find an alternative exit from the boarding house, be it down the back stairs or through a window. Venden casually went out through the front door and returned to the stables in order to ready the horses.

Calfain, Peltene and Dennel waited in their room for Twill's return.

He did so within several minutes, giving a light tap on the door and furtively sneaking in,

'Window at the end of the hall is the best way out,' he whispered.

'Right,' Calfain said, standing up, 'let's go.'

Twill opened the door and stuck his head out, searching and listening carefully for movement. There was none. The three, loaded with their saddlebags, followed behind.

The window opened silently and easily, Twill was through and made the jump to the ground easily. He looked up just in time to see Calfain dropping the bags. Twill had to jump clear to avoid being hit by them. He kicked them out of the way and then beckoned for someone to follow. Peltene swung her legs over the sill and hesitated for an instant.

'Pel,' Calfain was close to her ear, 'it's just like when you were a child in the apple trees.'

'Yes, but then – I had no sense of the danger and wasn't anywhere near as heavy.'

'Don't worry,' he said lightly, 'just aim for Twill he'll cushion your fall.' And then, he gently pushed her out.

Next, Dennel was out and down on the ground quickly. Calfain was just lifting his leg when he heard a noise behind; he turned to see Rendin approaching with a large tray of food.

Calfain quickly retracted his leg and turned fully to greet the house owner.

'Ah! Master Rendin, how kind, thank you.'

Rendin gave him a quizzical look, glancing past him to the open window.

'Just taking a breath of air,' Calfain explained lightly, 'please – would you put the tray in my room?' He moved to the door and opened it for the boarding house owner to enter.

Rendin went straight to a table and put the tray upon it, straightening, he asked if there was anything else Calfain required,

'Well, actually, now you come to mention it,' Calfain put an arm around the man's shoulder and led him to the bed, 'this bed seems a trite lumpy.'

'Lumpy, Master Calfain?'

'Lumpy, Master Rendin, pray, try it. Lay upon it and see for yourself.'

Rendin gave his guest a quizzical look but Calfain was already gently squeezing on his shoulder, forcing him to sit upon the mattress. As he sat, Rendin began to feel his eyes growing incredibly heavy. He could hardly keep them open. It was a terrific struggle even to hear Calfain's soft voice. It seemed to drift in and out of his head. Then, Calfain's voice came to him clearly. It told him he should lie on the bed and sleep for at least ten hours. Rendin heard himself agreeing with the dreamweaver. He was indeed very tired and overworked. Yes, he would do as Master Calfain suggested. He would sleep now.

Within seconds, Calfain was out of the room and out of the window, dropping lightly to the ground.

'What happened?' Peltene asked anxiously.

'Oh, I just stopped for a bit of supper, Pel, that's all.'

'Calfain, this isn't the time...' she began to admonish him.

'Yes, I know – come on, let's find Venden.'

In little more than a quarter-hour they had cleared the city limits and were heading north towards Pa Old City. After half an hour of hard riding, Calfain slowed his horse to a trot. Peltene pulled alongside him.

'Cal, where are we going?'

'North to Pa City,' he answered without looking at her. His attention was focused along the deserted moonlit road.

'North!' she exclaimed, 'Shouldn't we be heading east towards home?'

He shook his head adamantly,

'No, Pel. North is our best bet right now.'

'Cal, I don't quite understand...'

He turned his full attention to her,

'Pel, if you were your husband, where would the first place be that you looked?'

'Ah! I see,' she answered; realisation dawning that Tennay would have his men search out along the eastern road.

'And besides,' Calfain smiled at her, 'I hear Pa Old City is a really romantic place at this time of year.'

Dawn began to break bringing pink tendrils of promise for a good day ahead. Venden suggested they should halt and rest as long as possible. He spied a vantage point about a third of a mile from the road. There they could sleep and take turns to observe the road for at least two miles in each direction.

Venden stood first watch. Dennel was asleep as soon as his head touched the ground. Peltene smiled down at him and spread a horse blanket over him, and then she gestured at Calfain to follow her to a small grassy hollow some thirty feet from the boy.

'Where's Twill?' Calfain asked as they sat on the grass.

'I saw him scuttle off around that big rock as soon as we arrived here.' She pointed in the direction of a large outcrop a hundred feet from them.

She turned herself to face the dreamweaver and reached out to take his hands in hers,

'Cal,' she said softly, 'I know it all went sort of wrong back on the island but I want to thank you for getting us all out safely and especially, Dennel.'

'Pel, it wasn't just me. We all did our part,' he squeezed her hands in his, 'I'm just sorry I didn't get to deal with your husband as I promised.'

'Well, that aside, we're all here now, all away from Cipeus Island and safe.' She leaned forward and kissed him tenderly on his lips.

As the kiss ended, Peltene snuggled against his chest and wrapped protectively in his arms, they both drifted into a deep sleep.

'Why didn't you wake me?' Calfain asked as he approached Venden, sitting on a rock overlooking the road.

'Mine own view was that ye needed sleep more than I, Calfain,' he replied smiling.

Calfain squinted up at the sky,

'Almost noon,'

'Aye.'

'Are you all right to ride?'

'Aye.'

'I'll get Pel to break out the rations we brought. A quick meal then off.'

Venden nodded and continued his vigil.

'Pel,' Calfain moaned, 'when I asked you to buy supplies, I meant rations, salted meat and stuff, not fluffy cakes and buns. These won't go anywhere.'

'*Oh hush,* they are full of sugar and we need our strength don't we? Besides, the cakes are not fluffy, they're rock solid now.'

Just then, Twill strolled into the little circle, 'Mmmm, sweet buns, 'aven't 'ad one of those in years.'

'Shut up, Twill,' Calfain snapped without looking up.

'What did I say?' Twill asked as Peltene handed him some food.

'Never mind, ignore him. He's just grumpy because I didn't bring his favourite... dried salted pork hide.'

Calfain ignored them both and went back to join Venden who was still at his observation post.

Without acknowledging Calfain, Venden began to speak, 'Mine own thought is that we shouldst perhaps veer off to the Northeast and skirt the lower Atan Mountains, ride across the plains and thence turn southeast and seek out Peane City.'

Calfain listened and pictured in his mind the route Venden suggested. Finally, he said,

'A sound idea, friend, or, we could travel to the Atans proper and stay for a few years.'

Venden shot him a withering look,

'Much as I doth relish the wild scenery of those mountains, Calfain, mine own body hair is naught as thick as the brown bears which doth inhabit that land.'

'You're just getting old and soft, Ven,' Calfain teased.

'Indeed,' Venden readily agreed, 'and as I do, I clamour for a more temperate climate.'

'Seriously though, Ven,' Calfain changed the subject, 'staying away from Pel's house for a while is not a bad idea. Tennay or his monks will surely go there and wait for her to return. So, I suggest Pa City for a while and then buy passage on a southerly ship and travel to say Tamlay. From there, we can travel up through Dolomes.'

'Dolomes?' Venden rubbed his chin thoughtfully, 'Interesting route, Calfain. How long wilst this journey taketh?'

The dreamweaver grinned broadly. 'Oh, the fat end of a year, I should think.'

'Pray tell, Calfain, who wilst pay mine wages throughout this period?'

'Well, if you're not willing to do it just for the fun of it and the pleasant company, then Peltene will of course.'

Venden rubbed his chin again, then suddenly grinned lopsidedly at Calfain, 'Pa Old City is a place I hath always had on mine list of places to see before I dost depart this old world of ours.'

'Excellent, Ven. Excellent.'

Five days of hard riding brought them to within a few miles of the ancient city of Pa. During that time, Calfain had insisted that they skirt any towns or villages they may chance upon. They slept under the stars and gathered food as and when they could, Venden doing most of the hunting, Peltene collecting nuts and any wild vegetables as she found them. Twill and Calfain occasionally made forays onto farmland and stole eggs from the farmer's chicken coups, on one occasion, narrowly escaping being shot by an arrow from a farmer's longbow.

Dennel remained silent unless spoken to. He listened intently to his mother as she had tried to persuade him of the need to rescue him from his father and the Cipean monks. He did however seem more at ease riding next to Venden. Calfain put that down to the big mans dialect, which was more in keeping with the monks own. Whenever possible, Twill would disappear into the bushes or behind a convenient rock for long periods of rest. Calfain did not care, as long as the addict emerged free of any plant induced ravings.

Pa Old City gradually came into sight. It was a magnificent, sprawling place by any stretch of the imagination. Said to be more than seven thousand years old it nestled on a broad plateau of granite looking as if it had been there since time began and would remain there forever.

The road that led them toward the plateau and then the city took them first through the overspill of the city's population. As their numbers had outgrown the walled area, they had moved out onto the flatlands below the plateau and built an intricate yet less dense urban sprawl.

After several attempts at asking passing citizens where they might find good lodgings, one, a tall man with thinning hair and a narrow but friendly face, took it upon himself to guide them to what he described as the finest middle-of-the-road hostelry in the city.

Calfain thanked the man for his generous endeavour and offered him a small token of appreciation. The man laughed and told the dreamweaver it was not necessary as he was by a remarkable chance of fate, visiting the establishment anyway. He bid them a good afternoon and hoped they would enjoy their stay. Then he and Calfain shook hands and the man departed.

'What a nice fellow,' Peltene said as he walked away.

'Hmmm' Calfain remarked quietly as he watched the man turn a corner.

'You don't agree?' she asked, watching the dreamweaver intently.

'He was too nice, Pel.'

'Cal,' she shook her head in dismay at his attitude, 'you're far too cynical.'

'Right now, Pel, my cynicism may be the only thing that keeps us alive.'

Peltene remained silent, in her heart, she hoped he would be proved wrong, but, her head told her he might just be right.

As they walked through the front door of the hostelry, Calfain glanced around. He shook his head,

'What's the matter now?' Peltene asked.

'Too grand, Pel.' He replied, still taking in the opulence of the place.

She followed his gaze for a moment, and then she said,

'Nonsense, it's wonderful.'

'It'll cost a fortune,' he argued.

'We deserve a little luxury after what we've just been through,' she argued back.

'I agree with the Lady,' Twill chirped from somewhere behind Calfain's back.

'Shut up, Twill,' the dreamweaver snapped without turning.

'Calfain,' Peltene said sternly, 'We're staying and that's final.'

As they walked across the thickly carpeted floor toward the desk, Venden lightly touched his friends shoulder and whispered,

'If tis any consolation, Calfain, I for mine own part, heartily agree with thee.'

'Right,' Peltene said smiling at the group as she had completed the transaction for rooms, 'Dennel and I have rooms next to each other which connect. Twill and Venden are sharing and you, My Lord,' she winked directly into Calfain's eyes, 'have your own. How's that?'

'Why do I 'ave to share with 'im?' Twill wailed, cocking his head toward Venden.

'Because someone has to keep you out of trouble, that's why,' Calfain snapped.

'Calfain, I'm clean. I swear it on me mother's grave,' he insisted.

The dreamweaver turned to him with such an intense look on his face that Twill took a step backward,

'Twill,' Calfain said in a low, menacing voice, 'What *was* your mother's name?'

Twill immediately glanced at the floor and began to fidget.

'Well?' Calfain persisted.

'Calfain!' Peltene snapped, 'That's enough!' Turning to Twill, she smiled apologetically, 'I'm sorry, Twill. That's all I can afford right now. If the hostelry had had rooms with three beds, then Calfain would have been sharing your room too.' She spread her hands signifying that she had done her best.

'That's fine, My Lady,' Twill gave her a wide grin, 'I just wondered, that's all.'

Calfain rolled his eyes heavenward and sighed loudly.

Whilst the others bathed and shaved, Peltene took her son to buy new clothes. Calfain had given him a pair of trousers and a shirt and Peltene had done her best to alter them to fit the boy. Now, here in the city, she had decided it was a good a time to get clothes that fitted properly.

Calfain was sitting, as usual in a reclusive corner of the bar when Venden entered. The big man glanced around and spotted the dreamweaver and then he went to the bar and ordered two tankards of ale.

'Thanks, Ven,' Calfain said, pushing his empty tankard away and accepting the refill. 'Where's our little friend?'

'He hath found a needle and thread and seeks to mend his torn clothing.'

'Well, as long as he's out of mischief.'

Venden nodded and leaned against the table with one elbow, eyeing the layout of the room and its occupants.

'Tis a thriving establishment,' he mused.

'Mmmm,' Calfain agreed, 'if all the rooms are full every night and this number of customers frequent the place, then I reckon it'll take about fifty or sixty gold crowns a week.'

'A tidy sum,' Venden nodded, sipping his ale.

'Would you fancy this line of work, Ven?'

Venden laughed, 'I am trained naught for this, Calfain. I couldst naught envisage mine own self serving food nor dispensing ales,'

'I always thought it seemed like a good way to make easy money myself. Especially if you hire trustworthy staff,' Calfain grinned, 'let them do the work, you reap the rewards.'

Venden took another sip of ale; 'Thou wouldst be bored within a year I'll wager.'

The dreamweaver smiled thinly, 'You're probably right at that.'

Changing the subject, Venden asked, 'How long dost thee thinkest we might stay in this fine city?'

Calfain shrugged, 'Perhaps a month. That should give us time to book a passage to Tamlay. Pa City is a big place; we can be anonymous here. If we decide to stay longer, we can move to other lodgings on the other side of the city. I think we're safe for a while.

Just then, Peltene walked into the room. She gazed around seeking out Calfain. He saw her and lifted his hand in recognition.

'Wouldst My Lady care to partake?' Venden asked as he stood and offered his seat to her.

'That would be lovely, Venden. Thank you.'

As he moved off to fetch her a drink, Peltene watched him go, then to Calfain she said; 'Now *he* is a nice man.'

Calfain nodded, 'One of the best, Pel. I wish I'd known him years ago. Anyway, did you get clothes for Dennel?'

'Mmm, yes. He's putting them on before we eat.'

'Hope he doesn't take as long as his mother, I'm starving.' He quipped with as deadpan a face as he could hold.

Venden returned with Peltene's wine and more tankards for himself and Calfain.

'I was just saying to Venden, I think we should hole up here in Pa City for perhaps a month, Pel.' The dreamweaver explained.

'A month?' she exclaimed, 'I don't know, Cal. We have been away for almost that already. I'd feel a lot more comfortable and safer, if I was in my home.'

Calfain had expected this much. He leaned forward in his chair, 'Pel, I know you miss your home, but I really do think we should stay away for a while. Give things a chance to settle down a little.' He leaned back, smiling, 'besides, consider it a vacation – a holiday if you will – away from all your cares. And, you get to be with good friends and pleasant company.'

Calfain saw the indecision on her face. He pressed home his point,

'Like I said before, Tennay won't give up that easily, Pel. He will – as sure as the night is dark - come looking for you and Dennel. All we have to do is wait until he either gets fed up of waiting or his plans for Paland can't wait any longer.'

'Calfain,' Venden spoke up, 'I fearest there be a fatal flaw in thine own plan.'

'Oh, what's that?' Calfain asked surprised.

'Whenst we overheard the Lord speaking with the abbot, the Lord did sayeth that he wouldst set sail to Tapp on the next tide, thence to execute his plans for subversion of the city elders. I doth thinkest that our escape wilst naught interfere with his mission.'

'So,' Peltene cut in, 'that means he won't be waiting for us at my house.'

'Nay Lady, mine own fear is that he will dispatcheth underlings to wait for us. Wait for however long it taketh us to arrive.'

Calfain looked up,

'I had already said as much, Ven. But even they will get bored and go home after a year.'

'A year!' Peltene gasped, 'I'm not going to stay away for a whole year. No! Definitely not.'

At that point in the conversation, Dennel joined them. Calfain immediately changed the topic and ordered food.

Later that night, Calfain lay on his bed in the darkness of his room. He was in the nether world of half wakefulness, half sleep. A gentle tap on his room door brought him fully awake. A slight creaking of the hinges was the only noise she made as Peltene entered his room.

'Cal,' she whispered.

'Over here,' he whispered back to her, rising to one elbow.

'I'm cold.'

Calfain smiled in the darkness and pulled down a corner of his bed sheet. She slid in next to him without a word and snuggled into his warm arms.

Sometime later, as they lay together again, she drew lazy circles on his bare chest.

'Cal,' she said softly, 'A year is too long.'

'No it's not, Pel. A year out of your life and you get to see sights and places you may never see again. And, you get home safe at the end of it.'

'You make it sound tantalising, but what about the others? Will they come too?'

'Venden surely will. As far as Twill is concerned, who knows? He is a bit of a liability.'

'He saved us back in the monastery,' she defended the addict.

'Yes, I know and I'll always be grateful for it, but, well, he will slip back, Pel. Trust me, he will.'

Peltene made her decision then,

'All right, My Lord let's go on a grand tour. Let's take the long way home.'

'Now you're talking sense, Pel,' he squeezed her shoulder.

'Cal?'

'Mmmm?'

'I do so love you.'

Calfain froze as her words burrowed into his ears. There they were. Those few little words. He recalled the times he had spoken them himself. They trip so easily from the tongue; they can be said in jest or with such shallowness that they mean nothing. And yet, when they are spoken during or after lovemaking, their meaning is unmistakable. He squeezed her comfortingly but he could not return her affection. He knew deep within that should he admit to her his feelings, and then he would be damned once again. To have one's heart ripped apart once was tragedy enough; three times was all a dreamweaver could take. A fourth was unthinkable.

The three loud thuds on his door made Peltene shriek in alarm. Calfain sat bolt upright. Before his mind came fully awake, the door had been forced open and two shadowy figures stood menacingly in its place.

'Calfain?' One of the figures shouted.

Peltene grabbed at the sheets to cover herself; Calfain sprang from the bed and lunged across the small space to where he had dropped his belt with his knife attached.

As the dreamweaver sprawled on the floor, one of the figures leaped at him, stamping a booted foot on his wrist.

'You will come with us.' The owner of the boot snapped.

The knife was already in Calfain's right hand. Now, he reached over with his left and transferred it across, stabbing down hard onto the man's left foot. The pointed blade sliced easily through leather and skin, crunching bone as it went. The man screamed and tried to yank his foot away. Too late! It was firmly pinioned to the floorboards, the knife having travelled through the boot sole.

Calfain leapt to his feet. As he did he landed an uppercut to the man's jaw hearing the satisfying crunch of bone. The man sagged and fell heavily. Calfain neatly sidestepped and scanned the room for his accomplice.

'Cal!' Peltene's voice rang out in the darkness.

Calfain could now see the other man standing at the opposite side of the bed, desperately trying to secure a hold on the struggling Peltene.

'Let her go and I won't rip your head off,' Calfain snarled.

The man ignored him and continued to grab at Peltene.

'Do as ye hath been instructed, friend,' Venden's voice cut through the darkness.

The man stopped trying to grab at her and stood very still, his arms at his side. Peltene scrabbled across the bed and into Calfain's waiting arms. He quickly covered her with the sheet and moved her into a far corner of the room. Then he advanced on her assailant.

Venden went to the room he and Twill shared. Twill was nowhere to be found. Calfain had cursed loudly as Venden returned to explain that the addict's bed was filled with pillows and sheets. The big farmhand had then checked Peltene's room to satisfy himself no other intruders lurked there before allowing her to waken Dennel and instruct him to dress.

Calfain now lit a lantern and looked down at the man he and Venden had tied to the bed with torn sheets.

'Who are you?' Calfain asked quietly.

The man remained silent.

'Did Lord Tennay send you?'

Still silence.

'Shalst I inflict pain upon him, Calfain?' Venden asked threateningly.

'No, Ven. There's a better way.'

The dreamweaver reached out and lightly touched the man's shoulder. Instantly, he closed his eyes and was asleep.

Calfain began to probe the surface of the man's mind. He knew from years of experience that would be the place where the last few days of the man's life would be stored. Confusingly, Calfain saw nothing. Only swirling mists of old memories, sorrow and fear. Calfain searched deeper. Still nothing. Then, suddenly, Tennay's face appeared before him.

'Dreamweaver,' the hollow voice thundered into Calfain's head, 'I see that my man has failed me. No matter, his was a hasty instruction to kill you. The next time, you *will* die, make no mistake. And I *shall* have my son returned to me. As for Peltene, make the most of her whilst you can.'

'Calfain,' Venden's voice boomed in his ear as he shook the dreamweaver, 'Calfain! Art thou awake?'

Calfain opened his eyes. Unusually, Calfain had become so absorbed in what he saw; he momentarily passed into a trance much like his subject had done. Now he was fully awake and a cold clammy sweat covered his face.

'What manner of evil didst thou see inside this fellow's head?'

'Tennay was there. He's wiped this man's memory clean and had left a message for me.' Calfain felt slightly sick as he realised the awesome power of the Cipean Lord.

'A message?' What kind of a message?'

Calfain looked directly at his friend,

'The kind that says we should get out of Pa City right now.'

Chapter Eighteen.

Everyone packed their meagre belonging as quickly as possible and assembled in Venden's room.

'Still no sign of him?' Calfain asked the big man stiffly.

Venden shook his head slowly.

'Then we go without him,' Calfain snapped, half expecting Peltene to come to the addict's rescue once more.

She remained silent as they left the room and headed for the stairs.

The lower level of the hostelry was deserted. Calfain led the way to the front doors without even considering paying the bill. Once outside, they moved quickly and quietly to the stables.

It was now, Calfain estimated, two hours after midnight. With a bit of luck, he thought they would certainly clear the city walls and probably get well out of the suburban area before first light.

As he and Venden saddled the horses, Peltene stood close by,

'How on earth did they find us so quickly?' she asked, almost to herself.

Calfain sighed, 'I really don't know, Pel. But I do know we're not staying around to ask them.'

'I thinkest I doth have the answer to that,' Venden muttered from within a stall.

Calfain glanced over the wooden rail and followed Venden's gaze. Sitting propped against the stall wall was Twill. The addict had clearly found a fresh and by the looks of him, large supply of fungi. He was leaning forward, grinning and burbling happily to himself unaware that he had been discovered.

215

Twill was holding something in his hands, twisting and turning the object whilst trying desperately to focus his eyes on it and hold some sort of conversation with it at the same time.

'What's he holding?' Peltene whispered.

'Hopefully a knife that he'll fall onto and save us all a lot of trouble,' Calfain hissed.

Venden walked over to the addict and gently prized the object from Twill's fingers.

"Oi,' Twill yelled, 'ya kin look, but don't take,' he slurred, grinning stupidly up at the big farmhand.

'Calfain,' Venden's shoulders visibly slumped, 'I thinkest we hath a serious problem.'

Venden handed the little object over the stall to Calfain and dropped it into his open palm. There glinting in the half-light was a green stone, slightly larger than the dreamweaver's thumbnail.

Calfain stared at it for a moment and then cursed softly.

'What?' Peltene asked, 'what is it?'

Calfain turned the gemstone between his thumb and forefinger and held it up for her to see.

'One of Tennay's emeralds. Twill stole one of his emeralds.'

Under her breath, Peltene repeated the same curse that Calfain had used. She stared at the shiny green stone and whispered,

'Now we really *are* in trouble.'

'He must have sold one,' Calfain said, 'or at least traded one for his habit. That's how they found us so quickly.'

'If thine supposition is correct, the city wilst be alive with Tennay's men.' Venden offered.

Calfain handed the stone to Peltene and passed through the gate into the stall. He grabbed Twill by his arms and dragged him roughly to his feet.

'How many more gems do you have you idiot?' He barked.

Twill giggled and sneezed loudly.

'How many?' Calfain demanded again.

This time, Twill began to retch. Calfain immediately let go of him and Twill fell to the floor in a crumpled heap, vomiting on the way. Now the front of his jacket was a mess of bile mixed with a red foul smelling concoction that made Calfain wince.

'Ya kin 'ave that wun, Calf, Calfwain. I got loads more 'ere,' Twill belched and tapped his soaking jacket grinning again.

Calfain held his breath and leaned over the addict, reaching out to pat down the jacket. It was a mass of lumps. It felt to Calfain as if the whole item of clothing was constructed of gemstones.

'Does he really have more?' Peltene asked from the other side of the stall.

'By the looks of it, probably every one that the monks have ever mined,' he answered grimly.

'Calfain,' Venden said, 'Tis thine decision, but we must start making distance from this place.'

'What do we do with Twill?' Peltene asked.

'We can't leave him here, Pel,' Calfain answered with a resigned note in his voice, 'They'll eat him alive.'

Between them, Calfain and Venden made ready his horse and hoisted the still burbling addict into the saddle. Twill leaned sideways and promptly fell out of it, crashing down hard on to the floor of the stable. Eventually, after two more attempts to secure him, Calfain decided to simply throw him over the saddle and strap him on tightly with leather lashes.

It was now more than three hours after midnight. The streets of Pa City were completely deserted. Venden led the way, instructing the others to follow his lead and ride the horses along the pavements so minimising the noise as their metal shoes clattered over the cobbles and save them from being entirely exposed in the middle of the deserted streets.

For almost another hour, they threaded their way along the winding, sometimes narrow, alleyways and streets that were synonymous of an ancient city. Then, the east gate came into view. The high wooden gates remained open and unguarded as they had for the last four or five centuries.

'Be alert,' whispered Venden, 't'wouldst be practical for them to hath watchers posted.'

They halted for several minutes. Four pairs of eyes scanning every nook and cranny of the fortifications. Twill, still bent double over his saddle, hiccupped and quietly drooled vomit down the flank of his mount.

'Let's go,' Calfain hissed, 'otherwise we'll be here till dawn.'

He urged his horse to move forward. The others followed silently.

* * *

'*Idiots!*' Tennay snapped. 'Seal the city! I want men on every gate – and put more out on the roads beyond the gates.'

'Yes, Lord Tennay,' a shaken monk replied and turned quickly to leave his furious lords presence.

Tennay turned to Persa, his second in command, 'I want those emeralds, Persa. I want them returned before dawn. And I don't want the dreamweaver or my wife or any of the others alive. Kill them! Kill them all!'

'What of your son, My Lord…?'

'If he chooses to return, then fine. If not, kill him! By now, he will have listened to his mother. She may already have corrupted him.'

'Yes, My Lord,' Persa said resignedly.

* * *

'Are you sure North is a good idea, Cal?' Peltene asked as they galloped passed the last cottages clustered at the roadside of the suburbs of Pa City.

'Yes, Pel, I'm sure. Hopefully Tennay will think we've headed straight back to your house and he'll be looking for us on the Eastern road, not this one.'

They rode without hindrance and spoke little. Their horses eagerly putting distance between them and Pa City. At sometime around noon, Venden called a halt, he was aware that the horses needed rest and water.

As the group dismounted, Calfain glanced toward Twill. The addict was still strapped across his saddle and looked decidedly uncomfortable and muttering to himself.

'Are you back in our world yet?' Calfain asked tartly.

'Get me off of this will yer?' the addict moaned.

The dreamweaver sauntered over to Twill and stood before him. Twill had to lift his head at an awkward angle just to look up.

'You really excelled yourself this time, Twill,' he said scathingly.

'It won't 'appen again, Calfain. I promise it won't.'

'You're right about that, friend. It most definitely won't.'

Twill twisted his head acutely to stare at the dreamweaver, 'Er, I don't think I like the sound of that,'

Calfain reached for the leather straps that bound Twill and untied them. Twill slithered from the saddle on the opposite side of his horse. The dreamweaver turned and walked back to the others who were by now, eating the remains of Peltene's cakes. Twill followed glumly behind.

As Calfain accepted an offered cake, Twill muttered,

'Lady Peltene, I promise that's the last time. I promise – on me mother's grave.' He looked toward Venden for some sort of sign that the big man agreed with him. Venden stared back stonily.

Growing more anxious, Twill turned again to Peltene,

'Lady – it was a stupid little mistake. I needed to get something inside me.' He held out his hands in an open gesture of desperation.

'Twill,' Peltene began heavily, 'this time you went too far. You endangered all of us. Tennay will never give up the chase now.'

'We can give the gems back;' Twill said desperately, 'I only traded one. 'E won't miss one little gem,' he glanced at Venden, 'Ven – we can give em back. Tell 'er.'

Calfain sighed and turned to face the addict.

'Twill, look. This is how it is. My job was to rescue Dennel and wipe Tennay's memory clean. I failed to get inside his head but we managed to escape and we might – just might have gotten away with it but now - because of you – we all face a death sentence. Every Cipean monk, his first cousin and his pet dog and cat will be looking for us, whether we have the emeralds or not.'

Twill stared at the dreamweaver, disbelief in his eyes as he tried to comprehend the enormity of his actions. His legs began to shake; he lowered himself to the ground to sit, staring blankly at the earth.

'I, I never thought…'

'That's my point, Twill,' Calfain snapped, 'your brain is so muddled with drugs you can't think.'

'I'll take em back to 'im.' Twill offered, lifting his head resolutely, 'I'll offer them to 'im as an exchange for our lives.'

Venden shook his head slowly, 'T'wouldst be a futile gesture, Tennay's monks wouldst cut thee down on sight.'

Once again, Twill cast his eyes downward, defeated before he had begun.

'I could do it,' Peltene suddenly said.

Calfain turned his head and stared at her. He already knew the answer, but he asked the obvious anyway,

'Do what, Pel?'

'Take the emeralds back to Tennay and persuade him to trade our lives for them.'

'No! Absolutely not. No!' Calfain said sternly.

'Cal, I...'

'No! And that's final.'

'Calfain!'

'*Peltene!* I won't allow you to do that.' He suddenly exhaled loudly, 'If it has to be that way, then I'll do it.'

'I wilst be the one, mine friend,' Venden said softly.

'No, Ven. I...'

'Calfain!' Peltene interrupted, 'I'm perfectly capable of...'

'I know you are, Pel. But you're not going.'

'I got us all into this,' she protested.

Calfain wagged his finger and then pointed it directly at Twill,

'No – *he* got us into this.'

Twill looked up. 'An' I'll get us out of it. I'll take 'em back. I said so an' I will.'

'No no no, I want you alive, Twill,' Calfain growled, 'So that when this is all over, *I* can beat you to death – slowly.'

Twill winced involuntarily and averted his eyes.

Having decided on this new course of action, the group moved a quarter mile from the road and made camp. There they stayed throughout the afternoon. The atmosphere was palpably strained.

Twill chose to sit alone as he ate a small meal of dried meat and bread. The others, a few feet away munched quietly on their rations.

'How wilst thou go about returning the gems, Calfain?' Venden asked through a mouthful of bread.

Calfain continued chewing his portion of meat for a few seconds before replying,

'The simple plans are always the best, Ven. That's my motto,' he answered blandly.

Venden waited patiently for the dreamweaver to explain further. After eating another mouthful, he did so.

'What's the nearest big town north of here?' Calfain asked.

Venden screwed up his face, concentrating hard,

'T'wouldst be Tain, about three, maybe four days ride.'

Calfain nodded and swallowed his food,

'Then you all head to Tain and wait for me – be in the market place everyday at noon - but absolutely no longer than a week. If I don't make it, head for Yarlis and seek the protection of the queen.'

'Calfain' Peltene blurted, but he was ready for her and cut her off,

'Pel. It *has* to be this way. If we don't meet up in Tain, then there's no point in waiting around indefinitely. It means I failed and Tennay is still looking for you.'

Venden had been listening to the exchange closely. Now he spoke,

Calfain, I doth understand the sentiment behind thine desire to partake in this mission but I hath to sayeth, thee shouldst naught be the one. The Lady her son and thineself shouldst be the one's riding to Tain.'

Calfain chuckled. 'Don't worry so, Ven. I have no intention of getting myself killed. Anyway, I still have a few tricks to help me.' He winked at Venden, 'Don't worry – I'm a dreamweaver.'

As darkness approached, Calfain relieved Twill of all the emeralds and for good measure; made him strip to his underclothes to make doubly sure the addict was hiding no more.

As he checked his saddle straps, Peltene came to stand close.

'Cal, this is silly.'

'I know.'

'I do not approve.'

'I know.'

'There has to be another way. If only…'

'Pel,' he stopped working on the saddle straps and turned to her, 'I don't care much for it either. My first instinct back in Pa City was to get you and Dennel out and run for safety. But even on the ride here this morning, I kept wondering where we could hide and how long we'd have to keep it up. Yarland is a big place but eventually they'd find us.'

Peltene nodded silently. She knew he was right of course, but that did not mean she had to like it. She reached for his face and held a hand against his cheek, gently pulling his head down to her own. She kissed him tenderly then broke away slightly.

'I love you, Dreamweaver.' She whispered.

Calfain leaned close to her and kissed her again, unable to reciprocate with the words he knew she wanted to hear.

Chapter Nineteen

Dawn broke crisp and clear. The air was beginning to take on a slight chill as the summer drew to an early close this far north. Venden was the first awake and almost immediately spotted that Twill and his horse were missing.

'Venden,' Peltene asked anxiously, 'you don't think he's gone after Calfain do you?'

The big man's lips turned down at the corners as he spoke in a grim tone.

'Indeed, Lady. I fearest that is precisely where he hath gone.'

Calfain rode hard and fast through the night. The full moon was providing more than enough light for him to see by.

As he approached the outskirts of Pa City, Calfain reined in his horse. He took several minutes to scan the area in front of him. The dawn light was behind him and shining down on the houses and other buildings that formed the suburbs. The city walls or what remained of them were, he estimated another half mile away.

Calfain carefully chose a spot to tether and hobble his animal. Next, he donned his old cloak and pulled on the hood. Searching around, he eventually found a stout stick that he could use as a walking aid and set off towards the mighty granite walls, which had protected the ancient city for so long.

The dreamweaver took his time walking the distance. Almost two hours, but in that time he noted ten of Tennay's monks. None, to his relief, recognised him.

Recalling the overheard conversation between the abbot and Tennay on Cipeus Island, Calfain reasoned that the Lord would use his time in Pa to continue with his corruption of the bureaucrats. All the dreamweaver had to do was position himself somewhere near the buildings of the seat of government and wait for Tennay to show up.

Calfain stood around pretending to beg money for most of the day. His luck or judgement was awry that day but he did manage to collect enough copper pennies to purchase a meal had he so wished.

As he stood, in the early evening, counting the money, thinking to himself that this could almost be a profitable occupation, four monks walked briskly passed without a second glance at him.

Calfain immediately glanced up and watched them enter one of the government buildings.

As he waited for them to emerge, he thought it odd that although the Cipean monks had been banished to the island long ago, here they were, openly walking the streets of Pa City. Still mulling over this oddity, he almost missed them as they suddenly exited the building.

Calfain carefully observed them from a safe distance and began to casually follow, as they hurried along the near deserted street toward the western half of the city.

Several times, the monks stopped and appeared to hesitate as if unsure about their whereabouts or the direction in which they were travelling.

These actions led Calfain into a few tricky manoeuvres, ducking swiftly into side streets or doorways.

After more than a half-hour, the monks halted once again, this time outside a large walled house. They waited only briefly before the heavy iron gates were opened from the inside by, Calfain assumed, more of the brethren.

The dreamweaver walked casually past and glimpsed the gates and gardens beyond as he did so. The house was old and large, possibly more than thirty rooms, he decided. This had to be Tennay's place. He continued on until reaching the cornerstones of the outer wall, he turned at right angles deciding to completely circumnavigate the entire structure.

Once done, he now had a reasonable idea of the house's layout. One set of gates at the front – the main entrance, a smaller set at the rear, undoubtedly the servants entrance and that was it, no other access.

Calfain sauntered away from the house and went in search of something to eat. He would wait until the early hours before he attempted to gain entry.

* * *

'Nothing, you say? *Nothing?*' Tennay was in no mood to hear that word. 'He may well be a genuine dreamweaver, but that does not mean he can make them all vanish into thin air! Expand the search! Twenty leagues in all directions.'

'My Lord!' Persa pleaded, 'Twenty leagues – sixty miles – is somewhat unreasonable. I fear we do not have the manpower to accomplish such a task.'

Tennay rounded on his aide; his eyes flashed wide, a small sliver of spittle trickled from the corner of his mouth. His voice dropped to a deathly whisper,

'Persa, those emeralds have taken the brethren - your brethren – years to mine from the earth. There is more value to those gems than the collective wealth of every citizen of Paland. Hire mercenaries if you have to, pay whatever the going rate is – and more – I don't care. I do care, however, about having those stones back – without further delay.'

'Yes, My Lord,' Persa said in a small voice.

Sometime later, a fire had been lit in Tennay's private room. He sat dozing in an armchair, fearing that should he sleep in his bed, he would perhaps miss the first news of the dreamweaver's capture.

Tennay, in his minds eye, caught fleeting glimpses of the man named Calfain. Tall, confident with a disarming personality, a showman, but there was something that set him apart. His eyes. Tennay forced himself to seek out the man's eyes. There, buried underneath that twinkle of empathy was a hardness that acted like a barrier to his soul. Tennay could not reach past it to discover the secret fears that all men harbour. Tennay searched his own mind for an explanation. It was as if this dreamweaver had been scarred deeply and now suppressed his feelings so well that it would be an impossible task to determine his weaknesses.

Suddenly, the scene in Tennay's mind shifted. Now he saw his estranged wife, Peltene and his son, Dennel. They were in the garden of Tennay's house in Yarland. The sound of Dennel's laughter rang out. Peltene too was laughing and looking happier than he had ever remembered. Into Tennay's vision Calfain strode and swept the Lords wife into his arms, kissing her passionately. Dennel moved into view again and he too embraced the dreamweaver. There the three stood looking to the entire world as a happy and contented family.

Tennay stared at the scene. The three figures returned his gaze. Only the dreamweaver smirked back at him - challenging Tennay with his deep, impenetrable brown eyes. Mocking, silently laughing and gloating over that which he had taken from the one time Lord of the Manor.

Tennay involuntarily shivered as he dozed in his chair by the fire.

* * *

At any other time in any other place, Calfain would dismiss the feeling he was now experiencing as senility slowly creeping upon him. Tonight however, in this location, he took it as a warning that Lord Tennay was indeed close by. The hairs on Calfain's neck were on end and his mind felt as if someone was trying to enter it.

The dreamweaver, having scrambled up and over the garden wall was now leaning against the cool stones of the house, waiting and listening for any sign that he had been observed. There was none.

Inside, Tennay continued to doze fitfully. The dreamweaver's face floated across his vision. Tennay could see him holding the bright green emeralds in his outstretched hands, several of the gems sparkled and shone as they tumbled through the dreamweaver's hands to fall lost into nothingness. Tennay let out an audible groan of despair.

'Pretty little things aren't they?' Calfain's voice spoke inside Tennay's head.

'You'll pay for this, Dreamweaver,' Tennay mumbled aloud, *'you'll pay.'*

'But I want you to have them,' Calfain's voice spoke again, 'I want to trade them for the lives of your wife and son and my two friends.'

'I will not trade, Dreamweaver.' Tennay mumbled adamantly, 'Never! You will all die and I'll still have my gems.'

Suddenly, the chair in which Tennay was sitting was pulled back sharply. Tennay's legs shot out to counterbalance himself, his arms grabbing at the rests. His eyes opened wide with shock.

'Well, actually, My Lord, no you won't get them back.'

'*You!*' Tennay gazed up and saw the living face of his recent dreams.

'Me!' Calfain half-smiled down at the man.

'*Per…!*' Tennay almost managed to shout the name of his aide before Calfain's hand smothered his month.

'Tennay,' Calfain whispered urgently into his ear, 'if your men take me, then you'll never see the emeralds again. I swear it.'

Tennay remained tense for a further few seconds then began to relax as he digested what the dreamweaver had just said.

Calfain slowly let his hand drop from the lord's mouth and returned the chair to its upright position. Walking around the chair, Calfain stood with his back to the fire, facing the other man.

'Can we talk like reasonable men, My Lord?' Calfain asked in a pleasant voice

Tennay glared at him then taking a deep breath, attempted to bring his outrage under control.

'Go On,' he snarled.

Calfain studied the man for a second or two whilst preparing his little speech.

'I'm not usually a gambling man, Tennay, but I'll wager what happened back on Cipeus would not have prompted you to want us all dead. I'm willing to bet you would have been ready to see the back of us.' He paused and gathered his thoughts again. 'The theft of the gems was a pure mistake. My idiot friend is a drug taker – a flower sniffer. He could not help himself. He just saw a leather bag and he took it. Neither the others nor I want any part of whatever it is you're doing or about to do with those emeralds. We don't care. Call off your brethren and I'll return them to you.'

Tennay listened intently. He took a deep breath,

'And if I don't call off my brothers?'

'Then your emeralds will remain forever in the hole where I buried them.'

'I could torture you.' Tennay said matter-of-factly.

Calfain grinned as he rummaged inside his cloak.

'Well, you'll have to hurry,' he extracted a small glass phial and held it up to the light, 'because if I don't get to the antidote for this in less than an hour, I'm dead anyway.'

Tennay peered at the glass tube,

'I don't believe you,' he sneered.

'You don't seriously think I'd let you get inside my mind again do you, My Lord? Once was enough. I have no wish to repeat that particular nightmare.'

On hearing that, Tennay could not help but be flattered by the backhanded compliment,

'It is a wise man who learns well.' He said graciously.

'Respect your betters is my motto,' Calfain retorted.

'Indeed, Dreamweaver, but tell me, what's to stop me from keeping you here and watching you die, then gathering your friends – and my wife and son – and beating the location of the gems out of them?'

'I brought the emeralds with me and buried them on the way. I'm the only one who knows.'

Tennay leaned forward in his chair and rubbed his chin thoughtfully,

'You say you're not a gambler, but you play with the cards tight against your chest, Dreamweaver.'

'All I ask is that you accept my terms and keep your promise not to harm any of us.'

Tennay finally threw up his hands,

'So be it. Bring the gems to me.'

Calfain grinned, 'Er, I think it more prudent that we – you and I – should meet alone somewhere outside this house. I respect your promise to spare my life, but also I'm a cautious man.'

Tennay nodded his understanding, 'Very well. When and where?'

'Noon would be a good time I think,' Calfain replied, 'on the long wooden bridge that crosses the river three miles east on the Yarland road.'

'So be it. Noon it is,' Tennay sighed, 'But Dreamweaver, heed me, any foolishness on your part and you *will* die.'

'I guarantee there will be none, My Lord.' Calfain moved to the door then paused as an after-thought struck him, 'My Lord, I wonder – would you be so kind as to escort me to the front door. I fear your men are not aware of our agreement yet.'

An hour before noon, Calfain was already sitting on one of the wooden spars on the city side of the great bridge. He scanned the open area before him. The road was deserted and it would be impossible for Tennay to send any men out before him without the dreamweaver observing their presence.

Calfain idly munched on an apple, occasionally glancing over the side of the bridge to reassure himself that the thin leather sack was still at the bottom of the deep river, secured by an almost invisibly thin cord, tied to a nearby stone on the riverbank.

As the sun climbed to its zenith, a small cloud of dust rose on the near horizon. A single rider was heading toward the bridge. Calfain waited patiently until he could confirm the rider was Tennay himself.

'Well met, My Lord,' Calfain said cheerily.

'Show me my emeralds,' Tennay snapped without preamble.

Calfain glanced past the lord, checking that no monks were following on. Satisfied that Tennay had kept his word and travelled alone, Calfain jumped lightly from his perch and unhooked the cord that held the leather sack. A small eruption of mud broke free from the river bottom as the heavy sack was dragged upwards and the surface water was discoloured momentarily.

Calfain stepped toward Tennay who had remained in his saddle and hefted up the sack.

'All there, My Lord, except for one small gem which my idiot friend sold for drugs. For that I apologise on his behalf.'

Tennay pulled open the neck of the dripping wet sack and peered inside. Satisfied that the emeralds were more or less all there, he pulled the drawstring tight.

Calfain stood looking up at the man as he sat above in his saddle,

'No hard feelings, Dreamweaver' Tennay held out his hand to seal the deal with a handshake.

Calfain lifted his own and took Tennay's offered hand,

'Well, actually, Dreamweaver – come to think, yes there are a few hard feelings.' He grasped Calfain's hand tightly. Calfain felt a sharp prick in his palm and struggled to snatch his hand free of Tennay's grip. As he did, Calfain saw that the ring on Tennay's middle finger had been turned around so that the diamond cluster faced palm inwards. Protruding from the centre of the cluster was a tiny needle. Calfain glanced at his own palm. A small speck of blood had pooled and then smeared in his hand.

The dreamweaver looked up at Tennay, ready to curse him. Tennay spoke first,

'You should get yourself a new motto, Dreamweaver. How about – Never trust anyone – ever!'

Tennay's features began to blur as Calfain's eyes flickered and his mind began to cloud. He was unconscious before he hit the ground.

Tennay appeared to float in the blue-black of nothingness inside Calfain's head. His features were bland, giving nothing away. He spoke with an almost serene lilt in his voice although his lips did not move.

'Tell me one thing, Dreamweaver and I swear I will not harm your friends or punish my wife. Tell me where my son is.'

Calfain was still feeling the effects of whatever Tennay had injected into him. His mind was not quite clear yet. Inexplicably, he could only think that Twill would have enjoyed the substance – possibly even relished it.

'Concentrate, Dreamweaver,' Tennay was speaking again, 'don't let your thoughts wander to that pitiful excuse for a thief you call Twill. *Concentrate* – where is my son?'

Calfain could feel his own face smiling,

'He's – somewhere – between – here – and – there,' he replied raggedly, forcing his mind not to conjure a mental picture of the conversation he had had with Venden and the destination they had decided upon.

'You really are making life difficult for yourself,' Tennay said testily.

Suddenly, the dull ache inside Calfain's head seemed to explode. A blinding flash of pain stabbed at every corner and crevice in his brain. The dreamweaver let out an uncontrollable yelp of alarm. He could swear his eyes were melting.

'I'm tired of your games,' Tennay's voice boomed inside Calfain's head, *'I will have my son returned to me.'*

Calfain now began to feel pain like never before. It was as if a hundred men were rampaging through his skull, searching, tearing at anything they found, slashing with swords and knives, pouring over his entire life's memories.

Calfain was powerless to resist. He could physically feel Tennay laying open and reading his private thoughts, stripping the dreamweaver bare of everything from his intimate moments with Peltene to his childhood fantasies and fears.

As suddenly as it had begun, the pain of the violent intrusion was gone. Calfain lay on the hard table in the cellars of Tennay's house, breathing hard and sweating profusely. He opened his eyes slowly and cautiously. A red mist swirling across his eyes masked the stark glare of several torches burning brightly in their wall sockets.

Back inside his head, Tennay spoke once more,

'That was not too difficult, was it?' he asked in a kind, almost fatherly way.

Calfain was completely numbed by the experience that he had just endured. His only thought was that of Tennay now knowing everything, everything about him. That terrified the dreamweaver above all else. Calfain's mind began to race as he desperately attempted to think of a plan of escape. He had to somehow remain alive and find a way of stopping Tennay from killing his friends.

'I know what is in your thoughts, Dreamweaver,' Tennay was there again, 'and I have decided to demonstrate to you the rewards of treachery. Dennel will be taken back to Cipeus and allowed to resume the calling of the brethren. Your two friends shall be put to death and as for my errant wife, she will learn the meaning of obedience – after she witnesses me strip you of your sanity.'

On hearing Tennay's words, Calfain began to feel an utter sense of despair within him.

Chapter Twenty

Twill peered through the darkness, across the gardens of the old house. His mind was more or less clear as he concentrated on how to gain entry. The scruffy little thief was exactly that – a thief – an opportunist, not a burglar. He picked pockets or stole from shop counters for a living. He had never, apart from with Calfain and Venden, attempted to break into a building. Now he was a little nervous at the prospect of sneaking across a garden and climbing through a window, alone and unarmed and unsure of where to locate the dreamweaver, whom he was only guessing, was inside this house.

* * *

'My wife and her accomplices are moving towards Tain,' Tennay told Persa and another ten of his followers, as they gathered about him in the large sitting room, 'They will show themselves every day at noon in the market place, expecting to meet with the dreamweaver. Bring the boy back to me, Persa. Kill the others. '

This was a stroke of luck, Twill thought, as he stood as motionless as a stone statue, behind the full-length drapes in the room. The little thief remained hidden behind the drapes for the next half-hour, until he at last heard the horses galloping out through the big iron gates of the estate. Now he moved, carefully at first, occasionally stopping, waiting, listening for any sound that would indicate the presence of any Cipean monks remaining in the house. He heard nothing, but he realised that did not necessarily mean the house was empty. Encouraged by the silence, Twill reasoned, although he did not know why exactly, that the dreamweaver would be held in the cellars. He moved around quickly, keeping within the shadows cast by the flickering wall lanterns.

At one point, he heard footsteps and he froze, pressing himself hard against the wall and desperately trying to make the stones absorb his body. The footsteps did not came towards him and he relaxed a little. A door came into view and Twill gently lifted the metal latch and pulled. The door opened silently and he saw steps descending into the bowels of the house.

Twill took a gulp of air and moved forward down the cold stone steps into the darkness. Twenty-five steps later, the addict saw the flickering flames of a torch and heard a soft, but nonetheless venomous curse from a voice he instantly recognised.

'Calfain?' Twill whispered as loud as he dare, hoping no monks were still in the cellars.

'Twill?' came the startled reply.

Twill crept closer to the voice from the darkness and began to see the outline of his friend, sitting upright, strapped tightly onto a large hard wooden chair.

Twill stood, looking down at the man, held securely to the chair with thick leather bindings.

'Twill?' Calfain hissed through clenched teeth.

'Dreamweaver,' Twill whispered, 'I 'ope I aint gonna be rescuing you every other day for the rest of me life. Me nerves won't stand it.'

Somehow, Calfain managed to grin at that, 'Twill, my friend. This is the last time. I promise.'

'Nah! I'm not so sure of that,' Twill mumbled as he began to pick at the leather bindings.

'Could you hurry along – just a tad – please?' Calfain asked anxiously.

'I'm doing me best 'ere, I don't 'ave a knife.'

'The last time you did this, you just ripped everything to bits.'

'Did I?' Twill stopped picking and asked incredulously.

'You mean, you don't remember?'

'Well, I do, but not all of it. I was – er – under the influence – sort of.' Twill admitted self-consciously.

The dreamweaver was about to add another barbed comment, but thought better of it and sat silently whilst his rescuer worked on.

'There!' Twill announced as the last of the leather bindings fell away, 'Now can we go please. This place is doing me no good at all.'

Calfain leapt from the chair, 'It's not exactly been a good night for me either, he said witheringly, 'Come on!'

* * *

As they made their way up from the cellars of Tennay's house, Calfain paused every few moments to listen for any signs that his escape had been noticed. The house was silent, a sure sign – he hoped – that everyone had either left or was busy with other tasks.

Slowly the pair made their way to the ground floor, to the door, which opened up into the room in which Calfain had first met Tennay. It was empty and silent. Calfain listened, cautiously waiting for any sounds. Twill, somewhat brazenly pushed past the dreamweaver and stood for a moment, gazing around, getting his bearings.

'This way,' Calfain whispered, making his way across the room to the door that he knew would lead to the hallway and eventually the outside.

Twill dutifully followed the dreamweaver, passing by a small wooden table as he did so. The addict glanced at it briefly, almost bumping into it, before he realised what exactly had been left carelessly laying upon it.

There, in plain view was the empty leather bag, which had, he knew, contained the emeralds that were the cause of his immediate problems.

'Twill!' Calfain's urgent whisper cut through the addict's consciousness. He moved towards the dreamweaver, ignoring the bag,

Swiftly and as silently as they could, the dreamweaver and Twill exited the house.

'My 'orse is down this way,' Twill said, taking the lead.

'Hold!' A voice cried out. Neither Calfain nor Twill was about to obey that or any other command this night.

'We'll not outrun 'em with the two of us on this 'orse,' Twill observed as Calfain added his weight to the animal.

'We only have to get as far as the bridge on the Yarland road, mine is hobbled there.'

Twill half turned in his saddle. 'Won't they look for us there?'

'It's a chance we have to take, now get this old nag moving.'

Once clear of the winding streets of Pa Old City, Twill's horse picked up speed, but not by much with the extra weight it was carrying.

Calfain continuously turned his head, attempting to ascertain if they were being followed.

'Anything?' Twill shouted over his shoulder.

'Hard to tell, but a snail could pass us at this speed.'

'She's doing 'er best,' Twill said, defending his horse. Then, he quickly shouted. 'I can see the bridge.'

They were less than a hundred yards when Twill's horse suddenly stumbled, its head almost touching the ground before it. The action was enough to throw both riders forwards, increasing the weight on the wretched animal's front legs. The horse sank to the ground neighing loudly as it did so.

Calfain threw himself from the animal before it could roll sideways, Twill, one foot still in a stirrup was not as fast. The horse came down heavily, pinning his leg under it.

Calfain quickly grabbed the reins, attempting to coax the startled animal into an upright position.

'Get it off, get it off.' Twill shouted, and then directed a few choice curses towards the unfortunate beast.

With a little cajoling, the horse eventually rose onto its four legs. Twill lay on the ground, probing and rubbing his leg.

'How is it?' Calfain asked, moving the horse away, watching to make sure that it too had not sustained any damage.

'Nothing broken,' Twill mumbled, still rubbing furiously, 'you go an' get yer 'orse, I'll be along in a minute.'

Calfain nodded and set off towards the bridge at a brisk trot.

The dreamweaver's horse was exactly where he had left it, hobbled and tied to a tree. As he approached the animal, it glanced at him, snorting either a welcome or its disgust at being left tied up for such a long period.

'I know, I know.' He whispered apologetically, rubbing its snout. The horse snorted again.

Calfain untied the hobbles and released it from the tree. As he placed one foot into a stirrup, the animal turned slightly, inadvertently allowing Calfain a view over the bridge. He could plainly see Twill limping along, almost pulling his horse behind him. Then, movement some distance behind Twill caught the dreamweaver's eye. He rapidly blinked and squinted into the dark distance, seeing three horses bearing down on Twill at breakneck speed.

Calfain shouted at the top of his voice. 'Twill. Move it. Now!'

Twill was no more than fifty yards from the bridge. He raised a hand in recognition of the dreamweaver's call.

Glancing past Twill, Calfain suddenly saw the glint of steel being lifted above one of the rider's heads. *'Twill! Look out.'* Calfain shouted.

Twill spun around and saw the riders thundering towards him. He immediately grabbed for his saddle in an effort to outrun them. Twill's horse, startled by his sudden movements neighed and refused to stand and allow him to jump into the saddle. He cursed the animal and tried again, this time managing to secure his foot in the stirrup. With one leap he was up and over and in a sitting position, digging his heels into its flanks and urging the horse forwards.

Calfain, by now in the saddle of his own mount, watched helplessly as Twill furiously shouted at his horse. The dreamweaver saw Twill and his horse cross the threshold of the heavy wooden bridge; he clearly heard the noise of the horse's hooves as they suddenly struck down on ancient timbers. Then, barely ten feet onto the bridge, the first rider drew alongside Twill, lashing out with his sword. The weapon connected with Twill's body somewhere around his shoulder, causing the addict to yelp and lean away from his attacker. In doing so, his weight shifted so violently that his horse was momentarily thrown off balance. It skidded on the wooden planks of the bridge, crashing into a side rail. Twill was immediately unseated from his saddle and thrown in one fluid movement out and over the rail into the fast flowing river below.

Twill's attacker reined in his own horse and jumped from the saddle. His two accomplices drew alongside and momentarily

240

stopped, waiting for instructions. The monk with the sword peered over the side of the bridge as if hoping that his victim would be still hanging there. Then, glancing along the bridge, he saw the dreamweaver, less than a hundred feet away. The monk raised a hand and pointed, issuing an instruction to his brethren. Both men peered along the bridge and saw Calfain. They lashed at their horses hard.

Calfain had been watching intently. He realised that there was little he could do for Twill and kicked at his own mounts flanks in an effort to put distance between himself and his pursuers.

The dreamweaver had the advantage of a fresh and rested horse. His mount, having been in the position of being pursued on several occasions before, knew what was expected of it and rose to the challenge. With the passage of several minutes, the gap between Calfain and his attackers grew steadily wider. After what Calfain estimated to be at least two miles, he eased his horse into a trot, turning his head, listening and attempting to see through the darkness as his horse moved slowly forwards. He heard nothing, not a sound, but that in itself did not mean that his pursuers had given up. He simply assumed they would be resting their horses. On an impulse, Calfain decided to turn off the road and head out across open country. As he did, riding at little more that a canter his thoughts turned to Twill.

After an hour in the saddle, Calfain rode into a small hamlet, consisting of six houses and a few storage buildings. He saw no signs of life, but could distinctly smell food cooking. He began to realise that he needed something to eat, when, from the corner of his eye, he saw movement.

Two children, possibly about twelve or thirteen years old, were watching him.

Calfain raised a friendly hand, 'Ho there! Good day to you both.' He said amiably.

The children smiled back at the stranger.

Calfain turned his horse slightly and spoke again. 'Would either of you know where I might buy some food?'

Before either of the children could answer, the house door opened and the head of a woman came into view. She snapped something at the children, that made them instantly disappear around the back of the house, and then she turned her attention to Calfain.

'Would you be wanting something?' she asked, seemingly defying Calfain to say yes.

The dreamweaver smiled his most disarming smile. 'Good day, Mistress, I was just asking the children if they knew where I might buy food,' for some unknown reason he quickly added, 'to take with me.'

The woman hesitated, not sure whether or not to believe the unshaven, unkempt stranger.

Calfain understood her dilemma. This type of thing happened to him all the time. 'Mistress, I assure you; all I'm looking for is a little food and some fresh water for myself and my horse. I'll pay whatever you think it's worth, then I'll be on my way.'

The woman finally made a decision, 'Leave your horse there and go round the back.' Then she hurriedly closed the door. Calfain clearly heard the thump of a wooden batten being slotted into place.

At the rear of the house, Calfain was surprised to see a large, well maintained garden, full of apple and pear trees that would be ripening their fruits in the coming weeks.

'Here, this is all I can spare.' The woman's voice floated out through an open window.

Calfain turned away from the garden and located her leaning out through the window. She handed him a hastily put together parcel of bread, ham and two hard-boiled duck eggs.

Calfain smiled warmly. 'Mistress, that's more than enough. I thank you kindly. How much do I owe you?'

She waved her hand dismissively. 'It's of no value. Take it and leave and you can get water from the well at the edge of the village.' The window suddenly closed tight shut with a loud bang, signalling that this was the end of her dealings with him. The dreamweaver sighed and slowly walked back to the front of the house to retrieve his horse.

At the edge of the village, just past the last little house, Calfain found, as promised, the water well. He dismounted and glanced around again. No one was around; it was as if the woman and the two children were the only people in the entire place. Shrugging, he leaned over the little stone edge of the well and lowered the wooden bucket down. Not too far down, he heard a splash, and then the bucket began to sink and become heavy as it filled. Calfain hoisted it back up to be rewarded with a bucketful of cool, clear fresh spring water. He took a sip with his cupped hands and sighed. 'Beautiful.' He said to himself as he placed his water bag into the bucket, replenishing it for his journey ahead. Next, he gave what was left to his horse and began to chew on a piece of bread whilst she drank her fill.

As he quietly chewed, Calfain ruminated on what his next move should be. He knew from what Twill had told him that Tennay had sent his men to Tain to intercept Peltene, her son and Venden as they waited in the market place each day at noon. He was also more than certain that Venden would be cautious, not allowing them to be captured. Because Tennay had not gone with them, then it was a fair assumption that he would be using those emeralds to buy the government of Paland.

Calfain did not know why Tennay was so anxious to undermine the government. He did not particularly care, inasmuch as he was not overly concerned with politics. As long as everything was quiet, and soldiers did not arrest him whilst he was attempting to earn an honest living, then why should he care? But, for some unknown reason, he did care. As Calfain saw it, Paland had survived for hundreds, if not thousands of years, so, he could not understand why a fanatic should be able to come along and upset what was, ostensibly, a peace-loving country. Calfain shrugged. What did he know? He was just an ordinary person, trying to earn a crust. Live and let live was his motto. It was none of his concern. He swallowed the last of his meal, drank from his water flask and decided there and then to search out and kill the Lord Tennay. He did not know why, he just knew it had to be done – if only to give Peltene and her son, a chance to live their lives without fear.

Calfain climbed into his saddle and turned his horse towards Pa City.

Chapter Twenty-one

As Venden entered their lodging house, Peltene quickly glanced past his head to a point beyond. Venden saw her gaze and shook his head slowly, as he had on each of the previous three days.

'Nothing? No sign?' Peltene almost whispered.

'Nay, My Lady, naught as yet.' Venden replied sombrely. The big farmhand had visited the marketplace as Calfain had instructed him to do each day at noon. Yesterday, Venden had easily spotted Tennay's men, watching for him and he had just as easily avoided them. But, there was still no sign of, or from, the dreamweaver.

'Mine own self wouldst recommend thee not to worry too much over Calfain, My Lady,' Venden said reassuringly, 'after all, he dost posses a great ability to survive whatever troubles and tribulations present themselves before his own self.'

Peltene nodded absently, 'I know you're right, Venden, but somehow it doesn't make it any better.'

Two more days, My Lady. Two more visits to the marketplace and still, if there is naught a sign of him, then as instructed we ride to Yarlis.'

'And then what, Venden?' Pelted asked, almost imploringly, 'do we carry on as if nothing had ever happened? Do we just assume he died in Pa City – at the hands of my husband? What if he's injured and in need of our help?'

Venden smiled sheepishly, 'Mine own self cannot answer thine questions, My Lady. We canst only do as Calfain hath instructed.'

Peltene's jaw stiffened. 'Well, Venden, you might only be able to do that, but I can try and do a lot more,' She stood, smoothing down her blouse as she did, 'I'm going back to Pa City.'

'My Lady,' Venden gasped, 'that might naught be the best decision that thee hath made today.'

'I don't care, I've made up my mind and that's that. Come if you want – or not – I'm leaving either way.'

'But, My Lady,' Venden began to plead, 'what wouldst happen if Calfain was successful in his endeavours and is travelling to meet with us as we speak?'

Peltene smiled, 'Then we'll meet him on the road I should think.'

Venden sighed, defeated by her feminine logic. 'When wouldst thou wish to depart?'

* * *

Calfain quietly sighed to himself as he rode slowly past Tennay's house for the third time that day. It was dusk now and still he had not returned. He moved on past and headed towards a small inn where he knew he could find a hot meal.

As soon as he had entered the city, four days ago, Calfain had searched out a shop where he might buy a large brimmed hat and a new coat. A simple disguise, he thought, after all, the brethren were looking for him as they had last seen him – dressed almost in rags.

The black leather storm coat suited his purpose, firstly it was long, secondly, it contained a multitude of pockets, both inside and out and thirdly, he rather liked the smell of it. The hat was big enough for him to easily disguise his features without seeming to do so purposefully.

Now, sitting at a small table in his habitual dark corner, Calfain stabbed at the chicken on his plate, seeing the face of

Tennay as he did so. After his purchases, Calfain had taken a walk passed Lord Tennay's house and was surprised to see at least fifty monks swarming about the gardens, obviously, it seemed to Calfain, Tennay was bringing in more of the brethren to facilitate his takeover of Paland, or, Calfain smiled wryly to himself, because the lord was a tad afraid that the dreamweaver might return to complete his unfinished business.

The next day, Calfain watched as Lord Tennay had ridden out early. He had followed at a distance and saw Tennay visit firstly the offices of the local militia and then on to what Calfain assumed to be the city's main army barracks.

Rightly or wrongly, Calfain now firmly believed that Tennay was buying off the country's generals and its senior militiamen, possibly to stage a coup, oust whomever was in charge – Calfain did not know – or particularly care, and declare himself emperor, or king, but most likely – dictator.

Now, as the day, which had been a dark and dreary affair drew to an early close, the dreamweaver was back – at a safe distance, waiting for the lord's return to his house.

Calfain's attention was suddenly drawn to the arrival of what he assumed to be a delivery of some sort. Two men carrying large sacks over their backs were being accompanied by one of the brethren. In the half-light, he casually observed them as they entered the grounds and turned towards the rear entrance. As they disappeared from his view, Calfain added them to his estimated mental list of how many people were now inside the house.

The sound of hooves approaching jolted Calfain from his reverie. For over an hour he had been plotting how to deal with Tennay and escape without alerting the whole house. Having decided that the simplest ideas are always the best, he would wait until Tennay was asleep, and then slit his throat. As the lord and his two accomplices dismounted, Calfain wondered how he had failed to see the two deliverymen depart from the building.

* * *

'Where is Calfain?' Peltene's voice quietly hissed into her estranged husband's ear. Tennay was instantly awake, having slept for no more than a half-hour, he thought he was dreaming. As he turned his head he suddenly felt the sharp prick of a knife at his neck.

'I beseech thee, My Lord, tell thine wife that which she wishes to know." Venden's voice was in Tennay's other ear and he immediately felt a second sharp point of a knife on that side of his neck.

Tennay took a long slow breath, keeping as still as he possibly could. 'Peltene,' he said almost casually, ' how nice to see you again, dear.' His eyes flicked to the other side, seeing only a large shape in the near darkness. 'I don't think I've had the pleasure, sir.'

'Just answer thine lady's question,' Venden growled back.

'Where is he? What have you done to him?' Peltene hissed again, pressing the knife harder against Tennay's skin.

'Truthfully, Peltene,' Tennay sighed, 'the last time I saw him was just before he escaped from my cellars.'

Peltene's mind was racing, if Calfain really had escaped from her husband, how had he been captured, what had Tennay done to him and where was he now? She glanced across the darkness to Venden seeking advice as to her next move.

248

Suddenly, Tennay's hand was on hers, snatching the knife away as he rolled towards her. His deft movement caught Venden off-guard and even as the big farmhand made a grab for him, Lord Tennay was free of the bed, wrenching the knife from his wife's hand.

A searing pain flashed into Venden's head making him yelp in alarm. He momentarily swayed, knees buckling. Then, it was gone. Tennay was on the floor at the opposite side of his bed, his arms wrapped around Peltene as he held her knife close to her chest.

'Stand still, my friend, or I swear, she will die here and now.'

Venden could only see shapes across the room, but Tennay's tone was enough to convince him.

Peltene was struggling furiously in Tennay's grip. 'Ven,' she screamed, 'Kill him! Kill him!'

'Persa! Persa! Tennay shouted loudly, attempting to summon his guard. In the darkness, Venden took two tentative steps towards the struggling pair. Tennay struggled to his feet, now clutching Peltene by her hair, dragging her up with him.

As suddenly as before, the pain was inside Venden's head again. He gasped and his step faltered.

'Drop the knife,' Tennay bellowed.

Venden gasped again, forcing his eyes to open, 'I willst pray for thine own soul, My Lord,' he hissed through pain-clenched teeth.

'Persa!' Tennay bellowed again.

No sooner had the name been shouted, the bedroom door burst open. Persa, Tennay's personal guard seemed to fill the doorway. A burning torch clamped against his chest illuminated the room, revealing the scene in lighted detail. For several seconds, Persa stood, as if surveying the scene, then Tennay snapped harshly, 'Persa, disarm him.' Tennay nodded towards Venden, seeing him properly for the first time.

Persa continued to stare straight ahead, until slowly his body fell forward describing an almost perfect arc as it fell into the room crushing the torch and spewing forth hundreds of lighted sparks across the carpeted floor.

Peltene gasped, Venden immediately saw the blade, which was embedded in the base of Persa's neck. He glanced up and saw the dreamweaver silhouetted in the doorway.

Tennay glanced towards the door and recognised Calfain instantly. He pulled Peltene closer to his own body, placing her knife across her throat.

'One wrong move, Dreamweaver,' he pressed the knife closer, emphasising his intention.

Calfain could barely see the man in the half-light, but he assessed the situation accurately. 'And if you kill her? What then, Tennay? Calfain asked calmly, 'do you seriously think I'll let you walk away?' Calfain slowly entered the room, stepping over the body of Persa. 'Let her go, Tennay, I'll take her back to Yarland – with her son and you get on with whatever it is that you were doing. No questions asked.'

Calfain could feel the hesitation. He pressed on. 'Tennay, be reasonable, this can end here with no more bloodshed. Whatever your ambitions are for Paland, we don't care. As far as we're concerned, it's the other side of the world and none of our business. Let her go, Tennay. Do the right thing.'

'You make a convincing argument, Dreamweaver,' Tennay said at last.

'I'm just trying to make sense of this absurdity.'

'Very well, ' Tennay said confidently, I accept your terms.' He relaxed his grip on Peltene slightly.

'Excellent,' Calfain said, relaxing his own grip on the dagger hidden in his belt behind his back.

'Except for the boy,' Tennay proclaimed, 'he stays with me.'

Calfain groaned inwardly.

'No!' Peltene screamed, wrenching herself from Tennay's loosened grip. She twisted her body around, making a wild grab for the knife. Calfain lunged forward almost colliding with Venden who had launched himself over the bed. As three pairs of hands grappled wildly with Tennay, the blinding pain struck again in each of their heads. This time Calfain had been expecting it.

The scene inside the dreamweaver's mind was chaotic. Swirling red mists punctuated with vivid blue bolts of lightening randomly zigzagging in every direction. Each time lightening flashed; Calfain believed his head had exploded.

In the far distance, through the angry mist, Calfain saw a blinding white light; it grew larger as it seemed to approach him at unimaginable speed before stopping sharply in front of him. It was the face of Tennay but with grotesquely contorted features that stretched and pulled in several directions at the same time. Tennay's mouth opened and Calfain could clearly see the head of a viper, its eyes staring intently at him, choosing its moment to lunge and strike.

Calfain recoiled, placing a protective arm to his head. The viper struck with such ferocity that its fangs snapped as they crunched on the bones in his forearm. Calfain screamed with the sudden pain and shock. He swung his free arm up, imagining there to be a long, sharp dagger in his grasp. There was and he took a careless aim at the face of Tennay. The dagger pierced his right eye and the apparition began to blur and wither.

As the pain inside Calfain's head subsided, he opened his eyes, blinking rapidly, trying to focus. His right arm felt numb and for a split second, he thought he had fallen asleep with his full weight on it. He attempted to push himself up from the floor where he was lying on his side. His arm gave way and he grunted loudly. He glanced at his arm and realised that his shirt was covered in blood and that it was flowing freely onto his hand. Then, abruptly, his mind sprang into life. He now remembered everything. He quickly looked around searching out Peltene and Venden. Tennay was slumped against a wall, his head twisted at a strange angle. A long bladed knife protruded from his right eye socket, blood still pumping from the terminal wound.

As Calfain struggled to his knees, he saw Peltene lying prone across the bed; blood was splattered down the front of her clothing. He pulled himself up onto the bed and shook her gently. "Peltene,' He said her name anxiously, praying that she was not hurt, 'Peltene,' he called again. She moaned softly, he eyes fluttering open.

'Cal, Calfain?' she whispered, realisation coming to her, 'Oh no, what have I done?'

'Are you hurt?' he ignored her question as he searched her body urgently for any sign of harm.

'I've killed him, I've killed him.' She muttered.

'No,' Calfain said, 'I did that.'

Peltene groaned again, struggling to sit upright.

'Nay, Calfain,' Venden's voice said from somewhere on the floor, 'Mine own hand is responsible for that.' His head appeared from below the bed. Calfain saw that he too was bloodstained.'

'Are you alright, Ven?'

'I canst recall better days,' he answered, slowly rising to his full height. 'Calfain, I thinkest we need to be away from here.' He added urgently.

Calfain glanced at him and noting that the big farmhand was staring past him, he turned to see what held Venden's attention. The room was beginning to fill with smoke. The torch that Persa had fallen onto had spread its hot sparks across the thickly carpeted floor to reach the window curtains where yellow flames began to eat greedily at the woollen fibres.

'Calfain,' Peltene cried, 'you're hurt,' she pointed at his blood stained sleeve.

'It'll wait, where's Dennel?'

'He should be outside with the horses,' she replied, slithering from the bed and attempting to stand. As she did, she saw the disfigured body of her husband, his one good eye lifelessly staring up at her. She gasped and began to sob.

'Not now, Pel,' Calfain said, harshly grabbing her and forcibly moving her away from the scene

Venden was already at the door, his head craning around the jamb.

'All clear, Calfain,' he said reassuringly.

"It'll be a miracle if it stays that way. I don't know how we haven't been stopped so far.'

Venden grinned lopsidedly. 'Young Dennel wouldst be the cause of that. He gaveth instructions to each of the brethren that his own father wished them all to spend the night in contemplation within the cellars. Thence bolting the doors behind them.'

Calfain nodded, 'That explains why I didn't see anyone when I broke in.'

' But it doth naught mean that a new arrival or two couldst be lurking.'

As Peltene had promised, Dennel was waiting with their horses. Calfain rode with Peltene the short distance to where his horse was stabled, then, after Calfain had secured a makeshift tourniquet around his damaged arm, they headed in the general direction of Yarland, intending to put as much distance between themselves and Paland as possible before dawn

Chapter Twenty-two

'Calfain, It doth surely need the attention of a surgeon.' Venden announced grimly as he inspected the dreamweaver's wound.

Calfain peered at the gash in his forearm. He could clearly see the white bone of his arm deep inside.

'As long as the broken blade is out and Pel can sew reasonably neatly, then it'll be fine,' he replied unconvincingly.

Peltene gazed at the gaping wound, 'I don't think I can do this, Cal,' she sighed nervously.

He smiled reassuringly at her. 'You'll do fine, just pretend you're sewing a tear in your favourite dress.'

'It's not the same,' she protested.

'Yes it is. Pel, just remember to put a lot of stitches close together and in a neat line. I don't want an ugly scar.'

Venden chuckled. 'Tis mine own belief that a vipers bite wouldst hath been better.'

Calfain looked at him curiously. 'How so, Ven?'

'T'woust only hath been two small teeth marks to stitch.'

Peltene knelt down beside the rock on which Calfain was sitting and began to thread her needle.

"Dost thee think we willst be followed?' Venden asked casually.

'I don't know, Ven. You know them better than I. Do you think they'll seek revenge for the death of Tennay?'

Venden watched closely as Peltene made the first stitch in Calfain's arm. The dreamweaver flinched uncontrollably.

Peltene looked anxiously at him, seeking his approval to continue or otherwise. Calfain nodded and smiled.

'What wouldst they seek to gain by pursuing us all the way across Yarland?' Venden appeared to be thinking aloud. ''Tis mine own considered opinion that the brethren wouldst seek to return to Cipeus, lick their wounds and carry on as they hath before Lord Tennay discovered them.'

'My thoughts exactly, Ven.'

Peltene took an agonisingly long time to stitch Calfain's wound, after which she announced that she would prepare a meal for them all. She tucked away her needle and thread and began to dissect the small amount of vegetables that they had. Venden and Calfain strolled a short distance away from the campfire.

'Painful?' Venden asked, nodding at the dreamweaver's arm.

'Just a lot, yes,' Calfain confessed, 'but don't tell Peltene. Anyway, do you seriously think that they'll let us just ride away, Ven?' Calfain asked quietly, a good distance from the campfire.

Venden answered truthfully. 'Consider the possibility, mine friend, that they willst attempt to regain control of young Dennel's mind.'

'Why? For what reason? Calfain asked glumly.

'Because the brethren couldst presume that Dennel be the natural successor to his late father and therefore wouldst assume – rightly or wrongly – that he doth hold all the knowledge required to continue their struggle.'

Calfain took a few seconds to digest what his friend had just said. 'So, if you're right, then they would pursue us wherever we go.'

The big farmhand nodded solemnly. 'On the other hand, Calfain, 'tis only supposition on mine own part. I hath been known to be wrong.'

Calfain's shoulders slumped as he sighed heavily. 'No, Ven, I have this terrible feeling that you may be right.' Calfain smiled weakly at the big man. 'And if you are then one of two things must happen. Peltene and Dennel spend the rest of their lives looking over their shoulders – or, I go and find the abbot and convince him that Dennel is dead.'

'If that be the case, it doth mean that we be in exactly the same position as before. We hath to return to Cipeus,' Venden shuddered, 'a prospect that doth naught fill mine own self with gladness.'

Calfain shook his head. 'Not you, my friend, not this time. This time it's me alone.'

'Calfain, that decision wouldst naught bode well with the lady.'

The dreamweaver inhaled a long deep breath. She is not going to know, Ven. We are not going to tell her.'

Venden glanced around the immediate vicinity and then rubbed his eyes. 'Thine tone suggests a finality in thine words.'

'Yes, Venden, because what I'm about to offer you will affect us all, probably for the rest of our lives.'

Venden scrutinised the dreamweaver's face closely. 'Explain,' he said finally.

'Well, up to now all I've done is to go around in circles, kill a man and get another one killed...' Venden lifted a hand to interject.

'Calfain, twas mine own self, naught thee, who killed Tennay...'

'No, Ven, it was my knife in his eye. I did it in my head and it turned into reality.'

Venden was about to protest again, but was cut short.

'When Peltene offered me the job of getting Dennel back, all I was supposed to do was make Tennay believe that he never had a wife and son. Then when that didn't work I tried to reason with the man. That didn't work either, so what I'm saying is,

256

well, Peltene and I could have had a life together – of sorts, even if it meant looking over our shoulders for Tennay, but, if the brethren are hell-bent on pursuing us all the way back to Peltene's home, then I have to do something about it. It has to end.'

Venden nodded grimly. 'And if the abbot chooses naught to believe thine words?'

'Then I'll kill him.' Calfain answered simply.

'And the brethren?'

Calfain glanced up at the sky and smiled. 'I can't kill all of them, Ven, but at least, if I make my escape, then I can lead them around the countryside until they either lose their passion for revenge or I can fake my own death.'

Venden stared at the ground, slowly shaking his head. 'It shouldst naught hath to come to this, mine friend.'

Calfain put his hand on the big man's shoulder. 'Venden, it would make my life a lot easier if I could count on you to deliver Peltene and Dennel back to their home.'

Venden sighed heavily and silently nodded his acceptance of the task.

'And – if you need a job, I'm sure the Lady can more than make use of your talents.'

'Employment is naught a priority...' Venden broke off as Peltene walked towards them.

She smiled as she approached. 'And what are you two conspiring about now?'

'Oh, we were just arguing about who takes first watch tonight. Venden said he will because my arm hurts.' Calfain gingerly lifted his arm and managed to show a pained expression at the same time.'

'Peltene nodded. 'Well, come and have some food. Then you'll feel better.'

Venden fell in behind them; a grim expression was set across his own face.

It was an hour before dawn. Calfain had not slept; his mind was in turmoil with what he was about to do. He knew that he wanted to return with Peltene to Yarland, to her cottage and, hopefully, have a long and happy life together. He also knew that if the Cipean monks did decide to search out Dennel, then they might possibly spend the rest of their lives running away from every shadow. As he had said to Venden, this time, it really had to end.

He took a long deep breath and turned his head to look at the sleeping form of Peltene. His fingers lightly brushed her cheek. Peltene's eyes opened and she smiled at him.

'I'm sorry, I didn't mean to wake you,' he whispered.

She smiled sleepily, 'That's fine, what's the matter?'

Calfain took another deep breath. 'I just wanted you to know...' his voice deserted him.

'Yes?' she asked, 'what do you want me to know, Cal?'

Calfain gently stroked her hair. 'I just wanted you to know that...that I love you, Pel. I always will.'

'Peltene's eyes fluttered. 'And I love you,' she said dreamily as the dreamweaver's fingers began to work their special magic.

As the sun struggled to gain its foothold on the day, Calfain had packed his saddlebags and was sipping from his water bottle.

'Is the deed done?' Venden's voice seemed harsh, almost accusing.

Calfain jammed the stopper into the bottle with unnecessary force. He glanced at the big man. 'Yes.'

Venden expelled a lungful of air. 'Hath her memory of thee been erased completely?'

'Not completely, no. She will remember hiring me and most of our journey across country and she'll remember me saying goodbye and that I did not want payment.'

'And the boy?'

'There wasn't much about me that needed to be removed.'

'How canst thee just remove all of her feelings for thee, Calfain? Dost it naught wrench at thine heart?'

'More than you'll ever know, Ven, but it has to be.'

'Nay, Calfain, tis naught the right and proper way and in thine own heart of hearts, ye knowest it to be true.'

'You're right, Ven. I do know it to be true, but this is the only way I can protect her and her son.'

'Calfain, I...'

'Venden – please - don't make it any harder than it already is. Take them home. Watch over them for me.'

Calfain held out his hand, Venden grasped it and shook firmly. 'In another life, my friend, you and I could have had adventures to be proud of.'

'They couldst still occur, Dreamweaver.'

'You never know, Ven, you just never know.' Calfain broke free of the big man's grip and climbed quickly into his saddle. He looked down at the sleeping forms on the ground. 'They'll sleep for another two more hours,' he said without looking at Venden. Then he tugged on the horse's reins and trotted out of the campsite.

Chapter Twenty-three

Calfain sat side-saddle, his left leg casually hooked over his right, staring out to sea. Somewhere, out there beyond his vision, lay Cipeus Island. He carefully ate the last piece of cold pork that he had purchased some two days ago from a trader making his way to a local market that Calfain purposefully steered clear of.

Wiping his mouth with the back of his hand, Calfain lifted his leg and swivelled into his saddle. 'Right,' he thought, 'no dancing around outside of the fire. This time, it's the direct approach.' He nudged his horse into a trot and headed along the coast road that he knew would take him straight into Tapp City in less than half a day.

'Good day to you, sir,' Calfain grinned at the man as he climbed from his sailing boat onto the stone quay.

'Ho there,' the man replied, glancing up at Calfain.

'A fine looking vessel if ever I saw one.' Calfain nodded at the little craft, bobbing up and down a few feet below him.

The man stood upright. Calfain noticed the fish in a wicker basket that had obviously recently been caught.

'Aye, she's not a bad little scow, for her age.'

The dreamweaver nodded towards the fish. 'And a lucky one too, if you haul a catch like that each day.'

The man turned to face Calfain. He looked the dreamweaver up and down, assessing the stranger's motives.

'What exactly can I be doing for you?' he asked without a hint of rancour.

Calfain smiled and placed a friendly hand on the man's shoulder. 'Well, now you mention it, friend. I was thinking to myself that I really need to borrow your boat.'

The man's eyes suddenly glazed over as if he had just seen something astonishingly beautiful.

'So, are you sure you don't mind me talking your boat out for a sail around the harbour?' Calfain asked earnestly.

'No, no, go right ahead,' the man muttered, still gazing at some wondrous vision.

For good measure, Calfain pressed. 'Can I take as long as I require?'

'Oh, that's alright, young fellow, take all the time you need.' The man replied blankly, his head tilting to one side as if attempting to see around an imaginary corner.

'Thank you,' Calfain said cheerily, 'now if I were you, I'd go and have a drink in that tavern over there and tell all your friends that I haven't stolen your boat. I'm thinking of buying it.'

The man nodded dutifully. ' Yes, that's fine. You carry on. I'm just going for a drink.'

Calfain patted the man's shoulder and let him attend to his business in the tavern.

Two hours later, after struggling with a single sail plus a tiller and desperately trying to recall what Venden had told him about sailing boats, Calfain had managed to point the little craft in the general direction of Cipeus and was now – as far as he was concerned, out on the high seas.

Calfain reasoned that the direct approach was going to be his best option. Land on the island, it did not matter exactly where, march up to the front door and demand to see the abbot. Simple and straightforward. If the abbot would listen to his argument for Dennel and agree, then fine. If not, then the abbot would meet his maker in the same manner that Tennay had.

As night descended, Calfain began to realise the stupidity of attempting to sail alone in the dark. More so when he considered the fact that he was not an able sailor, nor did he know how to navigate accurately by the stars as Venden had, but a grim determination made him continue.

At first light, to Calfain's astonishment, he saw the outline of an island that he forced himself to believe was Cipeus. Within the space of a few minutes, he became convinced that it was indeed the dreaded island, not least because he could clearly see the foreboding tower, silently demanding that visitors should keep away.

Ignoring the tower, he trimmed the sail as Venden had shown him and steered the boat along the eastern side of the island, seeking out the wooden jetty that he had hoped he would never have to see again.

A short while later, the jetty came into view. Calfain pulled down the sail and fixed the oars. He intended to arrive with some sort of elegance and he reckoned that rowing in would avoid any sign that he was an incompetent sailor and would also minimise damage to the boat, should he require a rapid retreat.

Glancing over his shoulder, Calfain judged the distance to the jetty at about twenty feet. He pulled twice more on the oars and brought them back inboard. He glanced again this time, as if by magic, more than ten brown robed monks had appeared and were standing in a line, waiting for him to make contact. Even if he had wanted to turn around, it was too late. The boat gently rubbed against the wooden jetty and Calfain flung the rope to no one in particular, but with enough effort to gain some satisfaction from seeing several of the brethren duck with surprise.

Standing up straight on the jetty, Calfain fully expected to be manacled or at the very least forcibly marched into the monastery and beaten. Incredibly, the monk nearest to him bowed slightly turned and lifted his hand, motioning the dreamweaver to freely accompany him inside.

Calfain sat in a comfortable chair patiently waiting for events to unfold. He had been sitting in the same position for more than two hours and was beginning to get bored, when the door quietly opened and the abbot of the monastery noiselessly walked in.

'Good day to thee, Master Calfain,' the abbot said in a businesslike manner, 'please tell me why ye hath chosen to return so brazenly to our island.' He lowered himself into a chair opposite and no more than three feet away from Calfain.

Desperately trying to appear unruffled by the abbot's sudden appearance and his immediate question, Calfain leaned purposely forward in his own chair and spoke smoothly. 'Good day, Your Grace, I have come to ask you about your intentions regarding the late Lord Tennay's son.'

If the abbot was surprised by the forthright response, he did not show it. Instead, he inhaled deeply, measuring his answer. 'I was naught aware that the boy was still alive.' He answered blandly.

Calfain gauged that that was a lie. By now, the old man must have been informed that Dennel was alive and with his mother still. 'Well, let us assume, Your Grace that he is. Then what would be your intentions for him?'

The abbot steepeled his fingers, gaining time and watching the dreamweaver closely. 'If the boy were still to be alive and well, then I wouldst conclude that he should return to us and continue his learning.'

Calfain leaned further forward. 'And if Dennel has decided that he no longer wishes to be a part of your, er, order, then what?'

The old man smiled thinly. 'Enough of these silly games, Master Calfain. Brinksmanship is for those who wouldst wish to be intellectuals. If the boy were privy to his father's intentions, then we wouldst seek to divest him of that knowledge.'

'What if I assured you, Your Grace, that the boy has absolutely no knowledge of any of his fathers plans, ambitions or intentions?'

'Then, I'm afraid that thine assurance is naught one that we couldst take at face value, Master Calfain. We wouldst hath to perform a thorough investigation ourselves.'

'And what if I told you that I would not allow such an investigation?'

The abbot almost chuckled. 'Then I wouldst say to thee, Master Calfain, that we wouldst still investigate the possibilities and whilst we were doing so, ye wouldst be held here as a guest of the brethren.'

'Your Grace,' Calfain's voice dropped to almost a whisper, 'Dennel *does not* know or understand *anything* that his father was involved with.'

'I'm sorry, Master Calfain, I hath a solemn obligation to mine fellow brethren to satisfy myself that what ye say is the truth.'

Calfain breathed deeply and sat back in his chair. 'I cannot allow you to bring the boy back to this island.'

'Ye hath no choice in mine own decisions.'

Calfain leaned forward again. 'I could kill you.'

This time, instead of a chuckle, the abbot actually laughed aloud. 'And what wouldst that gain for ye, sir? An untimely death for thineself I wouldst dare wager.

Calfain sighed. 'Your Grace, as you said earlier, arguments like these are for supposed intellectuals. Let's whittle down to the notch. I assume that you have your emeralds back here on the island. And I said to Lord Tennay, I truthfully don't care what your plans are for them. It's not my business and is of no consequence to my friends or me. All I ask is your assurance that you will not pursue the boy for information that he does not possess.'

'And as I said to thee, Master Calfain, I must assure mine own self that the boy hath indeed naught any knowledge of his fathers intentions.'

Calfain sat back. 'Then we are at an Impasse, as they say.'

'Indeed we are.'

Calfain placed his hands on the arms of the chair and pushed. 'Then I am truly sorry, Your Grace. I honestly hoped it would not come to this.' As he stood, Calfain's left hand reached behind his midriff searching out the double bladed knife, which he habitually kept there strapped to his belt in a horizontal position.

'No hard feelings, Your Grace,' Calfain smiled as he held out his right hand.

The abbot sighed as he rose to his feet, 'Master Calfain, I meant what I said about staying here until...'

As the dreamweaver's hand touched the abbot's, the two men felt the simultaneous jolt inside their heads. The abbots head snapped back momentarily as he fought to gain control of his mind. Calfain gripped the old man's hand more tightly, pushing him back into the chair.

'This will gain thee nothing,' the abbot's voice spoke inside Calfain's head.

On a whim, Calfain had decided not to kill the abbot, but to try an experiment that had been niggling at him since he had selectively erased Peltene's memories of him.

'Perhaps,' Calfain replied, 'then again, perhaps everything.' Suddenly, the dreamweaver was deep inside the abbot's mind, sifting through the man's memories both past and recent, delving into his childhood, seeing his parents, his friends and relatives.

Calfain flipped through the abbot's mind until he found the first meeting that the holy man had had with Tennay. Satisfied that this was where he wanted to be, he mentally forced the abbot into sleep whilst he set to work.

'Well, thank you for your hospitality, Your Grace,' Calfain waved cheerily and closed the heavy oak door as he let himself out. One of the brethren was standing close by and moved to restrain the dreamweaver.

'It's all right, my friend,' Calfain smiled at the cloaked man, 'His Grace has instructed me to set sail for the mainland and retrieve the boy, Dennel. Er, we have an understanding. Oh yes, and he instructed me to tell you that he wishes to take a hot drink in about an hour. Not before mind, he wants to rest and contemplate a few things.'

The monk took a step away from Calfain, unsure as what to do next. He nervously glanced at the closed door and then at the dreamweaver.

Calfain shrugged, 'It's up to you friend, disturb him if you wish. Just don't let me be in earshot if you do.'

The monk turned, allowing Calfain to pass unhindered.

Out on the sea, Calfain breathed a sigh of relief. He turned; looking back at the island of the Cipean monks. It began to seem smaller. He sat back against the tiller and considered what he had just done to the old abbots mind. Calfain had no regrets that he had just erased every last memory that the man had of everything from the day that he had met the Lord Tennay. There were now only echoes in the old man's head.

Calfain glanced up at the scudding clouds, they seemed to be heading towards the mainland and may even speed his journey. He looked back at the receding island one last time and muttered to himself, 'Never underestimate a Dreamweaver. That's my motto.'

www.ingramcontent.com/pod-product-compliance
Lightning Source LLC
Chambersburg PA
CBHW020613260626
47157CB00003B/989